A FATAL
GLASS of BEER

The Toby Peters Mysteries

A FATAL GLASS OF BEER
DANCING IN THE DARK
TOMORROW IS ANOTHER DAY
THE DEVIL MET A LADY
THE MELTING CLOCK
POOR BUTTERFLY
BURIED CAESARS
THINK FAST, MR. PETERS
SMART MOVES
THE MAN WHO SHOT LEWIS VANCE
DOWN FOR THE COUNT
THE FALA FACTOR
HE DONE HER WRONG
CATCH A FALLING CLOWN
HIGH MIDNIGHT
NEVER CROSS A VAMPIRE
THE HOWARD HUGHES AFFAIR
YOU BET YOUR LIFE
MURDER ON THE YELLOW BRICK ROAD
BULLET FOR A STAR

STUART M. KAMINSKY

A FATAL GLASS OF BEER

THE MYSTERIOUS PRESS

Published by Warner Books

A Time Warner Company

3 1336 04323 3999

Mysterious Press books are published by Warner Books, Inc.,
1271 Avenue of the Americas, New York, NY 10020.

Ⓦ A Time Warner Company

The Mysterious Press name and logo are registered trademarks of Warner Books, Inc.

Printed in the United States of America

First printing: May 1997

10 9 8 7 6 5 4 3 2 1

Library of Congress Cataloging-in-Publication Data

Kaminsky, Stuart M.
    A fatal glass of beer / Stuart M. Kaminsky.
        p. cm.
    ISBN 0-89296-630-0
    1. Fields, W. C., 1879–1946—Fiction.   I. Title.
PS3561.A43F35   1997
813'.54—dc21   96–49494
                                                            CIP

To Barbara and Danny Sullivan

A FATAL
GLASS OF BEER

Chapter One

I think it was in Tierra del Fuego that I first began my search for the dreaded tsetse fly.

A pair of Amish men with well-trimmed beards, black suits and hats, engaged in conversation, came around the corner toward the bank. They were followed by a thin woman of no clear age, wearing a plain white Mother Hubbard dress and a tiny white bonnet. A boy and girl who looked like twins trailed the woman. The girl was dressed like the woman. The boy wore breeches, a long-sleeved white shirt, and suspenders. Both children appeared to be about ten.

I glanced at W. C. Fields, who sat beside me in the backseat of his Cadillac. He was sipping a drink from his built-in bar—plenty of gin, ample vermouth, large jar of olives, and box of toothpicks the size of a cigar box. He was also squinting in the general direction of the Amish family, which now entered the bank.

Fields was over sixty and wore what he described as a "fool-proof disguise," a gray jacket and trousers, a white shirt with a large bow tie, and a cheap Hitler-style mustache clipped to his nose, which had the effect of making the already admirably sized appendage look even larger.

"Might be him," said Fields, pointing toward the bank. "Disguised as a Mormon."

"They're Amish," I corrected.

We were in Lancaster, Pennsylvania. It was April the first, 1943, a Thursday. The war was going well. The day before, U.S. flying fortresses had bombed the harbor and shipbuilding area of Rotterdam, the chief port of call for German coastal convoys. It was the ninth March raid on the Axis in Europe. Down

Africa way, the English Eighth Army, under General Sir Bernard L. Montgomery, continued to advance against Rommel in Tunisia. In addition, six Axis ships were sunk in the Mediterranean by British subs. Elmer Davis, director of war information, issued a warning against over-optimism, but predicted Rommel's defeat in time for an invasion of Europe before 1944. On the home front, a musical called *Oklahoma* had opened. It starred Alfred Drake, Celeste Holm, and Howard Da Silva. On the airplane to Philadelphia, Fields had confidently predicted that a musical about a state, and one with a dwindled population and almost impossible to find on the map, was doomed to failure within the week.

Now Fields was as certain of the people who had entered the bank.

"Of course they're Amish," Fields retorted, disgusted at my ignorance. "Amish Mormons, a rare sect, shunned by most in this community, living quiet lives of confusion and conviction. I have a distinct fondness for real Amish."

"I believe you mean Mennonites," Gunther corrected. It was a serious mistake on Gunther's part.

Fields took a long sip from his martini glass and placed it on the bar in the back of the Cadillac. I had flown with Fields from Los Angeles to Philadelphia. Fields had hired me to help him recover money that he had stashed away in various bank accounts all over the country, a practice he had engaged in for over forty years. He estimated that he had over a million dollars "all over the place," plus a few hundred thousand in Europe, even fifty thousand in German banks, "in case the little bastards win," he explained.

Haggling with Fields over my fee had almost taken enough out of me to send me to the loony bin. When I brought this up, he had seriously suggested the sanitarium that he, himself, visited frequently.

"Maybe we'll check in together," he said. "After we complete our sojourn."

Fields's car had been driven willingly across country by my friend Gunther Wherthman, a Swiss midget—or "little person," as he preferred to call himself—who made a comfortable living as a translator of several dozen languages. Gunther was about a yard high. He always dressed impeccably in three-piece suits and drove quickly and with expertise.

After a few moments of suspicion, Fields had reluctantly taken a liking to Gunther, but insisted that whatever Gunther was paid would come out of my salary. The opportunity for the trip had come just as Gunther was about to drive off someplace on his own to brood for a few weeks or months over a lost love who had just received her graduate degree in music from San Francisco State and would soon be taking a teaching job in Vermont. He was also doing his best to avoid an aggressive film publicist who had a thing for very small men. Both women were more than two feet taller than Gunther, but that had not stopped him. He had pursued both relationships with courtly dignity.

The pedals on Fields's car had to be built up and a special wooden driver's seat inserted, both Gunther's, both removable. Fields had viewed Gunther with mistrust from the beginning of the case.

"The midget sounds like a Nazi," Fields had whispered to me when the two first met in Fields's home on DeMille Drive in Los Angeles the week before.

Gunther had heard the comment but chose to act as if he had not.

"Gunther's Swiss," I'd said. "Great driver. Used to be in the circus. He was in *The Wizard of Oz.*"

"I should have been the wizard," Fields had said. "Was up for the part. Had it all wrapped up. Forget what the problem was. Frank Morgan stole the picture. Think I was in that sanitarium we discussed earlier." Now he said, "Send the midget into the bank."

There was a plate-glass window between the driver's seat and the backseat of the car. It was, supposedly, soundproof or close to it. Fields could communicate with Gunther, or whoever was driving, with a microphone that hung on a hook right next to the built-in bar.

"What?"

"You heard me, Peters. Send in the midget. He can't tell a Mormon from a Mennonite, but maybe he can spot a thief. One of those two Amish may have been in disguise."

"Don't you think Gunther will be a little . . . conspicuous?" I asked.

"Nonsense," said Fields, taking another sip. "The Amish are a respectable lot. Probably invite him home for dinner and a discussion of sexual misconduct among Methodists in the circus."

I failed to understand the logic, but I was learning not to question it. Once a conversation with Fields was begun, its sense and direction were almost impossible to keep up with.

"I will go," said Gunther from the driver's seat when I slid back the glass window and relayed Fields's order. He opened the door and got out, straightening his jacket and brushing back his hair.

"Clean little fella," said Fields with admiration. "Still not convinced he's not a Nazi. Someday I'll tell you about the time I was in search of the dreaded tsetse fly in Tierra del Fuego, where I was thwarted in my scientific endeavor by a Nazi who looked suspiciously like Goebbels."

Gunther crossed the street. A few people looked in his direction. Fields and I watched him enter the bank.

"When I was a lad," Fields said, "back in Philadelphia, I had a set-to with my father when I was eleven. He hit me in the head with a rake. I dropped a crate on his head. Left home. Never went back. Lived in a hole in the ground for a while, then a loft over a blacksmith shop. Finally got a job cleaning up at a bar with a pool table. Slept in the men's room for a while and then on the pool table. Made a more-than-fair living by the time I was twelve, hustling on that table and splitting the take with the management. At night I taught myself to juggle billiard balls, balance pool cues, and do tricks with empty cigar boxes and hats people had been too soused to remember to take home.

"There were early times on the open road when I set out to make my fortune when I came through this part of the state. Amish were always good for a meal and they never tried to Christianize me."

One of the Amish men, along with the woman and two children, came out of the bank.

"Where's the other guy?" asked Fields, putting down his martini glass.

He was halfway out of the car before I could say something to slow him down. Traffic was light, a few cars, a few Amish horse and buggies. Some people on the sidewalks.

I went after Fields, who shooed off oncoming traffic with his bamboo walking stick as he crossed the street. He stood back to let a young woman with a small child come out of the bank and reached up to tip his hat to her. The woman tried to ignore the strange but somehow familiar figure with the large nose in the bizarre disguise, but the boy, who was no more than four, said, "Mommy, why does that man have such a big nose and a toy mustache like Teddy Sykes?"

The mother tugged the kid down the street, but he looked back over his shoulder at Fields.

"Highlight of my film career was when I got to kick Baby LeRoy twice in the ass when we were doing *It's a Gift*," said Fields, pausing, a large smile on his face.

I was about to say something about being careful, when Fields suddenly trotted into the bank. I followed. There were only a few customers and the bank was small. Two teller windows on the left, a high wooden desk in the center of the room for customers to fill out their deposit or withdrawal forms, and a wooden railing on the right, behind which were four desks, all but one inhabited by women. Behind the desks were three doors: two were for offices, one was a steel vault with an impressive lock in the middle.

"Godfrey Daniel," Fields hissed. "He's absconded. And he's stolen your midget."

"Mr. Fields," I said, looking around, not knowing what to say when I saw no Gunther and no Amish man. "It might be a good idea to follow this up calmly."

Fields ignored me and moved to the wooden railing on the right, addressing the lone, business-suited, elderly man at the nearest desk.

"Excuse me," Fields said, pointing his bamboo cane at the man.

The man looked up, startled at the sight before him.

"Yes, sir?"

"What's your name?" Fields demanded as I looked around for Gunther.

"Titus Trebblecock," the old man said. "Can I help you?"

"Trebblecock," Fields said. "You have a fine name. Do your powers of observation match your de plume?"

"I don't see the correlation between—" the confused Trebblecock began, but Fields cut him off with a wave of his cane.

"You see a midget and a man disguised as an Amish walk in here a minute ago?"

"Disguised as . . ." Trebblecock began again in confusion.

The women at the other desks had stopped working and were watching the drama.

"Fake beard, clothes," Fields explained. "Came in here to steal my money."

"Your money?" asked Trebblecock.

"Thirty years ago, or was it forty," said Fields, "I opened an account in this bank under the name of Otis J. Raisincluster. Ten thousand dollars. Disguised bastard just came in here after my money."

"I'm sure, Mr. Raisinclasner—" the man began.

"Cluster," Fields corrected. "Raisincluster. Why would I

make up a name like Raisinclasner. Any man named Titus Trebblecock should make a point of knowing the proper pronunciation of his patrons' names."

"You wish to make a withdrawal?" the man asked nervously, looking at Fields's fake mustache.

"Every penny," he said.

"You have a bankbook?"

"Hundreds of them," said Fields. "Desktop full at home. But some thieving, blaspheming amateur stole about half of them and plans to go around the country cashing in."

"I'm a bit confused," said the man, looking around in embarrassment.

"A bit?" said Fields. "I'd say you show every sign of either being sober or having a recurring bout of tremors from the bite of a dreaded tsetse fly."

"Mr. Fields," I said, touching his arm.

He brushed me away, and I gave up and went in search of Gunther. One of the tellers, an older woman who was watching Fields across the room through the bars of her cage, had no customers. I moved to her and asked if she'd seen a midget come in.

"Yes," she said, not taking her eyes off Fields and Trebblecock. "Followed an Amish gentleman back to the rest rooms."

She pointed to the rear of the bank where there was a door for ladies and another for gentlemen. I ran to the men's room. The door was locked. I knocked.

"Gunther?" I whispered.

No answer. I called again, louder. "Gunther."

This time I thought I heard a groan. I hurried back to the teller. "You have a key for the men's room?"

"Certainly not," she said. "It locks from the inside for privacy but not the outside."

"Is there a window in there?"

"Yes," she said.

I glanced across the room. Fields was whispering loud enough for everyone in the bank to hear.

"I want this kept secret," he said. "Spies everywhere. One lives across the street from me. Walks around at night in a Nazi helmet and claims to be Cecil B. DeMille, Air Raid Warden. The Amish man who claimed to be me, which I assume he did, was he a Jap?"

Fields was right in Titus Trebblecock's face now, demanding satisfaction. I ran out the front door and made a dash around the corner onto another street. Behind the bank was a wide alley. I found the bathroom window. The window was open but too high for me to look inside. I found a trash can and moved it under the open window. The can felt empty and I wobbled. I almost crashed to the pavement as I climbed up on it and looked into the men's room. The can began to give way under me. I went through the window headfirst and landed on Gunther, who sat on the closed toilet seat. We tumbled to the floor. My head missed the sink by a few inches.

Gunther didn't look his best. His suit was disheveled and there was a dazed look in his eyes as if he were just waking up from a confusing dream.

"I'm sorry I fell on you," I said.

Gunther said something in a language I didn't understand.

"English, Gunther," I said.

"I'm sorry," he said, sitting up and holding the back of his head with his right hand. "He struck me on the head with something. The Amish. Mr. Fields was right. The Amish made a withdrawal, a big one. I got close enough to see that his beard wasn't real. It was good, but I've been in show business long enough to know. He put the money in a small black bag and went into the men's room. I attempted to follow him. He was waiting for me inside and hit me on the head, perhaps with the bag. That's all I am able to remember. I think I heard the door lock and then you fell on top of me."

"You need a doctor," I said.

"Not necessary," Gunther answered, standing and examining himself in the mirror. He adjusted his jacket and vest, produced a small comb from his pocket and used it. I could see the rise of a bump under his dark hair, but it wasn't bleeding.

"Come out of there," Fields suddenly shouted from outside the door. "I know you're in there and I intend to beat you into a state of permanent discombobulation."

I started to pick myself up and made an unpleasant discovery: my chronic backache had returned. I had earned it years earlier when a large Negro fan had tried to get too close to Mickey Rooney at a movie premiere. I was supposed to be protecting Rooney. I suppose I did, but the bear hug I got from the big Negro had done something to my back that sent me to bed for a week and came back every time I did dumb things like falling through windows. I managed to get up and open the door. Fields, Trebblecock, and another older man in a suit and pince-nez glasses stood looking at us.

"Son of a bitch got my money," said Fields.

"He had a bankbook," said the man in the glasses apologetically.

"So does Hitler," Fields responded.

"And he signed his name. The match is nearly exact."

"Worthless," said Fields. "Any man who can't forge the signature of another has had a misspent youth." He pointed to the open window with his cane and went on. "What kind of a bank is this? Windows without bars."

"We have an alarm system that goes on at night," said the confused Trebblecock.

Fields twitched his fake mustache and shook his head.

"But in the light of day a fraud, a miscreant, a double-dealer, a cad and a thief can simply take my money and escape through a toilet window."

"I don't know what to say," said the man with the pince-nez. "Trebblecock, call the police."

"You don't have a bank dick?" asked Fields.

"Yes," said the man softly, "but Mr. Demeringthal phoned in

ill this morning, and I can't see that his presence would have had any effect in this situation."

"Easy for you to say. It's not your money." Fields looked down at Gunther. "Bopped you one, did he?"

"I was taken by surprise," said Gunther. "It will not occur again."

"I admire your zeal if not your pugilistic prowess, but the fault was mine," said Fields. "Never send in a midget to do the job of a sumo wrestler. Unfortunately, we don't have a sumo wrestler, and they're all Japs anyway. Well, Peters, what now? Leap through the window? Run thither and yon in search of the thief? He can't have gotten far."

I looked at Fields, who unclipped his mustache and put it in his pocket. My back throbbed, but I did my best to hide it. I had some pills from Doc Hodgdon in my suitcase. The suitcase was in the trunk of the car alongside Fields's two suitcases and a supply of gin that would be enough to get the entire First Army drunk.

What now, I thought. I was in no shape to chase anyone, and by this time he could be anywhere in Lancaster County. Would I even know him if I saw him? He was tall. Not heavy. That was about it. He had probably dumped his Amish beard and suit by now and was on his way to the next bank. Nothing came to mind. But that had never stopped me before.

"Back to the car," I said.

Fields shook his head in frustration and I helped Gunther to his feet, though it didn't do much for my back. We headed through the bank, followed by the confused Trebblecock.

We left him at the door and the three of us crossed the street, Fields mumbling to himself. We could all see it as we moved toward the car, a shirt board in the front passenger-side window. We stopped; there was a single word neatly printed on it: Altoona.

Chapter Two

Never trust a man who puts cash on the table, or one that doesn't.

Five days earlier, I had come back to my office in the Faraday Building to find a message from W. C. Fields. The note on my desk told me to come to his house immediately.

Violet Gonsenelli stood across from me as I sat looking down at the message she had taken. Violet was dark, young, a beauty with a husband who had been working his way slowly but steadily up the middleweight rankings when the Japanese bombed Pearl Harbor. For at least the duration of the war, Violet planned to continue working as receptionist for both Sheldon Minck, DDS, and Toby Peters, Private Investigator.

Violet's desk was in the reception area, where patients unaware of the danger they were letting themselves in for with Minck the Merciless, and people in need of a cheap, honest, and tenacious detective who could keep his mouth shut, could tell her their immediate needs. There was barely enough room in the reception area for Violet to inch her away around her small desk with the telephone on top of it, but she seemed content.

The only problem with the arrangement was that Shelly's wife, the Wicked Witch of the Southwest, was suspicious about what might develop between her short, fat, myopic, and bald husband and the beautiful receptionist. Shelly assured me he was working on that.

My office was a bit larger than a broom closet. It had once been a small storage room with a window. To get into it, a client had to go through Sheldon Minck's dental chamber of horror, which was why I did my best to meet potential clients at a restaurant or bar.

Not that my office was completely without charm. I had a

desk and chair. If I looked out the window behind my chair I got a beautiful view of the alley six floors down, where my Crosley was parked and being guarded for two bits by the latest in the series of homeless and often alcoholic or semi-mad wanderers who camped for days, weeks, or months in the shells of an abandoned truck and two abandoned cars.

There was barely room enough on the other side of my desk for two wooden chairs. Past the wall behind the chairs lay Shelly's domain. On the same wall, where I could look across at them from my desk, were two items hanging from nails. The first was my license to practice. The second was a photograph of a man, two boys, and a dog. The man was my father. The older boy with the big shoulders and sullen frown was my brother, Phil. The other boy, thinner, his nose already broken once, was me, wearing something that looked like a smile. Our father's head was tilted slightly to one side, toward Phil, and he had his arms around our shoulders. The picture was taken in front of my father's grocery store in Glendale. This was our family. My mother had died giving birth to me. Jeremy Butler, my landlord at the Faraday—who had once been a professional wrestler and was now a self-published poet who bought up shabby houses on the fringes of the city and personally renovated them—felt that Phil blamed me for my mother's death. Our father worked sixteen hours a day and died doing inventory at the age of sixty-four.

I had changed my name from Tobias Pevsner to Toby Peters and dropped out of the college where I had almost finished two years, earning grades that approached the fine edge of despair. Two more reasons for my ill-tempered brother to be upset with me. By then he was an L.A. cop and not yet married. He had come back from the war we hadn't won filled with anger over anything that resembled a threat to the laws of the nation in general and Los Angeles County in particular. His rise in the ranks over the years had come in spite of his frequent abuse of suspects. His marriage and two children had tempered him, but only at home. There were two Phils. One of them had paid my way through those two years of college. To try to make it up to him, I had joined the Glendale Police Department. After a couple of years of being blind-sided by drunks, covering for a drunken partner, I had taken a job on the security staff of Warner Brothers and been fired after a few years by Jack Warner himself after I flattened a famous cowboy star who was doing his best to molest a pre-starlet. I had enough of uniforms and became a private investigator. That was about the time my wife, Anne, left me and got a quick divorce.

"You are a child," she had said. "You've always been one. You're irresponsible and you'll be that way till the day you die. And the problem is that you like being a child. You're never going to grow up and I don't want to be your mother."

She was right. I loved Anne. Still do, though she was about to take her third husband, a rising movie star named Preston Stewart, who was ten years younger than she was. The wedding was in six days. I had been invited to the reception; I don't know why. Probably a mistake, but I was thinking seriously about going, at least to get a good off-screen look at Preston Stewart.

"He's out there," Violet said, jerking a thumb back at the door as I scrutinized the message in front of me.

I looked up at her and glanced over at the painting of the woman with two small boys in her arms. The painting filled the wall to my left. It was a genuine Dali, a gift of the artist. Madonna and two children. Dali and his dead brother on one wall, me and Phil on the other.

"Who's out there?"

"Fields," she said. "Says he has to see you *now*."

I opened my top drawer, swept old letters, flyers, thumbtacks, notes, and this morning's *L.A. Times* into it before I got up. Violet was reaching for the knob when she paused and said, "Beau Jack and Henry Armstrong Thursday."

In the six months Violet had been working for us, I had made five bets with her. She had won them all and had destroyed my opinion of myself as a boxing expert.

"Henry Armstrong," I said. "No contest."

"I'll take Beau Jack, even," she said. "Ten dollars."

I shrugged an okay. I had money in the bank from a job I'd just completed for Fred Astaire and I could handle the loss of a ten spot. I don't know how many more losses to twenty-two-year-old Violet my almost-fifty-year-old ego would take. But the Armstrong bet had to be safe. Beau Jack was a California fighter, the champ—Violet's husband wanted a crack at him when the war was over. But Armstrong was nonstop energy with a great punch. He never seemed to get tired and he never stopped coming at you. He was the most fascinating fighter I had ever seen. All out from the first second to the last. Few could withstand his almost insane attack.

Violet and I went into Shelly's operating room and I closed the office door behind me. The place was fairly tidy, thanks to Violet. The first thing I saw was Shelly straddling someone in his dental chair. A woman's legs were wrapped around him. I couldn't see her but she was groaning.

"Almost," Shelly was saying to her. "Almost got it."

A nicely chewed cigar had been set carefully on the porcelain worktable for the duration of the procedure. His bald head was beaded with sweat and his ample rear writhed under his stained white laboratory coat.

The second thing I saw was a man standing in the corner near the reception room. There was no mistaking him. He wore a matching jacket and slacks, casual shoes, a blue shirt, and no tie. A straw hat rested on his head. I'm around five-foot-nine; Fields was a little shorter. He carried a cane in his hand, which I later discovered was more a prop than a walking aid. At one point during our later flight, he would confide that he had begun smoking at the age of nine and had taken to carrying the cane when he was about fourteen. When in doubt, he would perform some balancing trick with a cigar or his stick or do his trick of putting the cane on his shoulder and then placing his hat on the cane instead of his head. I had seen him do at least five variations on this trick in movies, including a feigned confusion over the loss of the hat and a few seconds of fruitless attempts to retrieve the hat from the elusive end of the cane.

But now the comedian stood entranced by the sight of Shelly and his patient. I moved to his side and whispered, "Mr. Fields, I'm Toby Peters."

"Fine, fine," he said without looking away from Shelly and the struggling woman. "A confident sense of one's identity is the cornerstone of sanity."

Everyone from General Patton to Marlene Dietrich did an imitation of Fields. It was a mainstay impersonation, like doing Cagney or Walter Winchell. But they were all exaggerations. His voice was not as harsh as the mimics made it, his movements not as frantic. He moved with the grace of the great juggler he had been, the great comic juggler I had seen at the Grace Theater when I was a kid.

"Man's a genius," Fields whispered.

Violet shook her head and went through the door back to the reception room.

"And the secretary is as fine an example of youthful pulchritude as I've witnessed in a decade," he added.

"Husband's in the army. Ranked middleweight. I hear he has a temper."

"Most of the husbands I have encountered would merit a similar description," he said, his eyes still on Shelly, who shifted as the woman's legs tightened around him.

"Had almost the exact scene in a short I did, *The Dentist*," Fields confided, pointing at Shelly and his patient. "Studio cut it out. Censored. Said it looked like a sexual act with the woman's legs around me and me astride her on the dental chair as she gurgled in pain. I never forgave the studio and I never forgot the woman."

"There," Shelly roared, with a yank of his right hand.

The woman released Shelly, her legs going limp in the chair. He stepped back and held up a small dental tong clinging to a small bloody tooth. He brandished the specimen at the woman in the chair in a show of triumph. Her eyes were closed and she was doing her best to breathe.

Shelly pushed his thick glasses back on his perspiring nose, placed tongs and tooth on his white table, and returned the cigar to his mouth. He was smiling broadly when he finally noticed me and my client.

"You look almost like W. C. Fields," he said.

"I have the distinct though dubious honor of being William Claude Dukinfield, long known professionally as W. C. Fields," said Fields, extending his hand as Shelly moved forward to shake.

"My patients say I do a perfect imitation of you," said Shelly.

"Shel," I warned, but the rotund dentist in the now-blood-stained smock ignored me.

"Sir," said Fields, "I am not a friend of the dental profession. Too many times have its barbaric practitioners charged me outrageously for piddling procedures. Even took one to court. Lost the case, though I kept my dignity. But I have been watching you and admiring your dedication to the fine art of excruciating extraction."

"Well," said Shelly, going into his W. C. Fields imitation, which I had heard several times before, each time telling Shelly that it was terrible, "I may have received my lugubrious training in the fine art of oral hygiene in Philadelphia, but I have learned to overcome that obstacle and, with the help of candlelight as I read many a tome of dental history and care, became what I am today."

Fields looked at Shelly, showing no expression.

"Pretty good, huh?" asked Shelly, returning to his own voice.

"Pretty good?" Fields said. "I thought I was listening to my own mirror."

"We have to go to my office, Shel," I said, touching Fields's arm and motioning toward my door.

"Besides," said Fields, "I fear the poor woman in your chair has passed out or is dead. If she's dead, I know a good lawyer. Or, I should say, I know a skilled and crafty lawyer. There are no good lawyers, only evil ones, the more evil the better. That is what draws them to their profession."

We moved toward my office and I heard Fields mutter to himself, "Just as the desire to inflict pain drew you to dentistry."

When we squeezed into my office, I caught a glimpse of Shelly smiling and relighting his cigar. The woman in the chair made a convulsive twitch, opened her eyes in panic, and then lay back.

Fields looked around my office and took a seat across from me, glancing back over his shoulder at the photograph of me, my brother, my dad, and the German shepherd.

"Dogs are not partial to me," he said. "They are ungrateful and stupid beasts who have never responded to my gestures of armistice."

"His name was Kaiser Wilhelm," I said. "He was really my brother's dog."

"Should have called him Bismarck," Fields said, putting his hat and cane on the chair next to him. "I'm a great admirer of old Otto."

"Aren't we all," I said.

"I have a series of questions to ask you," he said, pulling a crumpled sheet of paper from his pocket and laying it flat on the desktop. I leaned back. "First," he said, "are you a man who takes pleasure in the occasional or even frequent imbibing of alcohol?"

"I like a beer once in a while," I said.

"What kind?" he shot back, leaning forward.

"Not particular," I answered with a shrug. "Edelbrew."

"What is your critical assessment of the martini?" he asked seriously.

"Sorry," I said. "Just an occasional beer. Most of the time I'm fine with a cold Pepsi."

Fields frowned and made a notation with a short yellow pencil.

"This is not going well," he said softly.

"Sorry," I said.

"Mae West recommended you," he said. "Damned fine writer. Little thing. Only woman besides Fanny Brice who ever successfully upstaged me. Pretends she's a man-eater. Probably still a virgin. I mean West. You agree?"

"I don't list my clients and I don't talk about them," I said.

"Good answer," he said, making another mark. "She says you're an honest man?"

"Is this the office of a dishonest man?" I asked.

He looked around, his eyes pausing on the Dali, and turned back to me. "An unsuccessful dishonest man, mayhaps."

"Mayhaps," I agreed.

"What do you think about marriage?" he asked.

"I tried it once. My wife left me and married a rich man. He died and she's about to marry another one."

"Good," he said, making a check mark. "I too was once married. Still am, though I haven't seen her in years. I believe I drove the woman mad, though we managed to bear a son. Do you have children?"

"No," I said.

"What are your fees?"

"Thirty dollars a day plus expenses," I said.

"Expenses?"

"Food, water, gas, bribes, parking fees, travel, hotels or motels if necessary," I said.

"You get paid twenty-five cash each day as a fee, and expense money as we go," he said, pulling a handful of bills from his pocket. "Here is one day or more in advance."

He handed me a fifty-dollar bill.

I thought I saw a bulge in his other pocket and the hint of the appearance of more bills. I didn't argue. Twenty-five dollars a day was my bottom-line fee. And, besides, this was going to be in cash.

"The case?"

He reached into another pocket and pulled out a letter. He handed it to me. It was postmarked Philadelphia. No return address. I opened it and took out the single sheet. It was typed and read:

Dear Bulbnose:

Humiliation is one thing a man cannot endure and call himself a man. You have humiliated me. I have spent years considering some form of humiliation for you but have come to the conclusion that you are beyond humiliation. However, you are not beyond pain, especially the pain of monetary loss. It is I who have taken your bankbooks. It is I who will take back some of my pride by taking as much of your money as I can. You can try to stop me, you sick old sot, but I'll prove the better man. The task begins in Philadelphia and will not end until I have at least a million dollars.

Lester O. Hipnoodle

"Who's Hipnoodle?"

"Never heard of him," said Fields.

"Sounds like a fake name."

"I am a collector of the odd, unusual, and creative name," said Fields. "No name surprises me. Many delight me. This nom de plume, if it is one, is not of the caliber that merits serious artistic consideration. Be that as it may, I have been, over the course of my long and honored career, stashing money in banks across the country, going back to the days when I joined the Keith circuit. I have kept the bankbooks on a table in my office at home. My secretary has of late attempted to put the books in order. In the midst of so doing, we both noted one morning that the stacks which overflowed elegantly like small works of art had significantly dwindled. There were only about half of them left. And then this letter."

I looked at the letter again and reached for the phone.

"We'll go to your house and take a look," I said. "After a couple of calls."

"Certainly," he replied, turning his hat in his lap and reexamining the Dali painting.

While I was putting my call through, Fields outlined his plan, said I should find a driver to take his car to Philadelphia while he and I flew, and that he trusted none of his servants.

"At least three of them are Nazi spies," he muttered. "And one is definitely a Jap, though he claims to be Chinese."

"Operator," I said into the phone. "I need a number in Philadelphia, Pennsylvania. . . . Thanks."

I held on while I waited.

"Why didn't I think of that?" Fields said. "Too much time in the damned sanitarium. I've got a slight case of mogo-on-the-gogo."

"Yes, operator. Do you have a listing for a Lester O. Hipnoodle?"

I waited while she checked and then I nodded to Fields. We had a bingo. I wrote down the phone number and then asked, "May I have the address?"

She gave it to me and I wrote it on the same envelope.

"Thanks," I said and hung up. And then to Fields: "New number. New address."

I told him the address and the number and, for one of the few times I was to know him over the next week, he sat completely silent and, for an instant, serious.

"That is precisely one block from the home I left when I was a boy," he said. "Hipnoodle is a fiend. He's not only going to get me back to Philadelphia but into the part of my life spent as a vagabond child, the most illustrious in that city since Benjamin Franklin, and the most unpleasant."

"Sorry," I said.

He sighed and said, "What now?"

"Hipnoodle is trying very hard to be found," I said.

I picked up the phone again and once more called the operator in Philadelphia, asking for the police. She gave me the number which I wrote on my envelope, and I thanked her and called. A very bored-sounding man answered.

"I'm calling from Los Angeles," I said. "I represent W. C. Fields. A man in Philadelphia just sent Mr. Fields a threatening letter claiming he has stolen Mr. Fields's bankbooks."

"W. C. Fields?" the bored man repeated as if this might be a rib.

"Yes," I said. "He is sitting right here with me."

"Give me the phone number at Fields's house so we can check this out."

I looked at Fields and mouthed, "Your phone number." Fields gave me the number, which I gave to the Philadelphia cop, plus the address and phone number of the man who called himself Hipnoodle.

"I'll turn this over to a detective," the no-longer-so-bored cop said. "We'll call you back at Mr. Fields's number. Tell Fields that Sergeant Roy McFadden is a great fan of his."

"I'll tell him, Sergeant McFadden," I said and hung up.

"We'd better get over to my place," Fields said. "You know there's a good chance Hipnoodle has already skipped."

"He'd be a moron if he hasn't," said Fields.

"Do you have the name of one bank he has the book for?" I asked. "A local bank would be easier."

"First Federal of Lompoc," he said. "Secretary made a list of the banks and the names under which I made my deposits." He pulled out a sheet of paper. "Used the name Quigley E. Sneersight in Lompoc."

I picked up the phone again and got the First Federal Bank of Lompoc. A woman answered.

"I'm a depositor with a problem," I said. "My name is Sneersight, Quigley E. Someone has stolen my bankbook and I don't want them to get into my account."

"I see," said the woman. "But how are we to know that you are the real Mr. Snoozeshot—"

"Sneersight," I corrected.

"Sneersight," she agreed. "If you come to the bank with sufficient identification, we might be able to do something. If, however, someone comes into the bank with your bankbook, presents proper identification, and has a signature that coincides with that on the account, we have no recourse but to honor the transaction."

"Can I talk to the bank president?"

"I am the president," she said.

"You think I'll get the same answer at other banks?" I asked.

"I would assume so."

"Thanks," I said and hung up. I looked at Fields and said, "I suppose you don't have identification as Sneersight?"

"None at all," he confirmed.

"If the Philadelphia police don't find Hipnoodle, we have to get to him before he gets all your money, or we can go to all the banks on your list and try to make the withdrawal, telling them you lost your bankbook. Without identification, that might cause some problems, but I guess we can try it."

"We pursue the rascal," Fields said, rising. "Even if it does mean going back to Philadelphia. If we don't trap Hipnoodle in his opium den, we'll try to get to the banks before him. Trap him or convince the banks to let me make withdrawals or close the accounts."

"How many banks?" I asked.

Fields shrugged. "This is not a case of the potential loss of ill-gotten lucre," he said, rising and patting his straw hat back on his head, "but of a man's savings, earned by painful hours of learning to juggle in frozen lofts and worse hotel rooms. We're talking about dozens of banks."

I nodded.

"You have a weapon?" he asked.

"Yes."

"Bring it."

I said I would. I didn't add that I had been the worst shot in the Glendale Police Department and had gotten decidedly worse since.

"Well, enough of this shilly-shallying, let's go to my house where I can pack and, if need be, be on our way to the scene of the crime before the day ends."

He led the way back into Shelly's office and looked over at the victim, who still sat in the chair. Her groans had turned to an eerie, distant low moan. Shelly was puffing away and washing his instruments in the sink.

"Man's a genius," Fields whispered to me behind his hand. "Don't want to praise him too highly. Might go to his head."

"I think we got the right tooth," Shelly said, turning to us and wiping his hands on his bloody smock. His eyes were huge behind his thick lenses.

"A consummation devoutly to be wished," said Fields. He tipped his hat to the barely conscious woman and headed for the door, while I told Shelly it looked like I was going out of town for a few days on business.

"Understand perfectly," Shelly said, reverting to his abysmal Fields imitation. "I'll hold down the corpus delicti."

In the reception room Violet smiled up at us from her desk, where she was confirming appointments for Shelly's patients. It would ever be a mystery to me why anyone allowed themselves a second visit to Sheldon Minck's Tower of London, but they did. Occasionally.

"Pleasure to meet you," Fields said.

"I'll write to my husband and tell him I met you," she said. "He thinks you're funny."

"Armstrong takes Beau Jack, ten bucks straight up," I reminded her.

Violet nodded solemnly; Fields and I left.

"Note," he said as we closed the door and stood on the railed landing of the sixth floor of the Faraday Building, "she said her husband likes me. It has been a source of irritation that women, as a gender, are not particularly responsive to my wit. They prefer a popinjay ballet dancer like Chaplin to honest misogyny."

"Hard to understand," I said, remembering that my former wife, Anne, had refused to see Fields movies with me, claiming that they made no sense, weren't amusing, were nasty to women and small children. I had agreed with her, but I still thought he was funny.

Fields moved to the railing and held his straw hat to his head to insure that some indoor breeze wouldn't take it down six flights to the lobby.

I was about a dozen feet away from him now and had a good look at the great man. I knew he was over sixty and that he had looked pretty much the same in movies for the last twenty years as he did now. His stomach was a bit larger, his nose probably a little more red, though I had never seen it in color before today.

"Long drop," he said.

The Faraday echo answered, "Drop."

Fields turned around, pleased.

"You came up on the elevator?" I asked.

"Indeed," he said, heading for the black steel cage. "Trip took almost as long as a Zambesi safari I was once on with Applejack Strainfinger, the great one-armed white hunter. Almost got me killed."

We got in the elevator. I pressed the button and we started slowly down.

"Rhino charged right at me when I wasn't looking. Applejack had a mastodon of an elephant gun which he had trouble bringing to his remaining good shoulder. The rhino stampeded closer and I gave serious consideration to addressing ancient and all-too-often fickle gods. The native bearers had all fled. It was just me, Applejack, and the rhino. When the beast was no more than two pool-tables' distance away, Applejack fired. The beast fell at my feet. Left the carcass to the natives, took the horn, had it pulverized into an aphrodisiac which dissolved admirably in a martini."

The noises of the Faraday accompanied us as we slowly ground downward in the steel-barred elevator cage. Arguing, musical instruments, laughter, singing, the clacking of an occasional typewriter came from offices on each floor. The Faraday was not the class location of downtown L.A. Just off the corner of Main and Hoover, it was home, often a very temporary home, to talent agents, jewelry distributors, quacks, music teachers, baby and publicity photographers, and a fortune-teller named Juanita the Seer, who was standing before the elevator when it came to its usual jerky stop on the main floor.

"W. C. Fields," she said as I opened the door. She held out her hand.

"Don't," I said, but it was too late. Juanita had touched him.

"Madame," he said gallantly as he stepped out, removing his straw hat, "I can say that, outside of the stage itself, particularly a certain Kitty Majestic who did a magic act, I have never witnessed a female as confidently clad."

Juanita was somewhere around Fields's age. She had gone through three husbands back in New York. Her second husband had been half owner of a trio of successful men's shops. Juanita was financially set, but a few years after her third marriage, to a candy distributor in the Bronx, she got the calling. She claimed that one morning she just woke up and knew things. Husband number three died two weeks later in a subway accident, and Juanita moved west.

And here she stood, ready for work, gypsy costume of yellow flowing skirt, billowing red blouse covered with a repeating pattern of fruit ranging from mangoes to bananas. She wore a massive string of multicolored stones around her neck and a turban of gold. Her earrings matched the stones in her necklace, and her dark lipstick came close to the cherries on her blouse.

"Confidentially—" Juanita said. "And Toby knows this—I wear all this stuff for the customers. They want a little show, a little color with a glimpse of their future. So, I've got a table, crystal ball, the whole *chozzerai.*"

"Garbage," said Fields. "Picked up a smattering of the Yiddish tongue in my sojourns."

"You got it," she said.

"We've got to go," I said, gesturing Fields onward toward the door, but he stood watching Juanita, who touched the stones around her neck and said, "He or she is dead."

"Dead?" said Fields.

"Let's go," I urged.

"The one you're looking for," she said.

"Hipnoodle?" he asked.

"Not yet, but soon. And another one. Two dead men. One's been dead for some time. The other soon will be. See it as sure as I see you now. There will be a quest," she said matter-of-factly. "Then you'll find out the one who's sending you on your journey is dead, has been for a while, can't say exactly how long. Wait, another one's gonna die. That's three. This death stuff is creepy. Gives me the *shpilkes.* Sorry, gotta go now, got a couple of Mexican brothers upstairs waiting for advice on how to stay out of the way of the cops."

She closed the elevator door and headed up.

"What in the name of Godfrey Daniel was she talking about?" Fields asked.

"I've come to believe in Juanita," I admitted as we walked across the lobby, the elevator rising behind us. "The trouble is that I can't figure out what she's telling me till it's over and too late."

"Cassandra," Fields said, nodding his head in understanding. "I too have witnessed soothsayers, one particularly in Mozambique who had such powers, probably from indulging in too much catawhowoo, a beverage so pungent and alcoholic that even I had trouble consuming more than a few moderately sized gourds of the brew. That soothsayer could truly see the future, but only when he was completely soused. Man couldn't hold his liquor."

His car was parked at the curb, a large Cadillac with a driver. We got in the back, closed the door, and Fields reached for the built-in bar as we drove away.

The driver was big, his head covered in thick, darkly matted hair, his neck a cord of muscles.

It wasn't far to DeMille Drive, where Fields rented a large house across the street from Cecil B. DeMille, an early settler after whom the street was named. The house and street were on a hill and when we stepped out of the car and closed the door, Fields grunted, "Gonna fire that driver. The Chimp's got a bad attitude. Good solid Christian, cross around his neck, the whole business. Disapproval in his eyes and an accent he claims doesn't exist but I'm sure is German."

We walked up a tiled path with arched trellises covered with flowers. The path was about fifty feet long.

"My Chinaman keeps the posies fresh," he said. "She's away visiting her sister for a few weeks. My hope is to conclude this business before her return."

"Chinaman?" I asked.

"Carlotta, my companion, my loyal rock in the midst of a turbulent sea of human thievery, chicanery, and wars both personal and national. She wore a Chinese outfit one of the first times I saw her. Called her Chinaman ever since. She retaliates by calling me Woody. My friends call me Bill, and the world at large is expected to call me Mr. Fields. Home."

We were standing in front of a big dark wooden door. He was fumbling for his keys when it opened. A large man in a black suit stood within. His face and body were definite and unfortunate reminders of a long-necked bird.

"How did you know I was here?" Fields demanded. "Spying again?"

The man didn't answer. He turned and disappeared into the house.

"Can't remember his real name," Fields confided in a whisper that echoed through the house, "but I call him the Baltimore Oriole. I've fired him and hired him and the Chimp at least six times. They display none of the respect I demand of my servants. I won't tolerate it, but it's the one thing I admire about the creatures."

Fields placed his cane gently into a hollowed-out elephant's leg and hung his straw hat next to about a dozen other hats on pegs in the front hall. We moved to the left. I expected a living room, and I think it was originally intended as one. Along one wall was a half-size bowling alley. In the center of the room was a pool table. There was a cue shelf on the near wall which included a variety of both straight and oddly twisted cues. The high chairs that are found along the walls of many pool halls lined the walls of the room. The ceiling above the pool table was definitely sagging. Fields caught me looking at it.

"Fella I rent this place from says I should repair it," he said. "I say it's his responsibility. We'll end it all with swords, pistols, or in court."

"What's upstairs, over the table?" I asked.

"Ping-Pong table," he said. "Best money can buy."

He led me through a bizarre labyrinth of rooms on the way upstairs, including a workout room with weights and a steam box. Another bedroom had nothing in it but a barber's chair.

"Sleep in that sometimes," he said, nodding at the chair. "Go out for haircuts. I've always had trouble sleeping, from the time I was a kid. I can usually sleep on a pool table or in a barber chair. Beds and I are in a constant state of combat."

Finally, we arrived at a far-flung chamber that Fields said was his office. He found a key, opened the door, and we stepped in. He closed the door behind us and moved to a battered roll-top desk. He rolled the top up. On the desk was a microphone, and next to it was a square speaker with a series of buttons.

"Place is completely wired, even the pathway to the house. I can hear what's said anywhere and, through hidden speakers, talk to people in any room."

He looked at me with pride and I made the mistake of asking why.

"Why? Thieves, glad-handers, salesmen, my own servants who might say dastardly things behind my back. Once caught a pair of dinner guests insulting me. I came on the speaker and told them there'd be no mooched dinner that night and they could turn around and go to the Tastee Pup."

Fields patted his microphone and smiled with satisfaction.

"And there," he said, "is the table where I kept my bankbooks." Twenty or more bankbooks were still strewn across the table.

"I figured it for an inside job. Fired all the servants except the Chimp and the Baltimore Oriole, the most likely suspects," he said. "I want to keep an eye and ear on them."

Fields went into a cubbyhole in his desk and came out with a black folder, which he handed to me.

"List of banks, names I used. Most of the amounts. Secretary put it together before the bastard took my bankbooks. Never used a bank in Philadelphia, though. I'm eccentric but I'm not crazy."

I took the folder, opened it, and found three pages of single-spaced, neatly typed columns listing the name of the bank, the town or city, and the name he used to make the deposit. A few of the accounts were actually in his name, but most of them were under names like Ogle P. Thurp, Dedalus Krim, Mahatma Kane Jeeves, and Cormorant Beecham the Third. The amounts, which seemed to vary from a few hundred to as much as ten thousand dollars, were lined up with each bank name. A few of the amounts were missing.

"And there," Fields said, pointing to the wall next to his desk, "is my map of the war." I looked at the map on the wall. It was covered in thumbtacks of different colors. There was a blotch of red over most of France. Fields looked at the map with pride.

"Secret code," he whispered. "I can predict the progress of the war from troop movements, sizes of armies, number of jeeps, the seasons. Red spot on France is my own blood. Stuck myself with a tack. Bled all over France for my country. Like some advice?"

I nodded and Fields continued to whisper.

"Hoard. Canned goods. I've got thousands of cans in the cellar. I tried eggs. Bought thousands. Don't particularly like the damned things myself and they all rotted. Showed them to Jack Barrymore before he died and he asked where they came from. From a hen's ass, I told him. I miss that son of a bitch Barrymore."

Fields turned away from me and looked at his war map. The phone rang. Fields was lost in thoughts of John Barrymore, rotting eggs, or the progress of General Patton.

"Phone," I said.

"Ah, yes," he said, coming out of his reverie and moving to his desk, where he picked up the phone.

"William Claude Dukinfield's residence," he said. "Yes, W. C. Fields. And you are?" He got his answer and covered the mouthpiece with his palm. "Philadelphia police." He looked visibly shaken. "You know how much I stole from Philadelphia merchants when I was a boy? They've probably been after me for decades."

I took the phone. "My name is Peters," I said. "I work for Mr. Fields."

"Detective Belcher," he said. He had a high voice and seemed to be in a hurry. "We checked your address and your Hipnoodle. No clothes, no bags, no food. Landlady says he called and reminded her that he's paid up till the end of April and she should leave the place alone. If he comes back, she says she'll call me. I doubt it. Sorry."

"Thanks, Belcher," I said.

"Belcher?" Fields asked. "Ask him his first name."

"Mr. Fields wants to know your first name."

"Gus," he said. "Augustus."

I repeated the name. Fields beamed, took out a notebook, and dropped some bills in the process. He made a note in the book, probably Augustus Belcher's name, put it back in his pocket, and picked up the fallen bills.

"Let me know if we can help," Belcher said.

I thanked Belcher and hung up.

"You always carry pocketsful of money?" I asked.

"Always," he confided. "Even in my pajamas. Somewhere in the neighborhood of ten thousand dollars. Never know when I might have to go out the back door fast and flee the state or the country."

I didn't pursue it.

"We'd better go to Philadelphia," I said.

"I'll have my secretary take care of the airline," he said. "Already checked. Plane going out in the right direction tonight. Questions?"

"How do I get back to my office?"

"My driver'll take you. Leave him the address of your residence and we'll pick you up at nine and head for the airport."

Fields leaned over to his microphone, flipped a switch, and said loudly, "My man, stop searching the upholstery for silver dollars and come back here to drive Mr. Peters to his office. Then leave the vehicle where he tells you and return by trolley."

"Okay, Mr. Fields," a voice crackled sullenly over the speaker.

"Modern technology," he said, turning off the system. "I remember when Philadelphia went from gaslight to electricity. I was a small child. My father in his ever-infinite wisdom proclaimed with the remnant of his Cockney accent that the whole thing wouldn't work and the city would be wise to leave the gas vents where they were. Met Edison once. Deaf son of a bitch almost drove me nuts. All he wanted to talk about was strip mining and the weather in Florida. You'll get us a driver who can drive the Cadillac across the country and meet us in Philadelphia?"

"Got just the operative," I said.

"I'll pick you up at nine in the Lincoln," he said. "Your address?"

I gave it to him and he wrote it and my home phone number on his pad.

"Nine," he repeated, pouring himself a glass of clear liquid from a thermos on his desk.

"Nine," I agreed. "By then your car should already be on the way to Philadelphia."

The Cadillac was waiting at the end of the tiled path outside. The Chimp looked like a sulking primate in the front seat. I didn't say anything to him on the ride to the Faraday.

Twenty minutes later I was in my Crosley, waving good-bye to the latest alley resident behind the Faraday after having given him a dollar to watch the Caddy and promising another when I saw him next. I had called No-Neck Arnie the mechanic, told him where to pick up the Caddy and what to do with it.

In the lobby of the Faraday I ran into Jeremy Butler, landlord, poet, former wrestler—close to three hundred pounds of bald power who always spoke softly and a little sadly, resigned to the inevitable decline of humanity. His tone, however, changed when he talked about his wife, Alice Pallis Butler, who almost matched him in size and strength, and his baby daughter, Natasha, dark-haired, smiling, delicate, and beautiful.

Jeremy was wearing a black turtleneck sweater. He told me he was working on a poem about the aromas of the Faraday. I told him it sounded like a great idea. I told him I didn't know when I'd be back, but it probably wouldn't be more than a week or two. We shook hands and I was on my way to Mrs. Plaut's boardinghouse on Heliotrope.

Chapter Three

Never show up for a job interview in bare feet.

Talking Gunther into driving to Philadelphia was no problem. I knew he was looking for an excuse to go somewhere, anywhere, to get away from the aggressive female publicity agent at R.K.O. who was coming close to smothering him. His full-sized girl-friend was going to move to Vermont. She had told Gunther that she was seeing a sociology professor socially.

Gunther had not complained. Instead, he had plunged into his translating work. I told him No-Neck Arnie was already putting the blocks on the pedals and filling the gas tank.

"You were confident of my doing this," he said as we stood in his room at Mrs. Plaut's.

"Reasonably," I said.

"You were right," he said. "I shall pack instantly, inform some people I am working for, and Mrs. Plaut, naturally. How shall I find you in Philadelphia?"

"Call a Detective Gus Belcher," I said, writing Belcher's number on a note pad on Gunther's desk. "I'll check in with him."

I went to my room, next to Gunther's. Somehow I had gotten by Mrs. Plaut, who usually caught me before I reached the stairway.

Dash, the big orange cat who sort of lived with me, was sitting near the refrigerator in my room, waiting. He blinked once as I turned on the lights. The room was the same as always except at night, when I'd move the mattress to the floor where I slept because of my bad back. I threw my jacket on the small sofa against the wall with the hand-stitched pillow saying, "God Bless Our Happy Home," lying against one arm. Near Dash, by the window, was my table and two chairs.

I checked the time on my Beech-Nut Gum clock on the wall. I had plenty of time. I fed Dash some milk and a can of tuna. I told him I'd leave the window open. Dash could fend for himself. He had sometimes disappeared into the night or day and not returned for a week or more. I didn't figure I owned him. We just roomed together.

I joined Dash for lunch, eating a bowl of Wheaties with what was left of the milk. Then I packed. Took me five minutes. I don't have much and my suitcase is small. It had seen better years. The suitcase had belonged to my father who, as far as I could tell, had never used it. I had banged it up a few times, but it was in pretty good shape and genuine leather.

I used the pay phone on the landing to call Anita Maloney at Mack's Diner and told her I'd be gone for a while and where I was going. She had worked and owned the place on her own since Mack Chirikides, her second husband, had died. Her first had been a hunk named Ozzie, who she had divorced. Then after a few years at Scripps College for Women, she got the acting fever and did her best to avoid casting couches while she lived with a guy named Harold who she caught necking in a car with her mother. Then she met Mack. He wasn't young, but he had been honest and faithful till he died.

Anita had been my date at the senior prom. Those were better days. Almost thirty years later I had met her again at Mack's Diner, and now we were in our second month of what might turn out to be something. It was already good. I hadn't quite forgotten Anne, but Anita, who had been through a bad marriage of her own, was just making it a lot easier.

"Busy?" I asked.

"A few regulars and a drunk who wandered in," she said. "I'll give him some coffee and head him down the street. So you're going to Philadelphia with W. C. Fields?"

"Yup," I said.

"If he's anything like he is in the movies, he'd drive me bughouse in less than a day," she said.

"He is," I said. "I'll try not to go bughouse."

"Call me as soon as you get back?" she asked.

"Before I unpack my bags," I promised.

We said good-bye and I turned on the radio, watched Dash clean himself, and heard a man's deep voice tell me that Old Gold cigarettes were now protected by Mellow Apple Honey. Then I listened to Jessica Dragonette sing a Victor Herbert medley. It was interrupted by the entrance of Mrs. Plaut. She never knocked. Her motto was clear. People shouldn't be ashamed of what they were doing in their rooms in her house, nor should they engage in acts for which they should be ashamed. The bathroom was the proper place for dressing and undressing.

She stood in the doorway. Dash made a low growling sound and disappeared through the window. Mrs. Plaut was about a foot taller than Gunther, who claimed three feet. She was thin as a chicken's leg and deafer than Edison, but she had the heart and determination of a worthy heavyweight contender, even if she didn't always grasp the situation the way others did.

"Things to discuss," she said.

In one hand was more of her dreaded manuscript, the endless book she was writing about the history of her family. Lined sheets with neatly printed words. She handed the pages to me. I took them. For some reason she had decided, in the wisdom of her eighty-plus years, that I was both a book editor and an exterminator, these being the reasons that the police and other unsavory individuals were frequently looking for me.

"I'm going out of town for a week or two," I shouted, seeing that she wasn't wearing the hearing aid Gunther and I had given her. "So is Mr. Wherthman."

"You're both paid up," she said, folding her arms. "If you're going on vacation, I suggest the Carlsbad Caves. That's where the departed Mister and I honeymooned."

"I'll take the pages with me and read them at night," I shouted, putting the sheets on the table.

She nodded. I had given her the answer she wanted, but she didn't budge.

"Stamps," she said.

I went into my top drawer and pulled out the quota of ration stamps I had picked up two days earlier: red stamps for meat, canned fish, butter, and cheese; blue stamps for canned goods and processed foods. She pocketed the stamps and remained rooted.

"Next, the cat," she said.

"You said he could come and go as long as he didn't go into any other part of the house," I reminded her.

"I still think he tried to eat Simon, gave him a nervous breakdown."

She had a pet bird in a cage in her rooms on the first floor. The bird was something that resembled a canary. The name she gave the fowl was constantly changing.

"It wasn't Dash," I said.

"Cat doesn't like me. I don't like the cat," she said. "Plain and simple."

"I'll see to it that he doesn't get out of the room," I said.

"And doesn't poo or pee on the furniture," she said.

"He does that outside," I shouted.

"He should do that outside," she said. "One more thing."

"Yes," I said, resigned to my lot until Gunther or Fields arrived to save me.

"You have a phone call."

She stepped out of the way and I hurried down the hall to the dangling phone. Whoever called had probably hung up, but . . . "Peters," I said.

"Don't go," came a voice that sounded as if it were being filtered through a bag of seashells.

"Go?"

"With Fields," the voice said. "You go, you die. Both of you."

"Hipnoodle?" I asked.

There was no answer.

"I saw the letter you sent Fields," I said. "I thought you wanted him to come after you."

"Come to Philadelphia and you both die."

He hung up and so did I, as the doorbell rang. Mrs. Plaut ambled down the stairs and opened the door. Fields stood in the doorway wearing his straw hat. He doffed it to Mrs. Plaut and said, "Good evening, madam."

"Fields," she said. "Mister and I saw you on the stage in Marietta, Georgia, back in '09."

Fields smiled and looked up at me on the landing. He stepped in and Mrs. Plaut closed the door.

"You juggled," she said. "Lots of stuff, boxes, hats, Indian clubs. Ad said you were the world's greatest juggler. You were."

"Still am," he said with pride. "Though there is little call for or appreciation of that skill in the modern world."

"I agree," she said. "Don't care much for seeing young girls with almost nothing on."

Fields looked up at me, perplexed.

"I'll be right down," I called and headed for my room. "You'd better shout if you expect Mrs. Plaut to come close to understanding what you're saying."

I checked the bed, picked up my suitcase, turned off the light, and went to Gunther's room to leave a note telling him that I had left. Then I went downstairs and found Mrs. Plaut and W. C. Fields seated in the living room. None of the other boarders were there. She had poured him and herself a glass of her famous elderberry *saft*.

"A dose of gin might give it an extra tang," he shouted.

"Fine by me," Mrs. Plaut said.

Fields took a flask from his back pocket and poured a generous amount into his glass, and Mrs. Plaut's.

I stood in the doorway, waiting. They drank.

"Exhilarating," she said with a smile, and emptied the glass.

"Not bad," Fields agreed.

"I'll give you a bottle to take with you," she said, getting up and moving past me.

"Admirable female," Fields said, finishing his drink. "Little twig of a thing should be staggering around the room, unable to locate a *saft* bottle or firm furniture."

"She comes from hardy stock," I said as Mrs. Plaut returned with an unopened bottle of *saft* and handed it to Fields, who had risen.

He took the bottle, stood back a few feet, threw the bottle in the air and, as it came down, took off his hat and threw that in the air.

"Good high ceiling," he said, juggling the hat, bottle, and the empty glass from which Mrs. Plaut had downed her *saft* and gin.

"Time was," he mumbled as the bottle went back in the air, "I could keep five separate items afloat and every so often pretend one of them was getting away from me. Now . . ."

He gathered the bottle, glass, and hat in, placed the hat on his head and the bottle and glass on the table, and bowed to Mrs. Plaut, who clapped.

"I take it then," he shouted, "that you have continued to be a loyal fan."

"No," said Mrs. Plaut. "I don't go to your movies. I don't see anything funny about them. You should go back to juggling."

Fields's smile froze as he strode past Mrs. Plaut and motioned for me to follow him. I did. When we got out on the porch, I told him the car was taken care of and would meet us in Philadelphia. Fields turned toward the door.

"Should have bashed the old bat with this bottle of elder-berry *saft*," he growled.

"I just got a call," I said.

"Strangling her might be called for," he mumbled.

"Caller said he'd kill us if we went after Hipnoodle," I said.

"Probably thinks Chaplin's funny," he said.

"Did you hear me?" I said. "Someone just called me and threatened to kill us if we go after Hipnoodle."

Fields went down the stairs. I followed, my father's suitcase in hand.

"If I counted all the times I've been threatened with murderous mayhem," he said, "I'd need all my fingers and thumbs and most of yours. Let's go, Peters. The game's afoot."

The Chimp drove the car to the airport, looking at us sullenly in the rearview mirror.

"He wants to drive the Caddy to Philadelphia," Fields explained. "I barely trust him to ferry me within the confines of Los Angeles County."

The plane ride to Philadelphia, with a changeover in Chicago, was reasonably uneventful—as uneventful, I discovered, as any trip with Fields. I sat by the window. He sat next to me on the aisle. I don't like airplanes. They crash and kill people. I like trains, buses, and cars. They crash and kill people too, but I feel some sense of control and connection to the earth. A crash on the ground is fast. Split second. No time to think. You lose control or get blind-sided and you're dead or in the hospital. In a plane you have all the time it takes from the moment you know you're going to crash till you hit the ground. I was miserable, but I kept my mouth shut and looked out of the window when Fields wasn't talking.

He had brought a huge thermos with him. "Filled with pineapple juice," he confided. "Only thing I drink when I'm making a movie or chasing thieves."

The thermos was filled with martinis. I knew it and everyone on the plane who knew who he was probably strongly suspected it. People came for autographs, which Fields generously gave, juggling a cup of his "pineapple juice" in one hand as he signed everything from autograph books to airline-ticket envelopes. One man in a business suit, at whom the great man beamed with pleasure as the plane suddenly and loudly dropped a few feet and I closed my eyes, actually had a copy of Fields's *Fields for President.*

Fields signed with a flourish and the man went back to his seat, examining the signature.

"Book sold like hotcakes," Fields confided in me as we hit another small pocket of turbulence and I wished I had gone with Gunther.

We hit frequent turbulence. None of it seemed to register on Fields, who never fastened his seat belt.

"No one buys hotcakes," Fields said almost to himself. "People buy cars, cans of tuna, millions of bottles of beer and scotch, hats, bacon and eggs, but not hotcakes. You can get them free at Shrine breakfasts and Sundays at church socials. You can make them at home for practically nothing. No one buys hotcakes and no one bought my book. Damned funny book too. You should read it."

"I will," I said, feeling decidedly queasy.

"A small libation will help your distress," Fields said.

What the hell. I took the cup, sipped at the gin. He urged me on. I finished the drink and handed him the cup.

"There," he said with a satisfied smile. "Feel better?"

I felt worse, but I said, "much better" and closed my eyes.

Fields had brought a copy of Dickens's *Great Expectations* and as I sat back in fear, he chuckled.

"Read this book maybe six times," he said. "Scene of Pip describing his home life is one of the great comic monologues of all time. 'Connubial missile.' Says his parents used him as a 'connubial missile,' throwing him at each other. Strikes me as a proper use of a child."

I grunted.

In the waiting area of Midway Airport in Chicago I felt sick. The martini had definitely not had a curative effect on my stomach. I left Fields to fend for himself, talk to passersby who recognized him, sign his name, and generally pontificate. After a few minutes in the men's room, I felt a little better and returned to Fields well before our plane was due to leave. He had purchased a newspaper, the *Chicago Sun*, and was reading the sports page.

"Says here," he said as I sat next to him, "Phil Rizzuto, the Yankee shortstop, is going in the navy. Plan is to replace him with George "Snuffy" Sternweis. Snuffy Sternweis, great name. Doomed to success."

"You're a baseball fan?" I asked, not really wanting to talk or look over at him and his thermos.

"A fan of the odd," he said. "Sports figures, particularly baseball players, have great names. Dizzy and Daffy Dean. Grover Cleveland Alexander. Boxers don't come close. They're always called 'Killer' or 'Battler' or 'Hurricane.' An occasional gem will emerge from one of the minor sports like football or tennis. Bronco Nagurski, Jinx Falkenberg."

I nodded. We got back on the plane in the middle of a Fields monologue about a kumquat farm he once owned in Florida.

"Not far from Homosassa," he said. "Crop flourished, then in one night, every damn kumquat was eaten by the alligators. I fenced it in and turned it into an alligator farm. Once had to wrestle one of the filthy beasts. I considered it a draw. We both lived. Couldn't get the smell of alligator out of my clothes for a week. Sold the ugly lizards to a shoe company, a luggage company, and a woman's handbag company. Made a tidy profit. Donated some of it to an organization dedicated to the eradication of all animals known to have and capable of killing human beings. Would have given them more if they could have taught the beasts to confine their attacks to Methodists."

Fields slept all the rest of the way to Philadelphia, clutching his thermos to his breast, snoring loudly. He had put a white salve on his nose and declared that he almost felt as if he were in a barber chair before he closed his eyes and was asleep instantly.

When we landed I was hazy from lack of sleep. Fields woke with a smile, stretched, wiped the salve off with his handkerchief, and declared that he was hungry "as an alligator deprived of kumquats or human appendages."

"Philadelphia," he declared as we went down the steps which had been rolled over to the plane. "City of my youth. Birth site of me and the nation. Home of the Liberty Bell and Independence Hall and Murphy's Saloon. Never thought I'd be back here again."

We ate breakfast at a counter in the airport terminal. I had tea to settle my stomach, scrambled eggs, and toast. Fields asked if they had shrimp or crabmeat salad. The uniformed woman behind the counter said, "No, what we got, we got on the menu. That's it."

Fields ordered two pieces of toast with no butter or margarine and two strips of bacon. He shook his thermos and told me that we needed a liquor store almost immediately. I nodded, ate, and said we'd stop if one was open this early.

"Drat," he said. "For an ecstatic moment, I forgot we were in Philadelphia. You know my entire family is buried here?"

"Mine's in Glendale," I said.

"Difficult choice," Fields said, pouring what must have been close to the last of his martini supply.

He ate one piece of toast. Took a bite of the other. He ate one strip of bacon and left the other. I felt better after we had eaten. I made a call. Detective Gus Belcher was in his station house. I got him on the phone and he told me to come over with Fields. I took the address, retrieved my employer, and found a taxi whose driver knew where we could find a liquor store open in the morning. We stopped, got what Fields needed, and proceeded to the station, paper bag of bottles and olives in his lap.

"Give the driver a generous tip," he said.

"Easier if you paid him," I said. "Then I don't have to bill you for the taxi."

"True, but I'm sure you would be more generous than I," Fields said.

I knew he had stuffed all of his pockets with cash. On the plane and in the Chicago airport, I had seen the bulges and the tips of crumpled bills. He was a flashing target for pickpockets, but I was sure that, even dead drunk, Fields could sense the presence of anyone who might dare approach his cash.

Fields glared glumly at his hometown as we drove.

"Damned place never changes," he said. "Cities are supposed to change. Get modern. Tear down buildings, put other ones up, engage in progress."

When we got to the station, the driver removed my suitcase and Fields's traveling bag from the trunk. Fields had a couple of suitcases in the trunk of the car Gunther was driving. Gunther was small, but his foot was heavy. I figured him well past Arizona by now.

The station house looked like it had been built by veterans of the Revolutionary War. It was two stories, made of red brick carrying about a hundred and fifty years of dirt.

"Life is a mockery," Fields declared as we looked at the building. "More than several are the times in my early youth when I was accused, brought to, and lectured by blue-uniformed officers in this very building. Entering, which we must, will be hell."

Inside we faced a corridor. On our right was an open door. The sign on the door said: Complaints and Inquiries.

We entered. Several people were sitting in a tired daze on the bench that ran along the wall of the stone floored room. A uniformed cop, too old for military service, sat behind a high desk, writing a report and singing.

"I'll be walking with my baby down honeymoon lane. Soon, soon, soon. By the moon, moon, moon."

I asked for Gus Belcher and the cop stopped singing, nodded, and picked up his phone. He looked a little like Andy Devine and even sounded like him, especially when he sang.

"Third door on your left," he said after making the call. "Aren't you W. C. Fields?"

"Thurston W. Ptomaine," said Fields. "I've been told the resemblance to Fields is almost uncanny. Alas, I'm a music critic for the *Tuscaloosa Times-Herald-Tribune-Star*."

The cop shrugged, went back to his report, and began humming.

We headed for Gus Belcher's office.

"The one thing that convinces me of the existence of the devil," said Fields, "is his whispering to Eve that she and her hubby might enjoy singing a ditty or two. The unholy practice has been passed down to us for more than five thousand years. I've thrown the Chinaman out for singing. And the devil has tricked me into renting a house next to Deanna Durbin. No amount of threats or shouts will get the vapid creature to stop caterwauling on her veranda."

Gus Belcher shared a small office with three other detectives, each of whom had a desk with a chair in front of it. On the wall was a reproduction of a painting showing the signing of the Declaration of Independence. Behind each desk, notes, posters, and photographs were tacked to the wall. The other three detectives were out. Belcher rose, held out his hand, introduced himself, and we shook all around after we put down our suitcases.

Belcher was around forty, cop physical-profile number two, like my brother, Phil, L.A.P.D. lieutenant. Built like a medium-sized tank, his hair was dark and curly and looked as if he had just been to a barber. Nose almost as flat as mine. Dark face reminding me of a bulldog that had once chased me across the lawn and over the wall around the estate of a gangster. Belcher's trousers and sports jacket were clean, dark, and they matched. His shirt was starched and his tie was wide, dark-blue and red stripes.

"Not gonna find much here," he said, sitting down and pointing to the chairs in front of us. We sat. "Hipnoodle—for chrissake, I feel like an idiot even repeating the name. The suspect, as I told you, is gone. No trace. Nothing. See that *in* box?"

Fields and I looked at the wooden box at the corner of his desk. It was piled high with folders, reports, letters, and notes.

"I've got no time to give you any more help unless the suspect returns home and the landlady calls me," said Belcher. "You want to look for him, be my guest. Go talk to the landlady, look at the apartment, talk to the neighbors, storekeepers. I don't have the time. Come back to me or Mickey Knox, my partner, if this Hipnoodle actually gets his hands on your money or if he kills somebody or commits a felony in Philadelphia. You get the picture?"

"Yes," I said.

Fields had said nothing. He sat stiffly, his eyes on the painting of the signing of the Declaration of Independence.

"One more thing," I said. "We're going to be at a hotel, the . . ."

"Continental, if it still exists and has a vestige of gentility," Fields said.

"It does," said Belcher.

"A Gunther Wherthman, Mr. Fields's driver, will be arriving in a couple of days. I gave him your number and said you'd tell him where to find us."

"No problem," said Belcher, glancing at the pile in his *in* box and putting on a pair of half glasses he pulled from his inside pocket. When he made the move, I saw the holster and gun under the jacket. We shook hands again and Fields and I took off.

Fields looked at everyone in the corridor as we walked, a look of anxiety on his face which turned to near panic when we passed a uniformed officer or someone who looked like a detective.

"What's wrong?" I asked as we reached the front door.

"Thought I might run into one of the constabulary that had arrested me as a boy," he explained. "Probably still warrants out for me for stealing fruit and sweaters."

The sky rumbled with the threat of rain.

"The police who arrested you are all retired," I said. "They have to be in their eighties."

I flagged a cab and Fields got in hurriedly, still clutching his suitcase and the paper bag into which he had stuffed his thermos and fresh bottles. Twenty minutes later we were at the Continental, registered in my name. Fields had conspicuously pulled his hat forward on his head in a vain attempt to hide his face. A few people looked at him. The desk clerk, a thin, suited man with a skinny mustache and a European accent, politely ignored Fields.

We got a suite. Two rooms. Fields got the bedroom. It had two beds. I planned to sleep in the other room on the couch, away from his threats of twisting, snorting, snoring, turning, and insomnia.

We cleaned up and went out again in search of a cab, which we got, in spite of the rain now coming down heavily with distant crashes of thunder.

When we got to the six-flat apartment building, Fields paid the cabby and we got out. There was a sign on the building, saying: Furnished Apartments for Rent. The rain continued as we ran into the lobby.

Fields was decidedly pale. "This place was here when I was a boy," he said. "Passed it frequently. Stole coal from the shuttle that dropped it in back."

On the wall, next to the bells, I found a neatly printed card that read: Carol Monahan, Proprietor.

All the cards were in the same neat hand, including that of Lester O. Hipnoodle, Apartment 3.

I rang Carol Monahan's bell and we waited, but not long. The inner door opened and a woman in her fifties, in a bright-yellow dress, looked at us with an expectant smile. Her hair was dyed black and her teeth too good to be real.

"Mrs. Monahan?" I asked.

"Yes," she said, still beaming as she looked at Fields and added, "I know you."

"I will make full restitution in cash for the coal," he said.

Mrs. Monahan looked reasonably puzzled.

"A joke," I said.

Mrs. Monahan nodded, and I told her that Detective Gus Belcher had sent us and that we'd like to see Mr. Hipnoodle's room.

"I'm a private investigator," I said. "We're here from Los Angeles. We have reason to believe that Mr. Hipnoodle plans to steal a great deal of money from my client."

She nodded in understanding.

"Okay," she said, her eyes still on Fields as she stepped back to let us enter.

"What do you know about Hipnoodle?" I asked as we went up a short flight of dark stairs made even darker by the rain-black sky outside.

"Tall, thin, about forty, good teeth, pimple on his cheek, right here." She paused and pointed to her cheek.

"Tall?"

"At least six feet," she said. "Probably more. Talked kind of refined, but it sounded a little phony. Don't know why."

"Hair?"

"Dark, short. Don't remember the color of his eyes. The other detective asked me all this," she said, stopping in front of a door on the first landing. There was a white number three painted in the center of the door. She opened it with a key from a chain she pulled from the pocket of her yellow dress.

"I've got breakfast on the stove," she said. "I'm going back down. Lock the door when you leave."

And she was gone. I closed the door and Fields let out a sigh of relief. "Thought I was a goner," he said.

"She was a baby or not even born yet when you took the coal," I said, looking around the living room we were standing in. "And even if she wasn't and she recognized you, though I doubt if you look anything like you did when you were a kid, you could give her a couple of dollars. No one's going to arrest W. C. Fields for stealing some coal when he was a kid."

"I can see," said Fields, "that you have never been in Philadel-phia."

"Let's look around," I said.

Fields moved toward the bedroom. I stayed in the living room.

The furniture was old and dark but looked sturdy enough

and reasonably clean. A sofa, an armchair. A table with a radio. A telephone. The reproductions of paintings on the wall were definitely of the same vintage as the furniture. Meant to brighten the place, the landscapes and still lifes looked faded and weary. There was one window in the living room, behind the sofa. It faced a brick wall about six feet away.

I began to search, not knowing what for. I heard Fields rumbling in the bedroom. After five minutes of looking behind pictures, under the once-orange faded rug on the wooden floor, under the cushions of the sofa and couch—which netted me forty-eight cents, a button, and half a pencil—I picked up the phone book on the table next to the telephone. I flipped through it slowly, looking for notes or marks or underlines, knowing that even if I found any they might belong to the last person who had rented the place. I found nothing.

As I put down the book, the phone rang. I picked it up after one ring and looked at the bedroom door. Fields was standing there, listening.

"Yes?" I said.

"No," came the answer. It was the same muffled voice that had told me to stay away from Hipnoodle.

"This is Lester Hipnoodle," I said. "Who are you?"

"Peters," said the voice. "You and the old man still have time to walk away alive."

"We appreciate that," I said.

He hung up. I looked over at Fields.

"I think it was our friend Hipnoodle. He warned us to stop looking for him."

"But the damned letter he sent said he knew we'd come after him," said Fields. "The man can't make up his mind. Sounds like a movie producer."

"Anything in the bedroom?" I asked.

Lightning cracked. The windows streamed with rain.

"Last three issues of *Collier's*, two used razor blades in the bathroom garbage, and an almost unused bar of Palmolive soap. Very green."

I moved to the kitchen with Fields and checked the refrigerator, which was empty except for three Hershey chocolate bars, a depleted bottle of milk, and a shriveled green pepper.

Nothing on the small table. The countertop near the sink was clear. I lifted the lid of the garbage can. There were two Hershey bar wrappers and a crumpled sheet of paper in the garbage.

I picked up the sheet of paper and flattened it on the table. The writing was clear. "Lancaster. Eleven in the morning. April Fools' Day."

"He wanted us to find it," Fields said.

"Counted on it," I answered, folding the note neatly and putting it in my pocket.

"Lancaster, Pennsylvania," said Fields. "I have an account there. When do you think my car will arrive?"

"Two days," I said.

"Man must drive like a maniac," said Fields.

"Yeah," I agreed. "We can go to Lancaster now, try to get your money out before he gets there."

"I want to catch the bastard," said Fields, moving to the sink and looking out at the rain through a small window. "We go to Lancaster. He goes somewhere else. You know how many bowling pins I dropped on my head and toes learning to juggle? I couldn't afford Indian clubs. Had to steal bowling pins. I nearly collapsed staying up till three in the morning, teaching myself to juggle, developing an act. I was the tramp juggler. You know why? Because I juggled in the only clothes I owned, wearing a fake mustache I made myself. I worked for that money. I'm not losing a penny of it."

"Your call," I said.

"Not one red Indian penny or one copper profile of the Great Emancipator," he went on. "Hipnoodle has declared war, and war is what Hipnoodle shall have. Let's go back to the hotel. I'm getting just a bit tired and in need of libation."

Chapter Four

I once lost a bald canary in Altoona.

"Lost a bald canary in Altoona once," Fields said, carefully examining the glass in his hand as we sat in the rear of his car, heading west, with Gunther remaining well above the speed limit on the two-lane highways across Pennsylvania.

We swayed, bounced. Fields managed not to spill a drop of his drink.

"Bird belonged to a midget," said Fields. "Much the same size as our diminutive driver but with none of his aplomb. While I was on the circuit, it was my accursed luck to keep running across the Lilliputian demon on the same bill. The chap had a bad disposition and thought himself humorous. Carried around a small bird cage with a canary that chirped merrily inside."

Gunther was listening to the radio quietly in the front seat, the window between him and the passenger compartment closed. I was leaning forward in the backseat every few minutes, checking the mirror to see if we were being followed.

"Well, to make a short story a bit longer than necessary, the little man kept interrupting my act, mugging behind my back when I juggled, made faces, audiences thought it was part of the show. I warned him. He decided the laughs were worth more than the promise of distress. One evening when I was juggling Indian clubs, hats, and assorted items supplied by the audience—the smallest being a railroad watch and the largest a cane—the tiny twerp came up behind me with his canary. I bopped him on the noggin—the twerp, not the canary. He fell and, without my missing a beat or dropping anything I was juggling, I grabbed the small canary cage and added the chirper to the items flying overhead. Audience roared with delight. Midget was out cold. I returned the various items, dragged the midget off with one hand, held the canary cage with the other, and left my remaining paraphernalia for the stage hands to gather. It was then I noticed that the trauma of being juggled had given the canary a complete nervous breakdown. Feathers had almost all fallen out. He was completely bald and didn't feel much like singing. I went out on a triumphant bender—at that time I confined my activity to reasonable quantities of beer—and when I returned, the canary's cage door was open and the bird was missing.

"The midget, looking more than a bit fearful but consumed by litigious anger, demanded the return of his bird. I assured him that I knew nothing of the strange disappearance and that he should ask Thurston the Magician, who was also on the bill."

Fields took a sip and looked out the window thoughtfully. I did as little moving as possible in the hope that my back would feel better. It wasn't as bad as it could have been, but I knew it was in no mood for further violent activity and I was running low on pain pills from Doc Hodgdon.

"I was always of the opinion that a merciful showgirl, in search of W. C. Fields to congratulate him appropriately, had come across the once-yellow-feathered creature and let it free, far from a blessing for the bird, given its condition and the fact that I know of no way a canary, even if he weren't bald, could survive in Altoona. Turn up the radio."

Gunther obliged. We picked up "The Ransom Sherman Show," with Charles Ruggles as guest, and listened for about ten minutes.

"Jack Benny is the only really funny man on the radio besides me," said Fields. "But Ruggles should have his own show. Charlie Butterworth too, underrated. Turn it off. Find anything but music."

Gunther found "The Bing Crosby Show." Victor Borge was his guest and announced that he was also appearing at the Capitol Theater in New York.

"Kid's funny," said Fields. "But I can tell from that accent that he's not Danish, probably a German spy like the fella back home who says he's DeMille."

I didn't say anything. A car had been creeping up on us along with the twilight. It was a small Ford, dark. Evening sun was hitting his front window, so I couldn't tell in the rearview mirror who was inside.

"I think we need a little speed, Gunther," I said, sliding open the glass partition.

"I see him," said Gunther calmly, pushing up to eighty-five miles an hour.

Fields twisted in his seat to look back at the pursuing vehicle and saw what I saw. The road was clear except for the two of us. The driver's left arm came out of the window holding a gun; he'd decided that his Ford was no match for the souped-up Caddy.

He was probably right-handed. The first shot missed by a country mile. The second skipped and whined over the top of the car. We were almost out of his range when the third shot clanged off the rear bumper.

Then our pursuer was lost in the distant background.

"Shall I slow down?" Gunther asked.

"Not unless you want to lose two or three inches, which you can ill afford," said Fields, leaning back. "I need a drink to steady the nerves. Suppose it could be that midget with the canary? Hanging around Altoona, driven mad by the blow of my Indian club, waiting to extract revenge should ever I chance to return?"

"I doubt it," I said. "I've had two telephone warnings now for us to stay out of this pursuit of Hipnoodle. I think this was warning number three."

"Number four," said Fields. "While you were packing and picking up our diminutive Barney Oldfield, a call came to me promising my demise if we should pursue this adventure."

"You could have told me sooner," I said, looking back to be sure the Ford wasn't gaining.

"Didn't know he'd called you," said Fields, his voice going low, speaking almost to himself. "Cured myself of tuberculosis. Carried on long persuasive conversations with my liver, but it was made of greater resolve than my lungs. Next time I go to that sanitarium, or the time after, will be my last. This, Peters, will probably be my last adventure. Besides, no son of a bitch is going to steal the money I've worked my ass off for all these years. What I can't figure out is why Hipnoodle leaves us clues so we can keep following him while at the same time warning us not to follow him or he'll cause our immediate departure from this vale of tears."

"I don't know," I said.

"I think, if I may say so," said Gunther, loud enough to be heard over the engine, which didn't require too much of a shout since the car was finely tuned, "I think we may be dealing with two criminals. One we are pursuing and one who is pursuing us so that he or they can procure Mr. Fields's fortune from Hipnoodle when he has amassed it, a task which will be much easier if we give up or are dead."

"Makes sense to me," I said.

"Hipnoodles, unknown pursuers with guns," Fields said. "There's a movie in this somewhere. I'll call La Cava when we get back to Los Angeles."

Gunther and I wanted lunch but Fields didn't want to stop on the road. He wasn't hungry. I discovered he was never hungry. Neither did he want our pursuer to catch up with us and shoot us to death as we emerged from Ma's Eats. He had a good point.

So we went into Altoona. There was no problem finding rooms for the night at the Altoona Majestic Hotel downtown, the war boom had not really caught up with the town. Its chief contribution, the ancient and philosophical desk clerk told us, was to supply cannon fodder, including two of his grandsons. Its chief import was the return of the dead young men.

The lobby was small and empty, with pots of flowers and straight-back chairs and a couple of octagonal-shaped wooden tables.

"Now," said the clerk as I signed us all in, "they're raising the draft age to forty-five, or at least talking about it. My son would go. They say the war's almost over. We'll see."

"Rest assured, old fellow," said Fields. "I have followed this conflagration closely, charted its course and lack of discourse, and come to the conclusion that it will end soon."

"Soon?" said the thin old man, fingering his blue-knit cardigan.

"No more than a year," said Fields with confidence.

"Lot of people could die in a year," said the old man, brushing back wisps of white hair and revealing a forehead freckled with age and experience.

"You've done an admirable job of containing your curiosity about our little trio," Fields said.

"Not often a prizefighter, a dwarf, and W. C. Fields come into the Altoona," he said. "Time was, during vaudeville, we had lots of stars. You stayed here more than once. Fanny Brice. Burns and Allen. The Byrne Brothers."

"The Byrne Brothers?" Fields said with sudden energy. "They were my inspiration to become a juggler."

"Lots of stars," said the old man. "Almost all polite and quiet. Too tired from running across the country and working to cause a ruckus. Wife handled show people mostly. She's gone now."

Gunther had brought in all the luggage: my suitcase, his, and Fields's two large bags. Gunther wasn't even panting. He had once been part of a circus act in which he leapt through flaming circles after sailing off a teeter-totter, picked up a full-size clown and stuffed him in a suitcase, and performed various other acts of lunacy in the hope of getting a paycheck, some applause, and the respect of his fellow workers. That was a while ago, but Gunther had remained in shape.

I had checked the registry when I signed in. There was no Hipnoodle, or any other name in the least bit suspicious.

Fields leaned on the counter and whispered to the old clerk, "We should prefer to remain incognito. Business."

"Suit yourself," said the old man, glancing at the hotel register.

I had signed it twice, writing once, printing the second time.

Fields had frowned at my lack of creativity, but understood that this was not the time to draw attention to ourselves if our pursuer or Hipnoodle happened to be checking the limited number of hotels in Altoona.

"Mr. and Mrs. Vernon Sawyer and Mr. and Mrs. John Welch," the old man read. "Sawyer?"

I raised my hand, pointed at Gunther.

"Which leaves me as Mr. and Mrs. Welch," said Fields. "Leave a call for us, bright and early, eight."

"I will do so," said the old man, closing the book. He handed us the keys and pointed down the hall to his right. The rooms were next to each other, and I told Fields that I would be happy to bring him something to eat, but that he and Gunther should stay in their respective rooms. They were a little too easy to spot. I wasn't exactly inconspicuous with my flat nose, battle-scarred face, and the look of an extra in a Warner Brothers B gangster movie, but I was the closest we had.

Gunther had told us that the car was parked and locked behind the hotel in a corner behind some trees, where it would be difficult to find.

I dragged Fields's suitcases into his room. He had carried his own picnic basket, which I was sure contained a thermos or two of martinis.

"A small crabmeat salad," said Fields, as he looked around his small room. "At least the chair looks comfortable. I shall, aided by the pages of Mrs. Plaut's memoirs with which you have supplied me, sit in my skivvies and silk robe until something that resembles sleep or at least rest overtakes me."

"I'll knock four times fast," I said. "Don't open the door unless you hear four fast knocks."

Fields nodded, took off his hat, and opened his trunk.

Gunther and I settled in quickly next door. There were two beds. I let Gunther have his choice and took his dinner order. He asked for a ham and cheese sandwich and hot tea. By the time I left, he was already sitting in a chair, listening to music on the radio, and reading a book in a language I guessed was Russian.

"Hungarian," he corrected when I made my guess. He offered no further information.

I asked the desk clerk where I could find a restaurant where I could get some take-out food. The old man headed me toward a Greek joint a few blocks away. Ten minutes later I was back with Gunther's order, a turkey on rye with mustard and a Pepsi for me, and a chicken salad and coffee for Fields, though I had little hope he would eat. The restaurant had nothing resembling seafood, unless you count catfish.

"Fascinating tome," Fields said with sincerity, pages of Mrs. Plaut's manuscript in his hand after my four quick knocks got him to open the door.

"Fascinating," I agreed. "Might be another movie in that."

"Might, indeed," he said. "My meeting with La Cava will be longer than I thought." He accepted the chicken salad and coffee reluctantly, but said that he might try to consume some of it.

"See you in the morning," I said.

"I want to be there when the bank opens," he said. "At least a minute or two before nine."

I agreed and went to Gunther's and my room and pulled the mattress onto the floor. Gunther was wearing a robe over neatly ironed pajamas. He ate his meal and went right to bed, reminding me that he had just driven across a continent, and that I had had a long day.

It was still early. I wanted to call Anita or go see a movie, but I did neither. I took a bath to ease my back, shaved and washed so I'd be ready in the morning.

I must have been more tired than I thought. I usually sleep in nothing. I wore clean underwear tonight and took the .38 out of my suitcase and placed it on the table next to my bed before I turned off the light.

I'm not much of a shot, and the few times I'd had to shoot I had done more bad than good and usually hit something or someone I wasn't aiming for. But a bullet or two certainly gets a person's attention, and if they were close enough, it might also get them shot.

I turned off the light and lay on the bed on top of the blanket rumpled on the mattress. I planned to lie there working out a plan. Gunther was asleep, breathing lightly. Before I could get a grip on the first step of a plan I was asleep.

The dreams came. Most of them I can't remember, except for bits and pieces. All of them were about Koko the Clown. I always had Koko the Clown nightmares. Sometimes Betty Boop was in them, but not often. This time Koko and I were running across a field and a giant head was floating after us, singing, "I'll Be Glad When You're Dead, You Rascal You." The head was Louis Armstrong and he smiled as he sang. Koko and I were suddenly in a hotel room. He motioned for me to follow him. We jumped into a drawer and he closed it behind us. We lay in the dark. Koko giggled. Outside the room came the sound of a door opening and heavy footsteps thumping around the room, opening doors, searching. I could hear a drawer above us open. I put my hand over Koko's mouth to keep him from giggling. A second drawer opened. And then our drawer opened and we looked up at Louis Armstrong, who grinned and said, "Gotcha."

I remember clinging to Koko, who shouted, "Scat."

Louis Armstrong disappeared. I looked at my hand as we climbed out of the drawer. It was covered in red greasepaint from putting it over Koko's painted mouth to stop him from giggling. The greasepaint looked like blood.

Koko without some of his makeup looked like someone else, someone I recognized but couldn't place.

"You're . . . you're . . ." I said and then felt myself being shaken.

"Toby," said Gunther. "It's time to get up."

I sat up. He was already dressed. Casually for Gunther. Pressed slacks, shirt and tie, and a tweed sports jacket.

My back felt a little better. I took two pills, used the washroom, brushed my teeth, checked to see if I needed a fresh shave.

I did, but I didn't stop to take one. I was still waking up and I didn't want to take the time to patch any razor cuts from my not-yet-steady hand.

When I was dressed and ready, it was eight-thirty. We were both packed. I knocked four times on Fields's door. He opened it, neatly dressed, bags ready. I glanced at the table next to the chair. Some of the chicken salad had been eaten. He was wearing his disguise mustache. I didn't bother to try to talk him out of it then, when we checked out, when we got in the car, or as Gunther started to drive. I needed coffee and at least a sinker. Gunther agreed.

"Long as we're at the bank before nine," said Fields. "I'll guide you there. It's not far, as I recall."

We stopped at the same restaurant I had been to the night before, got two carry-out coffees, and we were on our way.

"It's the Chimp," said Fields as we drove. "Figured it out last night. Couldn't be anyone else."

"Is he Hipnoodle or the guy who's trying to stop us?" I asked, not looking at his face or his ridiculous mustache.

"Perhaps both," said Fields triumphantly. "Perhaps the accomplice of Hipnoodle, who is his twin brother or a fiendish cousin. No doubt about it. It's the Chimp, my traitorous driver. Evidence that you should never trust anyone, even a man in the electric chair with nothing to lose. The human mind has a penchant for dissembling. I learned that when I was twelve."

I nodded and wondered about my Koko dream, tried to see clearly the face under the greasepaint. It wouldn't come clear and I knew if I didn't get it soon, I'd lose it forever.

"Finished your Mrs. Plaut's chapter," Fields said, reaching for a morning drink, probably not his first. "Woman's a clear match for Thurber or Perlman. Want to read the whole book. Listen."

He fished Mrs. Plaut's manuscript from the picnic basket on the floor and began to read:

Cousin Antonio Pride who fancied himself special because he came from the Kingman branch which boasted of few who were feeble of mind and several who had finished high school, was a salesman of some stature in Goldfarb's Haberdashery in Steubenville, Ohio. Antonio was short of build, dark of color, and even of white teeth, a full and radiant mouthful that dazzled customers and pleased Mr. Goldfarb. One morning Cousin Antonio Pride, who had a wife and three children, fell prey to the family curse. He was thirty-nine years of age. He was in the process of fitting a stylish derby on the head of a customer whose hair was parted in the middle leading Mr. Goldfarb later to surmise that the customer was a bartender. Cousin Antonio Pride left the customer, walked out of the front door of Goldfarb's Haberdashery in Steubenville, Ohio, got on the four o'clock train heading west, held up said train with a pair of weapons originally belonging to his stepfather Hugo Arthur Slade, not his real father, Mario Pride, who had similarly departed several decades earlier never to be heard from again. Antonio's booty was from passengers and train personnel. (He did not take any goods or cash from the porters, though the conductor was not exempt from his criminal outburst.) Two bags full of cash, watches, jewelry including rings, and odd mementos later, Cousin Antonio Pride leapt from the train as it slowed at a turn onto a trestle over a river. Word came back years later that he had gone to Tampico, Mexico, converted his booty to cash, and opened a bar where he could thrash obdurate and noisy drunks with impunity. It was said that he had taken a young Indian girl of passable looks as his illegal wife. Exactly twenty years to the day he had walked out of Goldfarb's Haberdashery in Steubenville, Ohio, he emptied his cash register and the safe in his office and, at the age of fifty-nine, leaving behind a second wife and two dark children, headed farther south carrying with him a book called *Basic Portuguese* according to the dry goods salesman who sat next to him on the train and drummed up a conversation. The salesman later related the conversation to James Earl Pride, Antonio's second son from Steubenville who had set out in search of his father with the intent of making him pay for his desertion. James Earl, who was twenty-five at the time, passed the information on to his mother and brother who still resided in Steubenville. He had learned of his father's departure from Tampico from the Indian wife his father had abandoned. James Earl took pity on the woman and her two sons, gave up his search, and returned to Tampico where he married her legally, took over the bar, and lived comfortably until the age of seventy-nine when he was shot by a jealous husband with whose wife he was caught in a situation. The husband was a member of the constabulary.

The town gave him a good mourning in Spanish. Upon his death, a novel was discovered in James Earl's hand concerning the bloody bandit life of Al Jennings of Oklahoma who James Earl claimed to have known. The book was sold to and published in both Mexico and the United States to poor reviews and even poorer sales. Antonio was never heard from again. These events, however, suggest that there is in the blood of our family a drive toward abandonment, carnal activity till late in life, and a desire to engage in the creation of literary works.

"The bank," said Gunther.

Fields had more to read but his head shot up suddenly and he stuffed the pages of Mrs. Plaut's manuscript back in his picnic basket. "Five minutes to nine," he said. "We've beaten Hipnoodle here, and today we shall have our satisfaction."

Fields was wrong on both counts.

Chapter Five

There's no room in the White House for a man with barber's itch.

While we watched the front door of the First Consolidated Bank of Altoona, we listened to "Aunt Jenny's Stories" on the radio. In the episode a woman had lost her husband and had to take over raising her three young children and running her husband's real-estate office. Love came to her in the form of a wealthy widower who was looking for a small house where he could mourn with a beautiful view. Fields listened attentively, his eye fixed on the door of the bank. He hadn't taken a drink yet.

"The gold digger's looking for a free ride," said Fields finally, pointing at the radio. "Taking advantage of a grieving man to stop working and sit home eating cashews and holding the old man's hand while she clothes her brats in diaphanous dresses and fine lace."

Aunt Jenny seemed to think the marriage of the widow and widower was the happy ending.

"Turn on the news," Fields barked.

Gunther changed the station.

"Never did find out what killed the first husband," Fields muttered. "Probably poisoned by the greedy wench."

We caught the tail end of the morning news and heard from the deep-voiced announcer that one hundred flying fortresses had battered Sardinia and destroyed twenty-six ships and seventy-one Axis airplanes.

"Gotta remember to put a pin up for that one when I get back home," Fields said.

People entered the bank and came out. None, even if they were wearing disguises, were tall enough to be Hipnoodle. Gunther and I kept looking back for the black Ford.

An hour passed. No Hipnoodle. No black Ford. Fields reached for his first drink of the day, a premixed martini from his backseat bar. He drank slowly, scanning the street for suspicious faces. He concluded that all the faces were suspicious.

"See that woman there?" he asked, waving his drink.

A young woman, slightly on the heavy side, held the hands of two children, a small boy on the right, a slightly taller girl on the left.

"I see her," I said.

"German face," he said. "Probably a spy, perfect cover. Two kids are probably rented."

"What would a German spy be doing in Altoona?" I asked.

"They're everywhere," he confided. "Besides, there's a secret bombsight development center in Altoona. That's what my barber told me. Always trust your barber. Especially when you're getting a shave. If he's good enough to run a razor across your neck, he's good enough to know if there's a bombsight center in Altoona. Come to think of it, he said Ashtabula."

None of us noticed the uniformed cop until he knocked at the curbside window next to me. I lowered the window. The cop leaned over, examined us. Fields pretended to ignore him and continued to look out the window at the bank.

The officer was too old for the draft, even if they raised the age to forty-five. His blue uniform was a little baggy and so were his eyes.

"Mind tellin' me what you're doing here, gents?" he asked.

"Watching the bank," I said.

"Mind if I ask why?" he asked, hands resting on the rim of the open window.

"It is your civic duty to ask why," said Fields. "We could be a bizarre trio of bank robbers—a midget, an ancient juggler, and Mr. Peters, who, I must admit, fits the description of half the felons described each week on 'Gangbusters.'"

"I know you?" asked the policeman.

Fields's face was still averted, drink in hand. "Ever been in Nepal?" he asked.

"Yep," said the cop.

The reply caught Fields's attention. He examined the policeman leaning into the window as if he might have discovered a worthy opponent.

"What were you doing in Nepal?" asked Fields.

"Searching for the elusive Tarabini bird," said the cop.

"Find him?" asked Fields.

"Found him, ate him," said the cop. "Tasted like chicken. Everything tastes like chicken—rattlesnake, alligator, chickens. You're W. C. Fields."

"I confess," said Fields. "But I categorically deny having outstanding warrants in Altoona."

"Don't figure you do," he said. "But I can't let you sit here parked in front of the bank. Chief comes by, sees you idling here, wonders what a big Caddy has on its mind and where the hell I am. Do my best to avoid the chief. Got two boys in the service. One in the Pacific. One flying missions over Germany."

"See that woman?" said Fields, pointing. "Two kids. Think she's a German spy. After the plans at the bombsight factory."

"Bombsight factory?" asked the cop.

"You don't even know about it," Fields said. "You should have a long talk with my barber."

"Woman with the two kids is Kitty Sinnet," said the cop. "Family's lived here for as far back as her great-grandpa. Her husband's a commander on a P T boat. Don't think she's a spy."

"Bismarck probably planted the family here half a century ago in anticipation of the propitious moment," muttered Fields.

"Good to meet you, Mr. Fields," the cop said. "Now, if you'll move your vehicle . . ."

"I'll do better," Fields said. "I'll enter the banking establishment and engage in a transaction of some substance."

"That'll be fine," the cop said, stepping back as Fields opened his door onto the street and almost into a passing moving-van.

"Look where you're going," Fields shouted, waving his cane. "Man's driving in an alcoholic stupor."

If he was talking to the cop with the two kids in the war, Fields was too late. The cop was gone.

Gunther stayed in the car as I got out on the curb side and hurried after Fields, who was groping in his pocket for something. When we got across the street, he pulled out his fake clip mustache, attached it to his nose, and pushed his straw hat forward in an attempt to shade his eyes.

"How do I look?" he whispered.

"Like W. C. Fields with a silly mustache and his hat pushed forward," I said.

"You're a detective," he answered.

"It doesn't take a detective," I said. "What are we doing?"

"Looks as if Hipnoodle isn't showing up," he said. "His clue was a sham, a deception designed to throw us off the scent while he went ahead to Beloit or Muscatine. We will enter this establishment and I will remove my assets and consider our next move in the chase."

I shrugged. We entered. It was a bigger bank than the one in Lancaster, bigger and newer. Business wasn't brisk, but there were a few customers at the quartet of barred teller windows on the right. Fields headed straight for a closed wooden door displaying the words, Mr. Cameron Farber, Vice-President, in gold leaf.

Fields knocked once and entered before receiving a reply. I was at his side.

The office was small, a lot larger than mine, but small by most human standards. Behind the desk sat a man with a round, pink face, wearing a dark suit. Across from him sat a customer, a woman who couldn't have been a minute under eighty years old.

"I must insist on putting an end to this hanky-panky," Fields said. "Farber, you ought to be ashamed of yourself. I know I'm ashamed of myself."

"What are you talking about?" asked Farber rising. "What do you want?"

"Business," Fields said. "Not monkey business like you. This woman is old enough to be your mother. Have you no decency?"

"Mrs. Boyston . . . ," Farber began apologetically, but the old woman held up a hand to stop him as she stood.

"This is W. C. Fields," she said. "Professional misanthrope. Supposedly humorous rudeness is essential to his less-than-respectable trade."

With that, she walked past us, closing the door behind her as she left.

"I've been bested by a cop and an ancient harridan in Altoona," said Fields, moving toward the desk. "My mood is sinister. You drink?"

"Well," said Farber. "I . . ."

"Top drawer, left," said Fields. "Saw your eyes move. Steady yourself and we're on to business. I can always deal with a man who's had a healthy snort in the a.m."

Farber looked at me and opened the drawer. He removed a half full bottle.

"Rum," Fields said, focusing on the bottle "I'm a martini man myself."

Farber poured a healthy dose of his rum into a paper cup, put the bottle away, downed the drink in one gulp, and dropped the cup in a wastebasket.

"Farber," said Fields. "I wish to withdraw my funds from this worthy establishment."

"Of course," said Farber, looking more in control of mind and body than he had before his drink.

"Deposited a sum of nine thousand dollars and fifty cents," said Fields. "That was back in nineteen twenty-two. With interest, I calculate that the sum is now close to eleven thousand."

"Quite likely," said Farber. "I hesitate to say this, however, but one of my responsibilities is to examine the accounts on which there has been no activity, deposit or withdrawal, within a year's time. I don't recall a W. C. Fields account."

Fields consulted a folded sheet of paper, which he extracted with the flourish of a presidential candidate about to make a speech.

"Used the name Hopencrotch," Fields said. "Sidney Barchester Hopencrotch."

Farber shook his head and smiled.

"You've made a mistake," he said.

"Many," said Fields. "But it's best not to admit them."

"Mr. Hopencrotch withdrew his funds this morning," he said.

"Couldn't have," Fields said. "My compatriot and I, with the aid of a small midget who dresses better than Doug Fairbanks, Jr., have been watching the door of this bank since it opened. The man who could have claimed to be Hopencrotch never came out."

"Tall gentleman in his late forties," said Farber. "Deep voice. Straight back. Nice smile."

"Sounds like the culprit," Fields said.

"Mr. Hopencrotch came to the bank almost a month ago," he said. "I spoke to him personally. He made a respectable deposit in his account, several thousand dollars, and then said he was thinking of entering the banking business. Said he was tired of traveling. Said he would return in about a month and would appreciate a brief apprenticeship, unpaid, if that were possible. I told him that it was irregular but it could be arranged. He called yesterday and asked if he could come in today. He was here on time, at eight, with the other employees."

"He's here?" I said.

"No," said Farber. "Shortly after opening, he informed a teller that he had a family emergency and had to withdraw all of his cash immediately. Miss Ochmonic had no choice. He had his bankbook, with a recent deposit, and his signature was an exact match for the one in the bankbook and on our deposit slips."

"We were watching the front door," I said.

"Mr. Hopencrotch asked to leave through the employee exit because he had parked in the back," said Farber. "I let him out myself and he promised to return soon with a large deposit. The account is still open. He left almost two hundred dollars."

"How long ago did he leave?" I asked.

"Ten, fifteen minutes," said Farber, glancing at his desk drawer. "It was all very fast. Family emergency, you know."

Fields removed his mustache, pocketed it, and examined Farber before saying, "You let the son of a bitch steal my money."

"Under the circumstances . . ." Farber began, but I was already dragging Fields toward the door. We left the bewildered Farber standing behind his desk with an apologetic look on his face.

"The ravages of alcohol," said Fields with a sigh.

"I thought you said you could trust a man who drinks," I said.

"Not rum," he said. "Drink of charlatans and pirates."

We hurried through the lobby, past the woman with the two children who Fields had pegged as part of a multigenerational German conspiracy, and out onto the street. The trail was worse than cold, but we had no choice. I motioned to Gunther, who followed us in the Caddy down the driveway to the bank's parking lot in the rear. There were seven cars. None familiar. We were about to give up when Fields moved to the rear door of the bank. Taped to it was a piece of cardboard, neatly printed in black: Coshocton, Next Stop.

"Man's a torturing fiend," said Fields, tearing down the cardboard.

"Where's Coshocton?" I asked.

"Ohio," said Fields. "Bend in the road. Played in the Elks Hall there in the general vicinity of nineteen-nineteen. Appreciative audience, as I recall, balanced the stuffed head of an elk on my nose while telling jokes and juggling beer bottles."

The parking lot adjoined a tree-lined alley. I watched Gunther maneuver the big car around to let us in and aim for the entrance. I was reaching for the door when a shot spat through the air and split Fields's cane. The bottom half of the cane twirled in the air. Fields caught it, ducked next to the car, and looked in the general direction from which the shot had come. Trees, fences, buildings, cars, plenty of places to hide. The second shot seemed to come from a little farther away, as if he were moving back. Gunther was on the floor of the car. Fields and I were doing our best to keep the car between us and the gunman.

"There," shouted Fields, pointing far down the alley.

I looked where he was pointing. A man darted across the alley from behind a tree. He was carrying a gun and running fast. Well, not exactly running, loping.

"It's the Chimp," said Fields. "I knew it."

My vision's not perfect but it's good, certainly good enough to recognize Fields's driver from Los Angeles; but at this distance, Fields was just guessing. All we could see of the man was that he was the Chimp's size and build. We got in the car and Gunther sat up.

"Knew I couldn't trust him," Fields said.

"But he wasn't Hopencrotch or Hipnoodle or whatever he's going to call himself in the next town," I said. "Hopencrotch is tall, thin, good-looking."

"Accomplice," said Fields.

It sounded reasonable.

"What's his real name?" I asked as Gunther pulled out of the lot. The three of us looked both ways when we hit the street, expecting a dark Ford or a primate-shaped man with a gun.

"Chimp," said Fields, reaching for a drink. "All I've ever called him. I'll call my secretary and get his name."

"We should report this to the police," I said.

"We should get our asses to Coshocton, Ohio," Fields replied.

Gunther, driving with one hand, looked down at the U.S. road map in the passenger seat. Gunther could read a map. Actually, Gunther could read almost anything.

"No nonsense this time," Fields said. "We will beat our tall enemy and the Chimp to Coshocton, get my money, and stay two steps ahead of him and catch him in the act. Foot to the floor as soon as we're out of city limits, my diminutive conspirator. We'll beat their black Ford to the bank by hours."

"Doesn't make sense," I said. "Why tell us where they're going next and then try to shoot us?"

"The human mind," said Fields, "is a ball of mush held together by the glue from horses' hooves. There are rare individuals who can actually use as much as five percent of the organ's capacity. Try to fathom the human mind and you'll find yourself in the room next to mine the next time I sign myself into that sanitarium."

Gunther drove, swiftly and smoothly. I was hungry. So was Gunther, but Fields insisted that he would buy us a lavish early dinner after we visited the bank in Coshocton. We ate crackers and olives, which Fields had in large supply, as he leaned with dignity over into the front seat to find New York on the impressive radio built into the dashboard.

A voice came on, speaking a language that I didn't recognize. Fields sat back.

"The news in Yiddish," he said. "Every day in New York. Twice a day, maybe more."

"You understand Yiddish?" I asked.

"A little," he said. "Fanny Brice said I was a quick learner when we were in the Follies. Couldn't make up my mind whether I loved or hated the woman. She was too damn funny. . . . Rommel," said Fields suddenly, catching the name on the radio. "He said something about Rommel."

"Rommel is fleeing, abandoning his tanks, about to surrender," said Gunther.

"You understand Yiddish?" said Fields.

"It's not a difficult language," said Gunther. "Mostly German. Some Polish and Russian with bits of other things. A language of proud wanderers."

"I think now's a good time," I said.

Fields and I had developed this ritual which took place anytime in the afternoon after lunch. I'd say it was a good time. He'd reach into one of his pockets and come out with my day's pay. It took him a little longer this time. Reaching into his pocket was awkward and he couldn't find small enough bills.

We hit Coshocton a little after four and had no trouble finding the bank. There wasn't much to Coshocton. It seemed like a nice enough small town. Gunther stopped the car at the curb and Fields and I rushed to the bank door. A burly man in a brown uniform and cap stood in the doorway, letting people out.

Fields tried to move past him. The uniformed man's arm came up to stop him.

"Bank's closed, sorry."

"Emergency," said Fields. "Wife's dying of quintaberry of the liver. Surgeon won't operate without cash. Can't get cash without going into the bank."

"Morning," the man said, with a definite accent.

"Morning will be too late," said Fields. "The better half could have gone to meet her maker before dawn. The medical profession is mercenary. Six children will be essentially orphans."

"They'll have you," the burly man said, unmoved, as he let a pair of customers leave.

"I'm a cad and a drunkard," Fields said sadly. "A glass of beer could be fatal and then where would the lovely urchins be?"

The burly bank dick looked at us with suspicion.

"Your wife is not dying," he said.

"You are not only a doorman," said Fields, "but you're also a telepathic diagnostician."

"You're the radio funny guy," the man said. "Make jokes with Charlie McCarthy and Mortimer Snerd. I read about you somewhere. Come back in the morning."

"The death of a sweet, innocent woman will be on your oversized cranium," Fields said as the man went back into the bank and locked the door. He turned back to me. "At least Hipnoodle can't get in," he said. "Sign says the bank opens at nine. We'll be here at six. Scant hours or less behind us speeds the Chimp and his partner, determined to steal my money and kill me . . ."

"Unless you give up the chase," I reminded him.

"That is not an option," said Fields.

"I didn't think it was," I said. "Let's find a place to eat and sleep."

In less than three minutes Gunther found a hotel, small, with a restaurant. In a corner of the lobby, dark behind glass windows and a glass door, was a barbershop.

"Are we too early for dinner?" I asked the girl who checked us in.

"Start serving at four-thirty," she said. "We'll get your bags up to your room and you'll be just on time. You might want to freshen up a little first, but that's your business."

She couldn't have been more than seventeen, long blond hair tied with a ribbon. No makeup, green dress. There was a sharp cry from behind the desk. I looked around expecting to see the Chimp with a gun in his hand. The girl disappeared behind the counter and came up with a baby in her arms.

"Mom and dad are in Canton," the young woman explained. "Aunt Claire is pretty sick. Sister and I are minding the place till they get back. Actually, mom is usually back here behind the desk. Pop's the barber. I keep the place clean."

She rocked the nearly bald baby, who stopped crying and gurgled softly.

"I'd best feed him," she said shyly. "My husband's a Seabee. Hardly had a chance to be together after we were married."

"A lovely child," said Fields with a smile. "Does he bounce?"

The girl smiled.

"Does he have a name, or do you wish him to remain incognito till he reaches maturity and can carry on a coherent conversation?" asked Fields while Gunther and I plopped into nearby chairs, abandoning the luggage in front of the desk.

"His name is Bill," she said. "William, same as my husband."

"That's my name," Fields said, looking at the child more seriously. "I have a son who's also named Bill."

"Wow," the child bride said. "Some coincidence."

"Indeed," said Fields.

"Are there any other hotels in town?" I asked.

"One," she said. "New Marion on Second Street."

"This is W. C. Fields," I said. "We're being hounded by one of Mr. Fields's former employees who mistakenly thinks he is owed money when, in fact, he stole some valuable property from Mr. Fields. So, we would appreciate . . ."

"Snake River Rock doesn't have to fall on me," the girl said with a smile, rocking her baby. "I won't let on to anyone you're here. Wow, W. C. Fields. My husband saw you in a movie where you kicked a little boy."

"Filmic illusion," said Fields. "Baby LeRoy enjoyed it. I'm actually very fond of the little creatures."

"Well," she said. "I've got to feed Billy. Leave your things there. Here's your keys. My little brother'll get everything up to your rooms."

I needed a shave, a shower, and some rest. But I was hungry.

"I prefer to change clothes and bathe before dinner," said Gunther.

"And I," said Fields, "will retire to my room to work out a plan to thwart the Chimp and his partner."

"And call your secretary to find out more about the Chimp," I reminded him.

Our rooms were on the second floor. There was no elevator. Fields and Gunther made an odd pair walking up the stairs.

"Bring me a shrimp-salad sandwich," said Fields, who carried his picnic basket. "No pickle."

When they were gone, I felt my stubbled cheeks and looked into a small mirror in the lobby. I straightened my jacket and shirt, ran a hand through my hair, patted the .38 in the holster under my zipper jacket, and looked at myself again. I looked tough, even to me. The stubble with touches of gray in it added to the image.

The restaurant had three booths, four tables, and a counter with eight stools. I was the only customer. A waitress who was probably the older sister of the girl at the desk told me I could sit anywhere. I chose the booth in the corner. I could look through the curtains onto the street and I could see anyone coming into the restaurant.

I ordered Fields's sandwich to go. The waitress said the closest they had was tuna. I told her it would have to do and said I'd start with coffee while I went over the menu. I wasn't waiting for Gunther. By the time he felt sufficiently groomed to come downstairs to eat, I'd be on my way upstairs to our room or already there.

I drank the water the girl had placed before me and then ordered as I held up my coffee cup.

"What's special?" I asked.

"Chicken pie and dumplings," she said.

"Sold," I said.

"Homemade pies for dessert," she went on. "Made 'em myself, at least some of them."

"You got apple?"

"Sure."

"Apple pie and, if you've got it, a scoop of ice cream."

She didn't bother to write it down. No one else came in while I waited. The radio was on and the waitress was listening to "Mary Noble, Backstage Wife." From what I could tell, Mary, with great determination and dignity, was warning a young actress to stay away from Mary's husband.

The waitress returned in a few minutes with the chicken pie and dumplings.

"You from New York?" she said, standing next to me as I started to eat.

"Los Angeles," I said.

"Can I ask you something?"

"Sure," I said.

"Are you a policeman or a gangster?"

"Somewhere in between," I said.

The chicken pie and dumplings smelled terrific. I felt better immediately and held back visions of apple pie and ice cream. She stood, wanting to say more.

"Married?" she asked.

"No," I said.

"Me neither. Gonna be in town long?"

"Just overnight," I said.

"I could close down at nine," she said.

I looked up at her. Cute. Maybe twenty-three. Bored. Someone looking dangerous comes in for the chicken and dumplings and she decides to take a chance.

"I'm old enough to be your father," I said. "Easy. Probably older than your father."

"So's Harold Winch," she said. "I go out with him. He stutters. Not many young men in town with the war and all."

"Look," I said, zipping my jacket down partway and showing my gun and holster to her. "I'm the bodyguard for a movie star. We just checked in for the night. I'm not going to be getting any sleep. I'll be sitting up all night with this in my lap. There's a guy following us, thinks my client owes him money. You're one cute kid but . . ."

"I understand," she said with a sigh. "You got a girl back in Los Angeles?"

"A woman," I amended as I continued to eat. "She's a waitress too."

She nodded. "Want some more?"

I grinned and said sure. She took my plate and came back with another helping.

"If I went to Los Angeles and looked you up," she said, "could you maybe get me into movies? I mean, this guy you're protecting. He must have connections."

"We can try," I said. "My name's Toby Peters. I'm in the

phone book. I'm telling you not to try, to take my word, but it won't do any good and, who knows, you've got the energy, looks, figure, teeth, and nerve. Look me up in L.A."

"I'll get your pie," she said.

She moved across the empty room behind the counter and someone appeared in the door of the restaurant. It was the Chimp. He spotted me right away. I held up my .38 in my right hand and worked on a dumpling with my left.

He glared at me for a moment, took a step toward me, changed his mind, and disappeared. I dropped four dollars and some change on the table as the waitress returned.

"I think I'll eat this in my room," I said. "Got to get back to work."

She shrugged, gave me a disappointed look, and handed me Fields's tuna sandwich, neatly wrapped in wax paper.

I put the sandwich in my pocket and, one hand holding the pie and ice cream and the other my .38, went into the lobby. Empty. I went up the stairs to Fields's room, gave him the knock, and waited while he opened the door. He was in his underwear and still wearing his hat.

"I saw the Chimp downstairs," I said, handing him the sandwich. "He saw me. Keep your door locked. I'll listen for anyone coming."

"Called my secretary," Fields said. "The Chimp is Albert Woloski. Forty-four years of age. Two prison terms, plus an overnight misdemeanor for purse snatching. Two felonies. Armed robbery. Did eight years with the Carnes Circus— roustabout, cook, tumbler, catcher for a trapeze act. Can't say he's the least savory character I've encountered in my travels, but the others weren't trying to steal all my money and kill me."

"Keep your door locked," I said. "And put a chair under the knob."

"Up at six," he answered.

I nodded and he closed the door.

I went to my room. Gunther was dressed. I told him about the

Chimp and recommended the chicken and dumplings. The ice cream was melting on my pie.

"Thank you," said Gunther, checking his pocket watch.

"Warning," I said. "Waitress is a nice young dish who doesn't get around much and isn't shy."

"I shall endeavor to resist," he said. "Chicken and dumplings?"

"Apple pie's good too," I added, taking a bite.

Gunther was back in about an hour. He ate slowly, even when he was alone. He had not seen the Chimp and the waitress had expressed to him a similar invitation to the one she'd given me, which he had politely refused.

We went to bed early. My gun was on the table near my mattress. The door was locked and a chair in place under the knob.

I fell asleep almost instantly and stayed that way until I heard the two gunshots a little after three in the morning. They were followed by two more.

Chapter Six

If man is made in God's image, does God have prostate trouble?

I fumbled for my gun and the light, found both, and saw Gunther standing next to his bed, waiting for direction. I was wearing boxer shorts, a white undershirt, and a look of bewilderment. I ran for the door, kicked the chair out of the way, opened the locks, and dashed out into the hall, where the chances of getting myself shot were pretty good.

The door to Fields's room was open. I ran to it, gun ready, breathing hard. The lamp was out but from the light in the hall I could make out a figure crouched next to the bed.

Behind me a few people were opening their doors just a crack to see what was going on. A hum of low voices murmured in a frightened blur. There was a switch on the wall. Gunther, at my side, hit the switch and I leveled my gun.

Kneeling beside Fields's bed was the Chimp—Albert Woloski—with a gun in his hand and confusion on his primate face.

He stood up and reached toward the bedclothes, still holding the gun in his hand.

"Drop it," I ordered.

Maybe it was the boxer shorts and undershirt. Maybe the Chimp thought I could shoot faster than he could. Whatever the reason, he went headfirst through the open window next to the bed.

Gunther and I ran after him and leaned out. It was a two-story drop, but the Chimp was up and running down the empty street. He was limping slightly but moving fast.

I turned to Fields's bed and pulled back the covers. By now

the young girl who had checked us in stood in the doorway in a pink robe, her blond hair down.

The bed was empty. A pillow lay under the blanket. Feathers were showing through the two bullet holes in the pillow. I checked the blanket. Two more bullet holes.

"How many shots did you hear?" I asked Gunther.

"Four," he said. "Where is Mr. Fields?"

"What's goin' on here?" the frightened girl in the doorway asked.

"Long story," I said, going for the washroom.

It was empty.

"Is there an all-night bar in town?" I asked the girl.

"No," she said as Gunther and I moved past her.

There were three people, a woman and two men, in the hall-way, tentative, close to the doors to their rooms. They were all over sixty.

"Any of you see or hear anything?" I asked.

They stood silently, stunned.

"I'm a detective," I said, feeling more like a half-dressed idiot with a gun in my hand.

"Shots," said the woman.

"Four," said one of the men.

"Running down the hall," said the other man. "Shots woke me up and I heard someone running down the hall and two more shots."

"Just go back to your rooms," I said as calmly as I could. "No one's hurt. Domestic squabble. Got out of hand."

The trio of guests went reluctantly back to their rooms. We could hear the chains being pulled and the locks snapping into place.

"What's happening?" asked the girl.

"We've got to find Mr. Fields," I said.

"Make more sense with your pants on," she said. "Is anything broken?"

"You'll need a new blanket and pillow," I said, heading back toward our room. "We'll pay for it."

Somewhere below a baby began to cry.

"Bill," she said. "I've got to get back to him. I'm calling Sandy Milch."

I pulled on a pair of pants. Gunther did the same. I put my gun down just long enough to slip on the shirt I had worn the day before. I didn't button it. I didn't stop to pick up my shoes. Gunther buttoned his shirt as I moved to the door.

"Kidnapped?" Gunther asked.

"I don't know," I said, leading the way.

I ran down the stairs to the lobby. The night-lights were on and baby Bill was whimpering somewhere in a room behind the counter. We looked around. The restaurant was dark, locked.

It was Gunther who noticed the door of the barbershop across the lobby, slightly ajar. He pointed to it and tugged my sleeve. We moved to the door and I pushed it open. In the dim light of the lobby, we could make out a figure in the single chair. A low growling sound came from the figure. I trained my gun on the chair and Gunther scurried in search of a light switch. He found one.

Fields, wrapped in his robe with the sash neatly tied, lay back in the chair, mouth open, snoring. There were no bullet holes in him.

I moved to the chair and shook him gently. He grunted but remained asleep and snoring. I shook harder and said, "Bill." Gunther tried. He was firmer about it than I and nearly shouted, "Mr. Fields, we have an emergency. You must awaken."

Suddenly Fields, his eyes open, sat upright in the chair and shouted, "Two crates of raspberries and one of oranges. You have my solemn word I'll have them delivered in the morning. Besides, I didn't know she was married."

He sat there blinking for a few seconds, rubbed his eyes, and then looked around the small barbershop, first at me and then at Gunther.

"First decent sleep I've had in a week," Fields grumbled, sitting forward. "And you have to wake me to play hide and seek."

"How did you get in here?" I asked.

"My maiden aunt Calliope could open this door with a paper clip," he said. "Couldn't sleep. Came down here. Opened the door and got into the barber chair. A good specimen. About the same vintage as the one I have at home."

There was some activity in the lobby. I didn't turn around to look. Gunther was doing that for me.

"You didn't hear the shots?" I said.

"Shots?" Fields said, rising.

"Someone tried to shoot you in bed," I said. "Shot a couple of holes in your blanket and pillow. Gunther and I ran into your room. Woloski was there, with a gun. He got away. Dived through a second-story window and ran away."

"Second floor, eh? Once the show-business training is in your blood, you never forget," sighed Fields, now standing, if not firmly. "I told you he was in cahoots with Hipnoodle."

"You did," I said.

Gunther touched my arm. Two men in brown uniforms with guns in their hands stood in the open door of the barbershop.

"Put the gun down gentle," said the older man, who had a belly almost as big as Fields's. "Right on the barber chair'll be just fine."

I did as I was told.

"Despite the events of the past half hour or less I was blissfully ensconced in the arms of Morpheus, officers," said Fields. "You are too late to help and too dangerous to be pointing loaded weapons at innocent people. If either of you is adept at needlepoint or sewing, you might go up to my room and try to repair the damage I understand has resulted in the puncturing of the bedding in my boudoir."

The older cop with the gut looked puzzled. "We'll get to all that," said the skinny younger cop. He looked like he was draft age, though he didn't weigh in at more than a hundred and twenty. He took a step forward, deciding to take command from his older

partner, and I could see it was probably the limp that had earned
him a 4F.

"You're coming with us," said the young skinny cop.

"We're coming with you," I agreed. "Can we go get dressed?"

The cops exchanged looks, examined us, and came to a conclusion. "If you make it fast," the young one said, moving forward to pick my .38 up from the seat of the barber chair.

We passed the girl with the baby in her arms in the lobby. She
looked frightened and confused. Both cops had put their guns
away but we were still a strange middle-of-the-night gathering.

"It'll be fine, Missy," the older cop told the young woman.
"No one's hurt. Maybe a few people got a little drunk and shot
off some firearms. That the way it looks to you, Bobby?"

"I say we leave that to Sandy," said the younger man as they
let us lead the way up the stairway and back to our rooms. The
younger one went with me and Gunther. The older one with
Fields. We finished first, though Gunther was not at all happy
about being urged to hurry.

When we stepped into the hall, Fields and the fat cop still
weren't out of the room. Bobby motioned us toward it; since I
was two steps ahead of him and he was limping, I was the first
to see the fat cop sitting on the bed. He had a couple of seconds
to put down an almost-empty glass before Officer Bobby entered the room. The older cop quickly busied himself examining
the wounded bed. Fields, standing nearby, was sipping a martini.

We stepped into the room as the fat cop got up and said,
"Two holes in the blanket. Two in the pillow."

"There were four shots," I said.

"Four," Gunther confirmed.

"Two in the blanket. Two in the pillow," the fat cop repeated.

"I'd say that's two shots, each went through both the blanket
and the pillow," I said.

"Get the bullets, Virgil," the young cop said.

The older cop was glad to be active. He pulled back the blanket and pillow and said, "He's right. Right through the sheet
and into the mattress. I can see 'em."

He pulled out a pocket knife and probed, smiling and showing us each bullet triumphantly as he extracted it from the mattress. "Looks like thirty-eights," Virgil said, straightening with a bit of difficulty.

"We'll leave that to Sandy," Bobby the 4F cop said. "Let's go."

The girl and the baby were still in the lobby. She was doing her best to comfort him, rocking him gently, waiting till her family hotel was free of police and gun shooters.

Fields paused in front of her, dug into his right-hand pocket, and came up with a handful of bills. He plucked out three hundreds and handed them to the girl.

"Should cover the damage and maybe a little left over for the little tyke's defense fund, should he ever run into difficulties with the law," he said, tipping his hat to her.

Less than five minutes later, after a quiet ride, we stopped in front of the Coshocton Police Headquarters, which took up about a third of a one-story brick building that also housed the library and the office of the mayor.

We all got out quietly. Virgil the fat cop led the way. Bobby the young cop kept up the rear. We entered the door marked *Coshocton Police* and found ourselves in a big room. On the right were two cells, both empty. In front of us was a low railing. Behind the railing were two desks, neat. On the walls were some awards and a large painting of FDR looking serious. Next to FDR was another painting, a chisel-faced man in profile, wearing a cowboy hat.

"William S. Hart," I said to Gunther, who was looking with some puzzlement at the painting.

"This way," said Virgil, pushing open a gate in the low fence.

We followed in past the desks to an office door marked *Chief*. Virgil knocked gently. "Come in," came a woman's voice.

Virgil opened the door and stood back to let us enter. The room was small, clean, efficient: a table with four chairs, all wood and simple; an almost-matching desk; more awards on the walls and another pair of paintings of FDR and William S.

Hart. Behind the desk sat a small woman in a zipper jacket with a badge on it. She was around fifty, dark hair cut short, no makeup, and a no-nonsense look in her dark eyes. She looked tired. I guess we all did, with the exception of Virgil and Bobby, who the woman dismissed with, "Two of you wait outside."

They left, quickly closing the door behind them, after Bobby placed my .38 and the two bullets from the bed on top of the desk.

"Sandy Milch," the woman said without rising.

"I'm—" I began, but she cut me off.

"Know who all of you are," she said, removing a large revolver from her desk drawer and placing it in front of her. "Just tell me what the hell is going on."

"It began in the autumn of nineteen-oh-nine or nineteen-ten," Fields began, examining the straw hat he had taken from his head and gazing at it as if it were a crystal ball that would bring up essential images from the past.

"Too far back," Sandy Milch said. "You tell it." She pointed to me, and Fields let out a small sigh.

I told her the story, everything, and she took notes on a pad of paper. When I was done, she looked up at the three of us. Actually, she looked up at Fields and me and down across at Gunther.

"So a man named Albert Woloski, also known as the Chimp, and another one named Hipnoodle, are trying to tease you into following them while they steal your money. They are also trying to kill you and warning you not to follow them?"

"Something like that," I said.

"Makes no damn sense," she said.

"We agree," I said.

"You can check the Hipnoodle part with a detective in Philadelphia," I said. "Gus Belcher. I've got his number in my notebook."

"Take it out careful," Chief Milch said.

"Never met a lady police chief before," said Fields politely. "Refreshing change."

"Husband was the chief," she said. "He's a colonel in the Big Red One. I'm holding down the job till he gets back. I used to be the dispatcher. Bobby, the one with the limp?"

I nodded.

"He's our son," she said. "Good boy. Bad motorcycle spill when he was fifteen. Lost control. Went right through Andy Morrison's barn wall. Almost lost his leg."

I gave her the number for Gus Belcher in Philadelphia. She looked at it for a few seconds and then up at Fields.

"My Henry, the soldier, thinks you're funny," she said. "I don't see it."

"Bill Hart," Fields said, gesturing to the painting on the wall.

"Henry's and my favorite," she said, looking up at it.

"Had the pleasure of meeting Bill on several occasions," said Fields. "Trained Shakespearean. Shy man but he could be brought out with the right coaxing and he had some good stories."

"You know William S. Hart?" Sandy Milch said, sitting up.

"Acquaintances," Fields said. "We had much in common. I liked the man. Knew the Bard as well as I know Charles Dickens."

"I'll be damned," Sandy Milch said. "Was he like he was in the movies?"

"Simply played himself to perfection, and did his own stunts," said Fields with a small smile that suggested he was recalling an especially intimate moment in one of his meetings with the cowboy star.

Sandy Milch sat silently looking at Fields, unsure of whether to believe him. The silence lasted an instant or two and then she said, "I'll call Belcher. Probably won't be there at four in the morning, but I can leave a message."

She placed the call and waved at the table and chairs, a suggestion that we take a seat. We did.

"Detective Belcher," she said. "This is Chief Milch in Coshocton, Ohio, and I don't have much of a budget for long-distance calls so I want to make it quick . . . right . . . okay . . . I understand. He have a partner who might know about his cases? . . . Knox? Got it. Mickey Knox. And he'll be on day shift in three hours. Can you have him call me when he gets in?"

She gave her number and hung up. Then she looked down at her pad and over at us.

"Hipnoodle?" she said, shaking her head at the lunacy of the whole thing.

"Yes," I said.

"Detective Belcher is off tomorrow," she said. "Fishing with his kids. His partner'll call me back in three hours."

"Meanwhile?" I said.

"We sit, have some coffee, maybe a couple of doughnuts or pound cake from Aggie's down the street, and we go over all this slow and careful, maybe leaving us a little time to talk about William S. Hart."

"The bank opens at nine," Fields said.

"If we're not done, Virgil will be there, and if Hipnoodle—that's one crazy damn name—if Hipnoodle shows up, Virgil brings him in and we all have another talk."

"Account's in the name of Melodious Quach," said Fields.

"And Hipnoodle has your bankbook and can forge your signature and your handwriting?" Sandy Milch said.

"Apparently with great skill and aplomb," said Fields, tapping the top of his straw hat resting on the table before him.

"Virgil, Bobby," she shouted.

The two policemen who had been waiting outside the door came in instantly.

"Bobby," she said to her son. "Drive around a little and see if you can find this acrobat who looks like an ape. If you find him, be careful. According to our guests, he's got a record and tried to kill Mr. Fields tonight."

"I'll be careful, Mom," he said.

"As soon as Aggie opens, I want you to pick up coffees all around, some doughnuts, and pound cake." She handed Bobby a couple of dollars and said to us, "Aggie makes the best damn pound cake in Ohio."

Bobby pocketed the money.

"After you bring the coffee and cake, go home and get some sleep. Give Jimmy a call and tell him to come in an hour early. He's gonna ask about getting paid an hour overtime. Tell him we can't afford it. He won't curse me to you. Call Frankie Tolliver. Tell him to come in an hour early too. Frankie won't complain."

"Right," said Bobby Milch, limping out the door.

"Virgil," Sandy Milch said. "You go home, set two alarm clocks for seven, and be at the bank before it opens. Tell Ray that if anyone tries to make a withdrawal from the account of a Melodious Quinch—"

"Melodious Quach," Fields corrected.

"Quach," she amended. "He's to tell you right away and you're to bring Quach here for questioning."

"Okay, Sandy," Virgil said.

"Last thing, and I don't like saying it in front of strangers," she said. "You're a good policeman, probably the best of the four I've got, but if I catch you drinking on duty again, you'll be selling Old Dutch Coffee at Gutterman's Grocery and tearing out ration stamps."

Virgil was about to speak but Fields interrupted with, "The officer was not at fault. He showed a sign of momentary weakness and was tempted by me with the offer of a small drink after I took one to calm myself after having barely missed dying in Ohio."

Sandy Milch nodded to show that she heard Fields's excuse but didn't give it much credit.

We sat silently as Chief Sandy Milch examined my gun and then the bullets Virgil had plucked out of Fields's bed.

"Your gun hasn't been fired," she said, looking up. "One point for you. Gun registered?"

"In Los Angeles. I'm a licensed private investigator."

"Bullets from the bed," she said, a little puzzled, rolling one of them on her palm. "Different story. What kind of gun you say this Chimp guy had?"

"I think it was a thirty-eight, too," I said, "but I'm not sure."

"These bullets came from a big gun," she said. "Probably made big holes."

She held up a bullet between her thumb and forefinger for Virgil to examine.

"Big weapon," Virgil confirmed. "Bigger than a thirty-eight."

"I'll let the state police worry about that one," she said. "I'll call them when Virgil comes back with your Hipnoodle, providing he shows up. Now, I want to hear whatever you know about William S. Hart."

"I would be delighted to tell tales about dear old Bill that will make you laugh, sigh, and even bring a tear or two to your eyes," said Fields, "but I left a thermos of medicinal liquid in my room, and after this encounter with the reaper . . ."

"Virgil," Sandy Milch said. "Before you go home would you mind bringing Mr. Fields's thermos of medicine back here?"

"Sure," said Virgil.

"Then go," she said. "And don't drink any of it."

Fields began to tell tales of Hart's wit, honesty, humor, and compassion for children, the aged, and the afflicted. He told of the silent-screen cowboy star's love of his horse and his mother, not necessarily in that order.

When Virgil came back and placed the thermos before a grateful Fields, there was a brief pause while Fields poured himself a drink and said, "Pineapple juice with a healthy dosage of liquid jumju leaf, a calming concoction that also eases my lumbago."

Gunther put his head on the table and fell asleep. Gunther was accustomed to taking brief naps during the day and working at his desk during the night. I was accustomed to staying up for a night or two in my car, drinking coffee when I could get it,

and watching the house or apartment of someone I was supposed to be protecting or someone I was supposed to be catching in an act of sexual frenzy or bliss, neither of which would
please my client. Coffee would help.

Fields went on and on, holding Sandy Milch rapt. She took
notes so she could get it all in her next letter to her husband,
Henry.

Eventually, light came through the window. Just a little at first
and then definite daylight. Bobby Milch appeared with coffee,
doughnuts, a couple of caramel rolls, and half-a-dozen slices of
pound cake.

"Home now, Bobby," Sandy said.

"No sign of the guy who looks like a gorilla," he said.

"A chimp," Fields corrected. "Entirely different face and
carriage."

"Not one of those either," Bobby said and left the room.

I nudged Gunther and he awoke almost instantly. Sandy
Milch had joined us at the table about an hour earlier. My .38
was now in her desk drawer along with the bullets. She was at
the end of the table with her weapon right in front of her.

Gunther ate and drank slowly, delicately. I tried to restrain
myself from scooping in everything and finishing my not-
particularly-hot coffee in two gulps. Even Fields nibbled at the
pound cake, and then took an entire piece.

"Best damn pound cake you ever had?" asked Sandy Milch,
leaning forward.

"No doubt," I said, my mouth full.

"Superior," said Gunther.

"Excellent," said Fields. "I'd say it barely inches ahead of the
pound cake of Elfreda Labaca Caz in Lima, Peru. Elfreda runs
a little café there, cooks and bakes herself. Claims secret ingredients. I'm trying to think if Bill Hart was with me at the time,
but it was a long time ago."

Within the next thirty minutes, things happened fast.

Belcher's partner Knox called and said that they had investigated a guy named Hipnoodle who was supposedly planning to steal money from a bunch of Fields's bank accounts. They had gotten a warrant, searched Hipnoodle's apartment, and came up with nothing.

That much I could get from Sandy Milch's end of the line.

"So far, so good," she said. "It looks like the way things happened."

Almost as soon as she hung up, there was a knock at her door and she told whoever it was to come in. It was Virgil. He had cut himself shaving and had a small dab of toilet paper on the cut. He looked at us, looked at the chief, and turned his cap in his hand.

"Hipnoodle got away," Sandy Milch said.

"It was all—" Virgil started and looked at FDR and William S. Hart for inspiration. "I was standing next to Dorothy's desk, you know, sort of out of sight so people coming in wouldn't see a uniformed police officer."

"And you couldn't see them," Sandy Milch said.

Virgil nodded. "Anyway, I had told Ray, and while I was talking to Dorothy, Ray comes walking up and says one of the tellers is making a withdrawal for Melodious Quarh. By the time we get to the teller, which is real fast, she—Wendy Douglas, Archie's sister-in-law from Massillon—points to a tall guy going out the door. I'm headed right for him. He's just standing there, looking both ways down the street. 'Halt,' I yell, pulling out my weapon. He hears me, turns his head. I can see he's wearing those old glasses with no rims. He turns right and runs. I go out right behind him, yelling at him to stop, warning that I'll shoot, which I wouldn't. He keeps going. I keep following him and with my weight and age on his side, I still start catching up. He's not fast. Sort of gangly. He turns the corner right in front of Quilly's Hardware and I'm right behind him, knowing I'll catch him in a few seconds. And then it happened."

"It?" asked Sandy Milch.

"Someone hit me from behind," Virgil said. "God's truth. Hit me with something to my head. Got the lump right here to prove it. Then he kicked me in the back. I lost my weapon and he hit my head again with his hand. I didn't know which way was up or what color was blue. Then he stopped. I got my gun and stood up kind of dizzy. Gangly guy from the bank was gone. No sign of the guy who hit me."

"You get a look at him?" I asked.

"The tall guy, yes. Whoever hit me, no. Sorry, Sandy. I think he was big."

"Go back to bed, Virgil," she said. "You did your best."

Virgil slunk out of the room.

"What now?" I asked.

"Got nothing to hold any of you on or for," she said, getting up and going to her desk. "I'll have the state police check the bullets. You'll have to make a statement, sign a few papers, and then I guess you'll be leaving town."

"As quickly as we can," I said as she handed me my .38.

After she took our statements, Chief Milch herself drove us back to the hotel. Our bags were packed and waiting for us. Fields had already paid the girl with the baby the night before, but she was out watching as Gunther brought the car around.

After we had packed everything in the Caddy and gotten in, I said, "Where now?"

"No idea," said Fields. "But I want to get that son of a bitch."

"Ottumwa," said Gunther. "Iowa. I found this on the windshield, under the wiper." Gunther reached over his shoulder and handed us a card on which was printed: "Ottumwa. See you there."

Chapter Seven

Of all the presidents' hobbies, I think General Grant's came nearer to my ideals . . .

Fields sat in silence, looking out the window, leaning on his cane as Gunther sped up the Interstate on the way to Indianapolis and, beyond that, Ottumwa, Iowa. The cane was a spare he had brought with him and had been pressed into service when whoever had shot at us had cut the other one in two.

Finally, Fields muttered, "There's more damn corn in this country than there are people. I eat two ears a year and give my neighbor's dog an additional one or two just to watch him struggle with getting the little bits out from between his teeth. I've sent more canines into dental madness than modesty permits me to disclose."

"Corn is used principally to feed cows, extract oils, and to make alcoholic beverages," Gunther said seriously from the front seat, where he watched the road carefully and managed to drive just above the posted speed limits.

"Fascinating," said Fields, putting down his morning drink. "Pull over, we just crossed into Indiana."

Gunther pulled over. Cars zipped by us as Fields got out of the car and moved to the driver's window.

"Out," he ordered, opening the door.

Gunther looked back at me and I shrugged. Gunther got out and Fields leaned over to remove the straps on the pedals and shove the padded seat over to the passenger side. Then he got in. Gunther stood next to the car with some bewilderment.

"I," said Fields, "will show you how to get to Iowa faster than it takes a man I once knew named Whalebait to down half a pint of distinctly inferior whiskey."

Gunther looked at me. I shrugged and opened the rear door. Gunther got in. No sooner had he closed the door than Fields took off, tires screaming, almost hitting a truck that had "Royalist Cigars" painted on the side, along with a large picture of a cigar and smoke curling up.

"Should look where he's going," Fields muttered as he glanced back in his rearview mirror at the truck and its badly shaken driver. "Did you know that eighty-three percent of the women of these United States put out ashtrays the size of thimbles, designed to embarrass the cigar smoker whose ash, of necessity, falls on the table or arm of the divan?"

Neither Gunther nor I answered. Fields gathered speed. Over the course of the next four hours we had six near collisions, were almost hit by a train, and came close to a fistfight with the driver of an A & P truck who Fields had forced partly off the road and very nearly into the Vermilion River just past the Illinois border.

Fields reached back through the open sliding window from time to time for a glass of liquid from his thermos. He didn't trust Gunther or me to mix a martini for him.

"Drinking and driving is the only reasonable thing to do," he said, passing a trio of cars on a two-lane highway and coming within a dozen yards of a collision with an oncoming Oldsmobile before scooting back into our own lane, almost toppling the Cadillac.

Gunther was pale and gripping the armrests. I was preparing for my death somewhere between Danville and Davenport. Fields had made it clear that there would be stops for bladder relief only. He had allowed us to pause before we got out of Indiana for a stack of sandwiches, some bottles of Pepsi, and some ice, which Fields said we could keep in his backseat cooler. Neither Gunther nor I felt much like eating or drinking.

At least a dozen times, Fields drove partly off the side of the road, sometimes hitting small stones that flew up and pinged off the windows or spitting up dirt and mud that made it hard to see.

"If he can beat us to Ottumwa," Fields muttered at one point, "the bastard must be part eagle."

Finally, I tried to eat a sandwich, ham and cheese, while we drove. It wasn't easy getting it to my mouth. Gunther opened a sandwich and daintily took small pieces of meat and cheese. I spilled some Pepsi on the seat, looked up to see if Fields had noticed, and then managed to drink.

"Keep the upholstery clean," Fields shouted. "Never know when I might entertain a studio executive or his secretary back there."

Fields flipped on the radio, carefully zipping past anything that sounded like music. We heard from a serious-sounding man with a deep voice that General Patton had wept after his aide, Captain Richard Jenon, twenty-seven, was killed. The announcer said Jenon was from Pasadena.

Fields listened attentively, barely managing to avoid collision with the rear of a small pickup truck full of crates of chickens.

The newscaster added that Rommel was still on the run, that Dorothy Lamour had married Captain William Ross II, and that Beau Jack had won a decision to keep his lightweight crown. The announcer said that the crowd had almost unanimously booed the decision. Once again I had lost to Violet Gonsenelli, girl handicapper.

"Pugilism," Fields pontificated, "is the sport of men, ancient, honorable. I once went three rounds with Jack Dempsey. Just a lark. Got him good and drunk before I stepped into the ring. Managed to elude the staggering champion and engage in several pirouettes and entrechats in the process. He never laid a glove on me. Never caught me. I, being a gentleman, did not lay a glove on him. The newspapers called it a joke. I called it a draw."

"We're going to go through that red light," I said as calmly as I could.

"It's yellow," said Fields calmly.

"It's turning red right now," I said.

Gunther was attempting to speak but nothing was coming out.

Fields ran the light, missing a green Chevrolet by no more than a few inches. Fields opened his window and shouted at the bewildered man, who had pulled to the side of the road.

"Go to a decent driving school," Fields yelled. "Or buy a bicycle." Satisfied, Fields closed the window.

"You want to go home when we hit Ottumwa?" I asked Gunther quietly.

"Decidedly," said Gunther. "However, I have always made it a practice to live up to my agreements, contracts, and obligations. I will remain with you in the hope that Mr. Fields approaches something resembling sense and allows me behind the wheel once again."

"I heard all that, you runt," Fields shouted over the roar of the engine at seventy-five miles an hour as we swayed forward. "You're a good man. Ever play any pool?"

"No," said Gunther.

"Ping-Pong?"

"No."

"Poker?"

"No," answered Gunther.

"Do you chase women?"

"I am fond of females," said Gunther. "But I find that they often disappoint me. Perhaps the novelty soon fades."

"You mean you can't hold your own?" shouted Fields.

"No," said Gunther. "I mean *yes*. I was referring to the novelty of my stature. I am, as you so sympathetically put it, a runt."

"Don't like me much, do you?" asked Fields, honking the horn and forcing an old woman in an ancient car off the road.

"Strangely enough," said Gunther, "I have grown quite fond of you."

"You are an appreciator of the comic art of conversation and the skills of a world-class driver," said Fields, looking down the road for further prey.

"No," said Gunther seriously. "I do not understand your wit. Perhaps it is a language problem. Your vocabulary is large, but your use of it is confusing. I find you, however, a very sad man."

Fields had a smile on his face as he turned to face us, ignoring the road. He was about to say something but his eyes met Gunther's and Fields's mouth closed. He turned around and drove with something approaching his idea of caution for the next hundred miles. He drove without speaking, other than to ask for refills.

"I should like to take up Ping-Pong or pool," Gunther finally said as we crossed into Iowa.

"And I should consider it an honor to teach you the nuances of the art of table tennis," said Fields.

Except for almost hitting the woman pushing the baby carriage in Burlington and the unintended brief detour off the road and into a field of some sort of grain when a deer appeared in the road, we reached Ottumwa, alive, late in the afternoon.

I checked the watch on my wrist. It said six-fifteen. The watch was a bequest of my father. It had its own mad sense of time and seldom came within hours of being right. I'd been told by three watch repairmen that there was nothing they could see wrong with my father's watch. One of them, an ancient Austrian, said that it was probably me—a force field or something. He had seen many such cases of perfectly fine watches that wouldn't keep the right time and even stopped for no reason. This had happened even when the wearer changed watches. "You have, I think," the Austrian watchmaker had said, "an electromagnetic field that is negative instead of positive."

When I asked him to explain, he said he was a watchmaker, not a physicist.

One thing I did notice as we slowed to the pace of a mad cheetah was that not many of the stores seemed to be opened, though it wasn't quite five.

"Town closes down early," Fields observed, looking for the bank, trying to remember, having little success.

Finally, we pulled into a Texaco gas station where a thin man with a drooping lower lip, wearing overalls, came out, wiping his hands on a dirty rag.

"Fill the tank, my good man," Fields said. "And point us in the direction of the bank."

The gas-station man nodded and said, "Which bank?"

"How many you got?" asked Fields.

"Three," said the man, moving to the rear of the Caddy to fill up the tank.

"All of them," said Fields, sticking his head out the window. "And hurry."

"Won't make any difference if I hurry or not," said the man, starting to pump the gas and looking through the rear window at Gunther and me.

His demeanor suggested to me that he thought we were the sad remains of the Dillinger gang out to remove all the hard-earned money of the citizens of Ottumwa before hurrying on to more easy pickings in Nebraska.

"What time do the banks close?" asked Fields.

"Five-thirty," said the man, still pumping.

"Gives us more than half an hour," said Fields with satisfaction and a smile, patting the steering wheel as if it were Ken Maynard's horse Tarzan, and he'd just carried us over the Rocky Mountains.

"Nope," said the man in overalls, removing the nose of the pump and closing the tank. "Banks are all closed. Saturday. Only open in the morning till noon on Saturdays."

None of us, not even Gunther, had noticed that it was Saturday. The days had begun to melt into each other.

"We can't get in. He can't get in," Fields said. "And I'm damn sure we beat him."

"Now," said Gunther softly, "we must spend tonight and Sunday here."

He sounded relieved.

"You can drive again after we catch Hipnoodle here in the heartland," Fields said.

"A buck-fifty, even, and gas-ration stamps," the man in overalls said.

Fields produced both, handed them to the man, and said, "Dare I risk it? Can you point us in the direction of the finest hotel in your fair city?"

"Two lights straight ahead," said the man, pointing. "Turn right. Keep going. You'll be downtown. Hotels there. Never stayed in one myself."

"I'll remember that," said Fields, touching the rim of his boater hat and heading toward downtown.

Not much was open as we drove slowly along, but there were cars parked on either side of the street, cars and a variety of small trucks. Fields spotted a hotel and pulled into a space, slightly scraping an already heavily scraped pickup truck.

When we hit the lobby, we all saw a modest banner across the wall, stating, "Welcome, County Grange Members, 12th Annual Meeting."

There were groups of men, probably farmers, talking in the corners of the lobby, around tables, at chairs drawn up so they could lean forward and hear themselves. There was also a table behind which sat a very heavy woman with thick glasses and a stack of papers before her. She looked up at us as we passed her and headed for the check-in desk.

We had to ring to make a young man in a neat, tan, but slightly worn suit appear behind the counter. He had no left arm, just a kind of mechanical pincer showing through the end of his sleeve.

"Yes, sirs," he said.

"Two rooms," said Fields.

"You with the Grange?" asked the young man politely.

"The Grange?" Fields repeated.

Gunther was already, with the help of an old bellman, dragging in our considerable stack of luggage.

"Entire hotel is sold out. Has been for months. Grange members only."

"We are farmers," said Fields, standing erect.

The counterman with one arm looked at Fields and me and over at Gunther, who had almost completed the task of hauling in the luggage.

"Darned if you don't look and sound like W. C. Fields," said the clerk with a grin.

"I've been told there is a faint resemblance," said Fields. "Perhaps an anomaly on my mother's side."

"Mr. Fields is my favorite," the clerk said. "Don't miss a movie or a radio show. Never saw him live." He reached below the counter and came up with a copy of *Movie Life*, flipped through the pages, found what he wanted, and turned the page to Fields. There was no doubt that the man in the picture and my client were one and the same. "I'd appreciate your signing this for me," said the young clerk. "I'll have it framed and put it on the wall."

Fields took the pen offered to him by the young man and said, "What's your name?"

"Alex Collins."

"To my dear friend, Alex Collins," Fields said as he wrote on the picture. "And to the secret we have promised to share with no one but each other. W. C. Fields."

Collins turned the magazine around and grinned.

"Rooms?" asked Fields.

"Gotta convince the Grange check-in lady," Collins said with a shrug. "Can't risk losing my job."

"How'd you lose your arm? War?" asked Fields.

"No. Tractor. I was twelve."

"Farming's dangerous," said Fields.

"That's why I'm behind this desk," said Collins. "Good luck."

We moved, now a trio, to the desk where the fat woman in glasses sat. She looked up, hands folded and smiling.

"We're farmers," said Fields, removing his hat.

The woman blinked at the three of us.

"Up near Clarinda," said Fields, pointing toward the hotel door.

"Names," said the woman, pulling a typed pile of papers in front of her.

"Pearlfender," Fields said. "And these are my partners, Mr. Whalebait and Mr. Pertwee. You'll not find our names on your list. We just purchased the acreage and the delightful house and barn yesterday."

"Terry Willans's place?" she asked.

"The same," said Fields.

"I'll be cracked like an acorn," she said, shaking her head. "Terry and his family have been trying to unload that place for years. You're city people."

"Your powers of observation are beyond normal human ken," Fields said, still smiling and leaning over. "And your eyes are the sweet brown of a cow I once had the pleasure of milking in Minnesota some years back."

The fat woman blushed.

"What are you gonna try to grow on the place?" she asked.

"Couscous, farfel, exotic hearty grains no longer available to the palates of the sophisticated city dwellers who have not seen a couscous bud since before the war."

"I never . . ." the woman began.

"But soon you shall, my little prairie daisy," said Fields.

"Two dollars each," the woman said, holding out her pudgy palm.

Fields fished into his pocket and came up with a twenty. The woman found change and handed Fields a receipt.

"Just take it to the desk," she said. "Dinner's at seven. James W. Kroft is the dinner speaker."

"James W. Kroft," Fields replied amiably, handing me the receipt.

"Designer of the Kroft Heavy-Duty Silo," she said. "Is that couscous stuff heavy?"

"No, but the farfel sits in your stomach like an anvil," said Fields and then added in a whisper, "I'd prefer you not tell any of our fellow tillers of the soil about our crop plans."

"Mum," she said. "And don't miss the dinner. You paid for it. Besides, we always get rambunctious afterwards."

"Irresistible," said Fields.

The one-armed clerk checked Mr. Pearlfender, Whalebait, and Pertwee in with a smile and said, "I knew you could do it."

"Professional," said Fields, plunking down cash for the night's lodging and signing us in.

Collins handed us three keys, separate rooms. I found out why when we got to the third floor. There was an elevator which was much smaller and about the same speed as the one in the Faraday.

I had just closed my door, dropped my bag on the bed, and started to take off my shoes when there was a loud knock at my door and then a series of knocks.

"Coming," I said, slipping back into my shoes.

Fields was standing outside. "He wants to talk to you," he said.

"Who?"

"Hipnoodle," answered Fields. "The phone was ringing when I went into the room. The fiend is uncanny."

I followed Fields into his room and picked up the phone. "Yeah," I said.

"At the end of the street where you are staying," he said, "there's a dead end. Turn left, keep going. On your right you will see a park. Inside the park you will find a fish pond. Be there alone at eleven."

"The bank," I said.

"I've already got the money out of the bank here," he said.

"I've got the money out of almost all the banks. I'd been at this for weeks before I wrote to Fields. Eleven, park, fountain. You alone."

He hung up. I hung up and looked at the waiting Fields.

"Well? How did he sound?"

"Articulate and scared," I said. "He wants to meet me in a park at eleven, alone."

"Demand total capitulation," said Fields, pointing his cane at the phone. "Every penny he's gotten of my hard-earned cash, or a life behind bars where he will be forced to live on grits and water and consort with people who are unable to read."

"He says he's already been to the bank here," I reported. "And that he's been to most of the other banks, went there before he wrote to you."

"Bastard is smart and drives like a fiend," said Fields, pacing the floor. "Well?"

"I'll go to the park at eleven and see what's on his mind," I said.

"Apprehend the cur," Fields demanded.

"We'll see how it works out," I said. "Meanwhile, I suggest that you and Gunther be downstairs talking feed prices and the price of a barrel of corn with your merry group. This may be a trick to get me away from you."

"Good thinking," said Fields. "I'll inform the little fellow. Right after I have a small drink to calm my nerves."

I showered, shaved, dressed in the best I had with me, and joined Fields and Gunther for the farmers' dinner and the lecture on silos. We sat at a table with four other men, who eyed us suspiciously but talked politely. Fields took notes on what the silo man was saying. He wrote on the back of an envelope with the stub of a pencil. I have no idea why.

When dinner—a good steak, sweet potatoes, salad, and the best peach pie I'd ever eaten—was over, I told Gunther and Fields that they had to be downstairs in the lobby from a quarter to eleven till I got back. If I didn't get back by midnight, they were to call the police and tell them I was last heard of standing in front of the fish pond in the park. I wrapped a couple of pieces of bread in a napkin and stuck it in my pocket.

Then I went back to my room and lay down to wait, and listen to the radio. I caught the last few minutes of "Can You Top This?," a joke from Joe Laurie, Jr., and another one from Harry Hirschfield. Then the news, followed by a dance band live from Des Moines playing war songs, including "The General Jumped at Dawn" and "The Bombardier."

I dozed in the middle of "The Bing Crosby Show" after catching a few jokes at the expense of the comic Ukie and John Scott Trotter, a duet of "Mexicali Rose" with Bing's guest Roy Rogers, and Marilyn Maxwell and Bing doing "Two Sleepy People." When I opened my eyes, "The Groucho Marx Show" was on, and Groucho was exchanging insults with Hedda Hopper.

I got up slowly. I wasn't late, but it was time I got moving. My back ached. The bed was too soft. I should have moved the mattress onto the floor.

I put on my holster, checked my .38, got into my shoes, zipped up my jacket, turned off the radio, and went to Fields's and Gunther's rooms. Neither answered. A good sign. I spotted them in the lobby, engaged in conversation and drinks with some of the farmers. Fields was animated, drink in hand. Gunther sat back silently and glanced at me, making it clear that he wanted me to be careful. I intended to be.

My .38 sat heavily under my arm. There weren't many people on the street at this hour. A few of the farmers in search of a place to get a late Saturday-night drink. An older couple getting into their car.

It took me ten minutes to get to the park. The directions had been clear. The park was small, but you couldn't see the street from the fish pond. Not that it mattered. There was no one on the street. A park light stood next to the pond. There didn't seem to be a lights-out or curfew in Ottumwa. I guess no one seriously thought the Japanese or Germans would have the fuel or inclination to fly to the middle of the United States to drop bombs on small cities and cornfields.

I shifted my gun from the holster to my pocket, took the napkin out of my pocket, and fed the fish. I was early. The fish were mostly big carp. They gobbled the bread, breaking the silence with their splashing. I'd thrown in the last of what I had when I heard the sound behind me. My hand moved casually to my gun.

If I was about to be killed, I'd at least be going out in my best clothes.

He stood in front of me, tall, erect, thin, and older than I had expected. He wore a suit and a knowing smile. John Carradine would play him if they ever made a movie of his life. He looked at the nearby trees and bushes and spoke softly, a touch of something that sounded like fear in his voice.

"Mr. Peters," he said.

"Mr. Hipnoodle," I answered.

"The name is Lester Burton," he said. "I'd like you to accompany me to my room in a hotel other than yours where I can turn over the money, bankbooks, and responsibility to you. Though my life has had but few clear examples of theatrical success, I would prefer that I not be shot at again. I regret that I cannot complete my mission, but I would like to live to perform Shakespeare once more. I've always wanted to play Iago but was rejected, even in community theater, as being too tall. I protested that I had a proper lean and hungry look. In any case, there are three more banks to go. They are in Ogallala, Nebraska; Rifle, Colorado; and Panguitch, Utah."

"Someone's trying to kill you?" I asked.

"Several times over the last few days," he said, looking around.

"Man look a little like a chimp?" I asked.

"I never saw the person who discharged his firearm, but I did feel the heat of death."

"What's this all about?" I asked.

He moved to the pond and stared down at the fish, reaching into his jacket pocket. I had my .38 out. He handed me an envelope. I took it, put my gun away, and looked at it. On the outside of the envelope was written, "To Bill."

I opened the envelope and moved closer to the park light to read it. The words were large, clear, and written with a flourish of curves:

My dear compatriot,

By the time you read this I will be imbibing with the angels if I make it to heaven and God is just and rewards my few good deeds. If there is no God, I shall simply and permanently be dead. The possibility exists, I understand, that you too will have joined me by now. However, I am determined to have one last April Fools' joke. I hope Mr. Burton has led you on a merry chase and has now given you the money and the bankbooks. Since it is yours, you may bury it in the backyard, deposit it in one or two banks nearer your domicile, or give it to the idle poor, an option I feel confident you will not exercise. It has been fun, even when you cheated at croquet. If it is possible to miss someone where I now am, I miss you. Give my best to Greg and the other survivors and drink a round for me.

Yours in eternal mischief,
John Barrymore

I put the note back in the envelope and pocketed it.

"What's going on? Who are you?"

"You have my name," said Burton, his back still turned. "You have the letter. I was hired more than two years ago by John Barrymore, with whom I had worked briefly in a film of no consequence to either of us. In the course of a lunch break, I gladly confided in him that I could perfectly imitate any signature after seeing it but once. It was a gift. My father had it before me and it earned him considerable money and several years in prison. I gave Barrymore a demonstration. Two days later he presented his plan, his final prank, to me. If he were to die before Mr. Fields, I should wait till

just before April Fools' Day, steal his friend's bankbooks, withdraw
all the money, lead Mr. Fields on, and then, when we were back in
Los Angeles, appear on his doorstep, hand him the letter you have
and a leather bag filled with the money I had collected. Mr. Barrymore paid me more than adequately by leaving me a sum in his will.
The family was confused about who I was and why I was left the
money, and I explained only that I was an old and dear friend. Two
years passed. I began the game. Rather enjoyed acting the role. And
then . . ."

"And then," I repeated.

"I realized that I was being followed, starting back in Pennsylvania a few days ago," he said. "I was shot at and was fortu-
nate to escape with my life on two occasions. I regret not
fulfilling Mr. Barrymore's task, but . . ."

"I understand," I said. "Let's go to your hotel."

"Of course," he said, turning to face me.

The night was silent and the shot clear, sharp.

Lester Burton tumbled backward into the fish pond. I turned
as fast as I could and leveled my gun in the direction I thought
the shot had come from. There was no one there. A second shot,
this one in my direction, chipped out a piece of concrete from
the walk around the fountain. I ran for the cover of the nearby
bushes. There were no more shots, but I didn't move once I got
behind a cluster of tight branches. I crouched, gun in hand,
breathing heavily. I could see the tall corpse of Lester Burton
lying on his face among the curious goldfish.

I waited for about five minutes, maybe more. No police
showed up. I came out of the bushes, low and ready, and looked
around. I couldn't see anyone.

I took a chance, holstered my gun, and moved to the pond,
where I illegally pulled Burton from the water. There was no chance
he was alive. I had seen the splot of blood on his white shirt, the
open-mouthed look of surprise on his face. His eyes had remained
open.

I double-checked for any sign of life. There was none. I

scrambled through his wet pockets. His wallet confirmed that he was Lester Burton. There were four hundred dollars in twenties in addition to his identification. I put the wallet and the money back in his pocket and then I went through his other pockets. A car key on a chain with another key that looked like it belonged to an apartment or a house. And then I found it. A hotel-room key. It was on a chain attached to a dark wooden oval the size of a half dollar. Etched into the wood was the name of Burton's hotel, the Grand. There was also, in smaller letters, the hotel's address and Burton's room number, 213. I dried my hands on my jacket, looked down at Burton, and turned away, mad as hell. I had known the man for no more than three or four minutes. I liked him. And someone had killed him, a man who was doing a job for a friend. Burton could have collected all the money and kept it himself, but it had been clear from our talk that he planned to keep his word to Barrymore. Lester Burton deserved better.

I ran out of the park and onto the street, looking for someone who could tell me where the Grand Hotel was—even a cop, though that wasn't my first choice. Then I remembered; it was on the same street we were on. My back told me not to run, but my anger told me to ignore my back and get moving, fast.

I passed a few people, key jingling in one pocket, gun in the other, and almost missed the Grand Hotel. It was small, barely a storefront. In fact, it did have storefront windows with the name of the hotel in gold lettering. The lobby was dark. I tried the door. Locked. I tried the key I had taken from Lester Burton's pocket. It worked.

I closed the door quietly behind me, took out my .38 again, and moved slowly to the stairway next to the small check-in counter. There was a dim night-light on the wall halfway up the stairs. I went up slowly. On the second-floor landing were a small corridor light and an illuminated exit sign at the far end. There weren't many rooms. I moved slowly, ready, and found room 213 almost immediately. The door was closed, but as I turned the knob carefully, I could tell it wasn't locked.

Two ways I could do this. Slow and quiet, or fast and loud. I went for fast and reasonably loud. I opened the door, went flat on the floor of the room, and searched with the barrel of my gun for the killer. The room was empty. The lights were all on. There was a closed window. The bathroom was dark. I moved to it carefully, but by now I knew he had been there and gone. While I crouched in the bushes near the fountain and went through the pockets of Lester Burton, the killer had gotten here ahead of me.

I closed the door of room 213 and looked around more thoroughly. There was a suitcase packed with clothes. The closet was empty. The giveaway was the absence of the Fields bankbooks and the cash from the accounts—and the trail of bills on the floor. There were two hundreds, four twenties, and a ten. I picked them up and pocketed them.

I left the room, closed the door, and went down to the lobby. The guest register was on the counter. I turned it around and squinted at the names of those who had registered that day. Room 213 was Lester Burton. There were three other men. Names I didn't recognize and none that sounded like Fields style humor. Burton had given an L.A. address and listed his profession as "thespian." The other men had all registered as sales representatives with home addresses in Chicago, Lincoln, and Milwaukee.

My guess was that one of them besides Burton had just checked out and was driving toward Ogallala, Nebraska. I could be wrong. He could be heading home with a satchel full of cash, but my guess was that whoever it was wouldn't be able to resist getting it all. He had killed for this much. Had tried to kill Fields. Had warned me to stay off the case or die.

If I was wrong, the killer had gotten away with murder and a lot of cash, so, really, I had no choice but Nebraska.

I went back to the lobby of our hotel.

Fields was holding court for a circle of five farmers. Gunther was half asleep but he perked up when I came in and smiled, happy that I was in one piece. Fields did not appear to notice my entrance. He was deep into his narration, which I picked up on as I approached.

"The secret," he said, "is in sowing the seeds by the light of the full moon. Works every time. Crops are healthy and plentiful. Don't care if we're talking corn, oats, farfel, or Liberian plantains. The secret was given to me by a Chinese tiller of the soil several hundred kilometers north of Chungking. Now I share it with my friends. It's the only way I plant."

Now Fields spotted me. He excused himself with a flourish and a smile and followed me and Gunther up the stairs to my room. When we were inside I took out the two hundred and ninety dollars and handed the bills to Fields, along with the letter from John Barrymore.

Fields pocketed the money and read the letter slowly while Gunther looked up at me questioningly. When he was finished, Fields handed the letter to Gunther, who read it and handed it back to Fields, who folded it slowly, returned it to the envelope, and tucked it carefully into the inner pocket of his jacket.

I told them everything that happened and they both listened quietly, asking no questions.

"The Chimp," Fields said. "If he had a neck, I'd choke the primate to death when we catch him."

"Nebraska?" I asked.

"Nebraska," he confirmed. "If that's where he's going, he's got a start on us."

"Tomorrow's Sunday," Gunther said. "The bank won't be open."

"Besides, Burton was an expert forger," I said. "Our man may have a little trouble in Ogallala. Let's say four hours' sleep and we're on the road?"

"Four hours," Fields agreed.

Gunther nodded his agreement.

"Who drives?" Gunther asked.

"You," said Fields in a definitely disheartened voice I had not heard from him before. "I'm going to drink a toast or two to Jack Barrymore in my room and I may want to snooze in the car on the way to Ogallala. The damn Chimp isn't getting away with my money and spoiling Jack's April Fools' prank. To our rooms, gentlemen. In four hours we're back on the road."

Chapter Eight

My favorite book is One Hundred and Thirteen Birdcalls and How to Simulate Them.

Fields was tired. We all were tired. Gunther drove in early-morning darkness while I dozed off an hour here, a half hour there. Fields, hands folded on his belly, head back, snored like a red Los Angeles trolley car revving up for a busy day.

Gunther had closed the sliding window between the front and back seats and listened quietly to the radio for company as we drove down Highway 34 through Osceola, Creston, Council Bluffs, and then out of Iowa and into Nebraska, bypassing Omaha as the sun broke clear over miles of cornstalks on both sides of the two-lane highway.

Every time Gunther tried to tune in some music, Fields snorted angrily in his sleep and Gunther changed the station. The news, no matter how good or bad, seemed to soothe the sleeping Fields.

According to Elmer Davis, the Nazis were accumulating something called "heavy water" to be used in a weapon with hidden atomic power. A heavy water plant in Rukan, Norway, was burned and bombed to the ground by saboteurs.

Almost in his sleep, Fields mumbled, "Knew water was dangerous. Avoid it at all costs except for baths."

Somewhere outside of York, Fields woke up. It was a slow process, involving looks around the car, examinations of both me and Gunther as if we were strangers, and a look of near horror at the sea of corn outside the window.

"Does the stuff never stop?" he asked.

"We're hungry," I said. "It's Sunday. The Chimp can't get into the bank till tomorrow and we'll be there in plenty of time."

Fields ran a hand over his gray-whiskered face and agreed to a small "pit stop" at the nearest establishment that sold sandwiches, razor blades, and replenishments for his supply of martini ingredients, though he had enough to get him across the country at least five times. He had counted on either Gunther or me joining him in drink as we traveled. Gunther did, several times in our journey, join the comedian in a cocktail. I hate martinis, don't like hard liquor in general, though I don't usually turn down a beer.

At first our lack of companionship had irked Fields, who clearly stated his distrust of adult males who did not consume "reasonable" quantities of alcohol. He admitted, however, at one weak moment, that he himself didn't like the taste of whiskey, which was why he had settled on martinis after a youth of beer and a few years of "the harder stuff."

We stopped in York, got gas, and were directed to the only shop the girl who pumped the gas thought might be open on Sunday morning. We found the place, a drugstore, and after the three of us dug out our razors, we went inside and sat down on wrought-iron chairs at a round table, where we were waited on by a dark, tall man who was definitely an Indian. The man wore denims and a plaid shirt. His hair was the whitest I've ever seen.

"Sioux?" asked Fields.

"About the only Indians you'll find around here," the man said, taking our order, an egg sandwich on white toast and a Pepsi for me, with a bag of potato chips; a cheese sandwich on toast, milk, and a scoop of vanilla ice cream for Gunther; a couple of pieces of toast and "just a dollop of jelly" for Fields.

"You got a name?" asked Fields.

"Yellow Buffalo," said the man, "but people call me Steve."

The man nodded and moved behind the counter to put some bread in a toaster. We were the only customers.

There was a phone on the wall next to a big sign that said there was a sale on Persona Precision Blades. Top Quality. Ten for a dollar.

"I'll have a package of those blades, Yellow Buffalo," Fields said. "And some rejuvenation for my dwindling supply of liquid."

When the man, who continued to work, said that the store sold no liquor and there wasn't anyplace he could get any in town on Sunday, Fields began to worry.

"No time to go in search of a liquor store open on Sunday in Nebraska," I said. "We've got to get to Ogallala, wake up the banker, beat the Chimp to your account. Besides, you've got enough to last you a week."

Fields nodded reluctantly, examining his straw hat and shaking his head.

"Be right back," I said, heading for the phone.

I had saved a pocketful of change for an emergency. I had run into such emergencies before. It was one of the little things you picked up being a private detective, especially one with a string of old cars that didn't care where they decided to quit.

I pulled the Philadelphia number from my back pocket, got the operator, and asked what the charges would be for three minutes. I counted my change and knew I could make that, plus a minute or two more. I placed my call and got a weary, "Forty-third, Sergeant Stinnett."

"Is Gus Belcher back?" I asked.

"I don't know," said Sinnett. "I'll ring up."

I stood there waiting, watching almost thirty seconds go by and looking down at the pile of dimes, nickels, and quarters I'd stacked on a case of Wildroot Cream Oil.

"Detective Conroy speaking," a voice came on.

"I need Belcher or his partner," I said. "I'm calling long distance and the operator's going to ask me for more money."

"They're not here," Conroy said, obviously not impressed by whatever distance my call was coming from.

"Will you get in touch with Belcher or his partner and have them call me at this number? Fast. Tell 'em it's Toby Peters. Someone's been murdered."

Murder didn't seem to impress Conroy either.

"Okay," he said. "Shoot."

I gave him the number on the phone and asked him again to please hurry.

"I'm zipping," said Conroy, who hung up.

When I got back to the table, Fields was asking Yellow Buffalo, "Own the place?"

"No," said the man. "Work here for the Simmses. Work alone on Sunday. Saving up to buy the place from Simms when he gets too old to work it during the week."

"That be soon?" asked Fields.

"Soon," said the Indian, buttering toast. "He's four years younger than me, but he's not well. Pretty good man. Wants a fair price. People around here know me. My son'll come back after the war. He'll get married, help me run the place. Make it grow."

"Son's a soldier?" asked Fields.

"Communications," said the Indian. "Speaks on the radio to other Sioux so Germans don't understand."

"You speak Sioux?" Fields asked Gunther.

"No," said Gunther, sitting straight, his mind far away.

Yellow Buffalo brought our food as the phone began to ring. The call was for me, from Philadelphia. It was Belcher.

"Who's dead?" Belcher asked.

"Hipnoodle," I said. "Only his name wasn't Hipnoodle. It was Burton, Lester Burton. Forger. He got most of Fields's money. Someone shot him in Ottumwa, Iowa. Whoever did it still has three banks to go unless he figures he's got enough and heads back home."

"Ottumwa is a long way from Philadelphia," Belcher said.

"Can't argue with that," I said.

"Suspects?"

"Fellow who works for Fields, nicknamed the Chimp, real name is Albert Woloski, did time for armed robbery, don't know where. He looks a little like an ape, used to work in the Carnes Circus."

Belcher repeated what I said, reading it back from the notes he was taking.

"And?" asked Belcher.

"Woloski tried to shoot Fields in his bed night before last."

"Fields okay?" he asked with real concern.

"Besides having no liver, eating nothing, and knocking back enough to get the entire Pacific Fleet drunk every day, I'd say he's doing fine."

"Man's a Philadelphia treasure," said Belcher, sighing. "I'll see what I can find out. Where are you?"

"Heading for Ogallala, Nebraska," I said.

"Spell it," Belcher said.

I did and he told me he would make some calls and that I should call him from Ogallala.

"If you need the police," he said, "tell them to call me for a rundown on what we've got, but I'm telling you now, you're way out of our ball park."

"Right," I said. "Catch any fish?"

"Older son caught a few," he said. "Too small, but I pan-fried them. Not bad. Wouldn't do any good to suggest you try to talk Fields into just going home?" he asked.

"None at all," I said. "Fields won't listen."

I didn't add that at this point I wanted to see the thing through. Lester Burton had gotten to me.

"Take care of Fields," he said. "And call."

He hung up.

We finished our meal, Fields bought a paper, had a brief discussion about going into partnership with Yellow Buffalo on the Simms pharmacy, with the possibility of getting a license to dispense drinking alcohol.

Yellow Buffalo wasn't interested.

Fields retired to the rest room, where he shaved and returned awake and grinning knowingly. Gunther and I were next, each shaving with a Persona blade carefully handed to us by Fields.

Fields tipped generously with a bill pulled out of his pocket and we were on our way. Or we thought we were.

"He recognized me," said Fields. "Saw it in his eyes. Indians don't give anything away, but if you watch their eyes . . . and Gunther. Notice how he didn't even pay attention to him? How do you not pay attention to a man three feet tall in a three-piece suit on a Sunday morning in York, Nebraska."

"Maybe you're right," I said.

"And," he said, pointing his cane, "we have a flat tire."

He was right again.

Fields supervised, free with his advice, concerned about his supply of liquid refreshment in the trunk that we had to move to get to the spare tire. Gunther managed to remain almost unblemished by the ordeal, at least physically. My back complained once when we pulled out the spare, and once when we took off the flat and wrestled it into the trunk.

Fields proclaimed that it was hot for this time of year as he directed our every move, warning us to be careful of the delicate finish on the Cadillac.

When we were done, Fields climbed into the car and began to read the newspaper he had bought. Gunther and I went back into the drugstore and washed up in the rest room. Yellow Buffalo was nowhere in sight.

We drove while Fields read us the highlights of the day, at least the ones that interested him.

"Senator Truman," he said, "the loud little Democratic hack from Missouri, finally said something I agree with. Fiorello La Guardia has no more business being made a brigadier general than Darryl F. Zanuck has being made a colonel. At least La Guardia hasn't written a book about his nonexistent war experiences."

Neither of us responded. We looked at the corn.

"Says here Conrad Veidt died," Fields said. "Playing golf. Got to be careful of how you play the game. Dangerous. He was only fifty."

"He played the Nazi colonel in *Casablanca,*" I said.

"And Cesare the Somnambulist in *The Cabinet of Dr. Caligari,*" added Gunther, who seldom went to movies.

"Irony," said Fields. "Man fled Germany because he was a Jew and wound up making good money playing Nazis. Like Preminger and von Stroheim. All Jews. All typecast playing Nazis."

Gunther slid closed the window between us and himself and turned on the radio so softly that Fields had to strain to be sure Gunther wasn't listening to music.

"Sporting news," Fields said, folding over a page. "Alfred Snyder, the one-armed fencer, won ten out of eleven bouts in a tournament. How many hands do you need to fence? Might even be an unfair advantage having one arm. Damn thing isn't there to hit or get in your way."

I hadn't anything to say to this observation, so Fields went on with, "Bad news. Five-year-old Bobby Hookey, the jitterbugging singer, is getting his own radio show. Not only is he a child but he caterwauls, jumps around, and gets paid for his acts of atrocity. If I ever have the displeasure of running into him, I will feign disorientation and sit on the little bastard."

Finally, Fields said, "Now, here's an item worthy of serious attention. You can get a live turtle mailed to you for a dollar with a name of your choosing on its back. Get it from Penscript Company in Boston. What name would you want on the back of a turtle? How long can the name be? If you have a longer name for him, do you get a bigger turtle? Will they let you give the foul-smelling little beast an obscene name? And what if I want my name on it? William Claude Dukinfield. Dare they reject?"

He tore the item carefully from the paper, pocketed it in his wallet, patted down the pocket, and sat back to consider turtles and feisty little senators from Missouri.

A little after two in the afternoon we got lost. A detour at the Hastings junction took us south into Kansas.

"We are, according to that last road sign," said Fields into the microphone to the front seat, "now in the great and sovereign state of Kansas. I have no aversion to the state. In fact, I remember several memorable nights in Kansas City, or was it Topeka, with a chorus nymph named Mimi, whose real name, as I later discovered, was Esther Pertwee. However, we are supposed to be in Nebraska, heading at nearly breakneck speed toward the hamlet of Ogallala where a man who looks like a chimpanzee may well be planning to steal another several thousand dollars of my money."

"We are lost," said Gunther into his microphone, with as much dignity as he could muster under the circumstances.

"I assume," said Fields, "you concur with my observation that we have wandered aimlessly out of our way in anti-Oz, and not that our souls have been doomed to purgatory or beyond by a wrong turn."

"We're not that far off," I said, opening the slider and leaning into the front seat and looking at the map.

I pointed a route to Gunther, who agreed and made a right turn at the next intersection.

"Was ever man so cursed," Fields muttered, taking a drink. "Kansas from a car is just as flat as Illinois and Nebraska. Tobias Smollett's picaresque wanderers were not as afflicted by loss of money, dignity, and direction as we. I am in need of sustenance."

He poured himself a fresh drink from his thermos and sat back, closing his eyes against the mind-numbing sea of grain.

Several hours and much mumbling later we saw a sign through the twilight indicating that Ogallala was ten miles away.

"We will rouse the local banker," said Fields. "We will beat that primate to my money and then I—we—will thrash him soundly. Or maybe we'll just turn him in to the constabulary."

We had moved into a small woods with low overhanging rock on both sides of the road, when the front window exploded. Glass flew. I covered my eyes and heard a grunt from Fields. The car swerved. I opened my eyes and saw us heading for a wall of red rock. Gunther managed to avoid the wall at the last second with a loud squealing of tires and brakes. We slowed to a near stop.

"You all right, Gunther?" I asked.

"A small cut on my right cheek," he said, checking his face in the rearview mirror. "Mr. Fields?"

I looked at Fields. He was calmly fishing a shard of glass from his martini glass and examining it for more small bits. His hat had tumbled from his head but he didn't seem to notice.

"Spontaneous fracturing along a weak fault line," said Fields, sweeping pieces of glass from his lap. "I shall have my cadre of attorneys seize upon this manufacturing outrage."

But it wasn't a flaw in the glass.

A second bullet tore through the open window and whumped solidly into the padded seat a few inches from my head.

"The damn Chimp is trying to kill me again," Fields croaked, leaning forward to squint out of the breezy front window.

"Us," I said. "He's trying to kill all of us."

Gunther composed himself enough to push his foot to the floor, but a third shot came through the front window and blew out the back window.

A sign, hand painted in red, large letters on a whitewashed piece of wood, pegged into the ground, read: Rally. An arrow pointed to the right.

"Take it," shouted Fields.

Gunther made the right turn, shooting Fields across the seat into me. He crushed me against the door. Gunther straightened out and headed down the road, wide enough for one large car or one small truck.

There were no more shots.

Gunther looked at the map in his atlas for an alternate road to Ogallala. Wind blew through the car and Fields awkwardly turned and began to throw glass out the rear window.

"He tries to follow us and the odds are good he'll get a blowout and die an excruciating death," said Fields with some satisfaction as he continued to discard glass of all shapes and sizes.

Ahead of us through the trees, a glowing red light filled the early night. We were headed right for it and by the time we realized what it was, it was right in front of us—a burning cross about twenty feet tall in a wide grassy opening in the forest.

Surrounding the cross were about twenty people in white sheets and white pointed caps that covered their faces except for two small circles for their eyes. The white-sheeted men stood on a low wooden platform, the burning cross behind them. On either side of the platform were speakers. A microphone on a stand stood in the center of the low stage. About forty people wearing street clothes were visible in the burning light, facing the platform and the burning cross. We had stumbled on a Ku Klux Klan rally. Every face was turned toward us.

"Shall I turn around?" Gunther whispered.

"Too late," I said as a pair of burly men in sheets strode toward us. "And not enough room without taking a few of them with us."

We didn't have to open the window. Bullets had already done that.

The two men looked at us through the front window, only their eye sockets visible. I think I would have preferred our chances with the gunman.

I looked at Fields. He smiled at the two men and said, "Where do we park?"

One of the men pointed to the right, where a line of cars stood in the low grass.

Gunther pulled the car into the line of vehicles, mostly old cars and battered trucks. There were a few newer-model automobiles but nothing like the Caddy we stepped out of.

The two burly ghosts in white were at the side of our car before we could get fully out.

The two men looked at the broken windows and with the

light of the burning cross examined the glass on front and back seats and may even have seen the hole in the seat.

"Accident," I said, getting out.

"Attacked by Indians," said Fields, climbing out, straw hat under his arm. "But we were determined that not even the threat of death would keep us from the rally."

The two men looked down at Gunther as he got out.

"Driver," said Fields. "Swiss. Doesn't speak a word of English. Really his idea to come to the rally. He is an ardent supporter of the Klan, trying to start a coven or a team, or whatever you call it, in the lovely town of Berne."

One of the two men motioned for us to follow him. We followed while the other man stood at our side as we moved through the small crowd, which parted as we were guided toward the circle of men in white sheets on the platform below the burning cross. The people who weren't on the platform were dressed in everything from washed overalls to shabby suits and ties. Some of them held the hands of little children.

We stopped as one of the burly men leading us moved up on a small wooden platform before the burning cross and whispered to another white-sheeted clansman who wore some kind of chain around his neck. The man with the chain spoke into the microphone.

The one with the chain, who I figured for the leader, looked at us.

I felt like the Cowardly Lion about to face the Wizard.

"I have spoken," the man with the chain said, holding up his hands. "Our numbers grow. Our cause is God's and the preservation of a white America under Christ. Now those of you who want to join can step up while our brothers take your names and we administer the pledge."

There was some movement in the crowd. A man in overalls and a cap with a weary face, led his family out of the crowd and toward the line of cars. The family included an equally tired wife, a boy about fourteen, and a small girl.

"Brother, stop," called the man in white with the chain around his neck. "We must unite or be mongrelized."

"Wife's part Sioux," the man said, turning, unafraid, as he motioned his family toward and into a pickup truck. "Guess that makes my kids a smaller part. Men are dying in places I'm too uneducated to say right. Men who are dyin' ain't just white Christians."

"Conscripted cowards," said the man with the chain. "They started this war and they manage to stay alive while we die for them."

"Ain't the way I see it," said the man with the family. "But I ain't got the words to argue."

A few of the hooded men had advanced toward the family getting into the pickup. There was a stirring in the crowd and a second man who looked like a farmer stepped out of the crowd with a woman and a teenaged boy.

"Brother, stop," said the man in the chain, pointing to him.

The second farmer was bigger than the first and older. He stopped and turned toward the burning cross and said in a deep bass, "All of God's children are equal. Christ preached love and forgiveness, not hate. I read the Bible every night with my family. There's nothing like this in there."

"You're not reading it clear, brother," the gold-chained Klansman on the platform shouted.

"I can read clear," said the man, turning his back with his family and heading toward their battered pickup as the first family pulled out. Others in the crowd followed them. I started to turn, but the second burly man barred our way. Over his shoulder I saw a new car pull in, just missing the family in the first pickup. The new car pulled over near a tree, not in line, and the Chimp got out.

I nudged Fields, who followed my eyes. Gunther turned to me and whispered, "We cannot remain."

A little more than half of the crowd stayed while the others got in their vehicles and pulled away. The Chimp was lost in the dark shadows at the rear of the gathering.

"Though we are small in numbers," said the talking Klansman, "yet are we strong in our faith and the righteousness of our mission."

Gunther looked toward the crowd.

"And," the Klansman with the chain went on, "our numbers throughout the land remain strong. We are joined constantly by even those of rank, power, and station, as we are tonight. Politicians, businessmen, factory workers, farmers, and farmhands. White, Christian, and united."

The cross continued burning and crackling. A few glowing splinters flew off, but the fire stayed bright. I wondered what they had doused it with.

"Tonight," said the head Klansman, "we are joined by an obvious sympathizer in our cause, Mr. W. C. Fields, the great comic actor whose interests tonight are not at all comic. We urge Brother Fields to join us and say a few words."

Fields smiled at the crowd, doffed his hat at their applause, and shook his head, saying to the burly man at our side, "I'm here only as an incognito observer seeking the truth."

The burly man took Fields's arm and led him toward the platform. I stepped forward and was stopped by two men in white sheets and hoods who folded their arms and blocked my way.

The man at the microphone stood back and let Fields take his place.

"Testing," Fields said.

There was a reverberation and a whine from the speaker.

"Friends," he said, scanning the small crowd for a sign of the Chimp and ready to hit the planks of the platform nose-first if another shot rang out.

"Friends," Fields repeated. "There has always been much I have admired about the Klan, particularly the uniforms. I've heard the muckety-mucks down South get to wear different colors as they move up the spectrum, but I've always been partial to the white and wondered at how you keep your sheets cleaner than the ones at the Boiler Hotel in Winnipeg, where Mrs. Bertha Crumpbunny takes such pride in her linens that she washes them daily, by hand, with a crew of chunky Ukrainian girls who can't speak English. But I digress. Canada is not on today's agenda. Another thing I have always admired about the Klan is the way you guys keep those hoods pointed. Knew a clown in the circus who wore a hood. Used wires to keep it pointed. Very impressive."

He paused to scan the crowd more closely.

There was some scattered and confused applause.

"I've made a few notes here," Fields said, fishing into his pocket and coming out with what I could see was the ad for turtles with their names painted on them. Fields made a show of pulling out a pair of rimless reading glasses and perching them on the end of his sizable nose.

"Ah, yes," he said. "In anecdotal support of your cause, I wish to draw upon a few examples from my own experience. When I was a lad traversing this great land, I found myself starving and cold in Lansing, Michigan. One night I slept in a church pew. The deacon found me, gave me some bread and coffee, said 'God bless you,' and sent me on my way. I was huddling in the doorway of a modest grocery during a storm when the door opened and I was taken into the establishment by a family I soon learned was named Rubenstein. Jews, all of them. They took me to the back of the store to a small storeroom, fed me hot soup, and made up a bed for me. Even as a child I could tell there was something cunning going on in their devious brains. They lived upstairs of the store. There was a small fireplace in the back room. One of the family, three girls and the mother, took turns staying by my side for three nights while I recovered. They talked to each other in a strange tongue."

There was a murmur, more of confusion than understanding, in the crowd.

"Well," said Fields, "after three days, the weather had broken, the temperature had risen, and I felt almost like my own self again. I told the Rubensteins I wanted to leave. They urged me to stay a while longer. When I insisted, they gave me an old but warm coat and some clothes and a shoebox full of food. The father, a fat man who wore one of those little black hats on his head, no doubt to ward off heavenly spirits, had been amused by my juggling. He told me about another Jew named David something, in Kalamazoo. I walked to Kalamazoo and the Jew named David gave me a job juggling between screenings at his movie house."

Fields looked over his glasses at his confused audience. His eyes opened wide and he nodded toward the crowd. The Chimp had slowly made his way forward.

"I had escaped from the Rubensteins with my life," Fields said. "I left on a Thursday night. The next night would have been Friday, the night of their dark Sabbath. What better to offer as a sacrifice to their false god than a homeless Christian boy who they had done their best to plump up in three days. Who knows how many babies and young virgins the unholy tribe had dispatched over the years? I shall never forget the evil Rubensteins and can only surmise that the Lord had saved me like Isaac for a purpose, maybe to stand up here today."

There was mild applause. A few of the Klansmen also applauded. Fields looked through his glasses at the turtle ad and went on. "Ah, yes. One day when I first started out and was stranded with a troupe of hapless performers in Cody, Wyoming, not far from Yellowstone National Park—you see we had been abandoned by our road manager, who had paid us nothing—I checked the contents of my small satchel, heavy with bowling pins, cigar boxes, various hats, a shirt, and a pair of socks of dubious longevity. We sat in the train station and those who could bought tickets and prepared to spend the night waiting for buses heading in whatever direction offered them hope. I had a total of a ten-cent piece and six pennies with the likeness of an Indian on them. On our small bill was a fellow of the Negro persuasion, every bit as devious as the dreaded Rubensteins. This fellow, known as Happy Smith, the World's Greatest Banjo Player, was an old man. False teeth clacked as he played his foot-tapping medleys on stage. 'Shine on Harvest Moon' was his showstopper. But I digress. This Happy Smith motioned me over to him and asked me if I had any money. I showed him my palm with the white dime surrounded by savage copper Indians. My friends, can you imagine what that former slave had the audacity to do then?"

Fields looked up. No one had the slightest clue of what Happy Smith had done. So Fields told them.

"With his gnarled black fingers, he took a small purse out of his pocket, opened it, and asked me where I wanted to go. I told him New York, where the work was, and he gave me the money for the ticket. While accepting money from his lowly race was beneath me, none of the other members of our troupe had made a similar offer. I took the money and promised to return it promptly. The mistake of a young, innocent lad. For it was at that moment, brothers and sisters, that I needed a staunch man with a clean white sheet and finely pointed hood to come to my rescue, to warn me about what I had gotten into by dealing with the creature of inferior race—who, by the way, was one hell of a banjo player. From that day on I was beholden to Happy Smith. The humiliation, which he had obviously intended, haunted me. I could see nothing but his black smiling face as he handed me the tainted money that got me back to New York and a well-paid job as the tramp juggler on the Keith circuit. Needless to say, I soon located Happy Smith with a troupe of entertainers in St. Louis and returned his filthy money with interest. Two days later, the interest was returned to me with a note saying he was glad I was doing well. Insidious. The man had managed to get his nails into me and make me grateful for the rest of my life. My friends, you should not underestimate the evil cunning of the Jew and the treachery of the Negro. The

Klan is dedicated to the demise of people like the Rubensteins and the ilk of Happy Smith."

There was more applause. Fields looked down. The Chimp was in the front of the line, looking around. He saw me, Gunther, and certainly Fields. The Chimp's hand was in his pocket. He knew he couldn't make his move surrounded by the crowd. I watched him inch his way to the edge of the crowd toward the line of cars.

"What about the damned Indians?" came a voice from the crowd.

"Yeah, this is Sioux country. They ain't white. They ain't Christian and they can't hold their liquor."

"We concur," said Fields, looking in the general direction from which the voice had come. "Something in their genes. Never knew an Indian who could hold his liquor. Even knew one Mohawk named Yellow Buffalo who keeled over dead from a fatal glass of beer. Indians. Savages. Not so long ago in our history, the red men by the hundreds armed with spears, tomahawks, and bows and arrows, along with a handful of rifles, savagely attacked thousands of gallant, uniformed American troops in act after act of bloody war in an attempt to thwart the white people in the rightful pursuit of their manifest destiny. These savages wanted to hold on to land they had lived on for several thousand years, to keep it from the hands of worthy white Christians like us. They murdered armed but innocent soldiers by the dozens, even attacked innocent settlers plopped peacefully in the middle of the Indian grazing lands. Thousands of the red heathens died. What was left were put in reservations, and yet you and I know that they are even now plotting to regain what is now the United States in secret pacts with other tribes—Navajo, Chippewa, Apache—and the Japs. It must be stopped."

This time there was real applause. Fields looked at me in bewilderment.

Some of the hooded Klansmen on the platform near the

flames of the burning cross stepped forward to usher Fields from the microphone. Fields should have known, and probably did, that some members of the Klan were far from fools.

"To prove my good faith in your cause," Fields said suddenly, as one of the Klansmen took his arm, "I'll point out to you a spy in our midst, a reporter from the *Daily Worker*, ready to distort our words. That man."

Fields pointed at the startled Chimp at the edge of the crowd. The Chimp stepped back while everyone looked at him.

"A Communist," Fields said.

The Chimp backed up as the crowd, and some of the men in sheets on the platform, moved toward him. The Chimp pulled out a gun and waved it at the advancing crowd, which stopped abruptly. The Chimp backed away after another look at Fields, who tried to stand behind the Klansman who had taken his arm.

After he had backed off a few dozen yards, the Chimp suddenly turned and ran for the woods.

"Careful," Fields said into the microphone. "There may be more Bolsheviks in the bushes, armed with rifles, swords, and homemade bombs."

The small crowd began to disperse in confusion, heading for their vehicles.

The Klansman with the chain repossessed the microphone and shouted, "Stop. We're not finished. There is no danger."

But it was all too late.

Fields carefully put his glasses away. The Klansmen were talking animatedly in small groups.

"Glad I could help," said Fields to the head Klansman.

Fields stepped down from the platform. I had the feeling that the boss with the chain around his neck was going to call for a lynching, but he was surrounded almost instantly by his fellow members asking questions, bewildered. Some of them leapt from the platform, took off their hoods, and headed for their cars.

"Come," said Fields out of the corner of his mouth as he

drew even with us. He patted the shoulder of the nearby burly Klansman and said, "Keep up the good work."

Gunther and I followed Fields through the confusion to the Cadillac. We got in. I looked up. The cross was still burning, but not as brightly. The head Klansman pointed in our direction. Gunther started the car and pulled in front of an old Ford. There were already a string of cars and trucks on the narrow road leading out of the woods. The Klansmen would have no trouble catching us on foot, trapped between slow-moving vehicles.

Gunther didn't enter the line. Instead, he headed the car directly at the platform with the burning cross. Klansmen on the ground scrambled out of the way, falling in the dirt and grass.

"Hard to get those stains out," Fields muttered.

Gunther made a sharp right turn and drove around the back of the cross and platform. He drove around the edge of the grassy clearing, saw an opening, and plunged the Caddy onto a narrow path, but not too narrow to crunch forward as branches scraped the sides of the car and leapt through the front window.

"We can get out and hide," I said. "Or head in the general direction of the highway to Ogallala. I've still got my thirty-eight."

"Speed forward, little man," Fields said, strangely exhilarated. "Forward to your destiny. How'd you like my speech?"

"You almost got us killed," I said.

"Might still," said Fields, "if we suddenly plunge into a river or a bog or a dead end."

With no spare tire, we hurtled ahead. In the lights we saw a large animal cross the path and then lope into the forest. A little farther in our headlights we saw, coming straight at us, the Chimp, a pistol in his hand.

He held up a hand to stop us, but Gunther pressed on and the Chimp jumped out of the way.

"Wouldn't shoot," said Fields. "Shot would draw the Klansmen like actors to a free meal. Excelsior."

I wouldn't call it a miracle, but I'd say we had a lot of luck with us. The path suddenly widened and a gate appeared in front of us. I got out and ran for the gate. There was a lock but the latch was wood and old. I kicked at it five or six times and broke the wood holding the lock. I pushed the gate open and guided Gunther through. The car was now a battle casualty, a scraped, scratched, dented, broken-windowed, and seat-wounded survivor.

I got back in and we drove down a wider road for about five minutes before we hit a double-lane road, probably the same one we had been on when we turned to join the Klan rally.

"We find a hotel," I said as Gunther speeded up. "I take a bath and tomorrow morning we go to the bank."

"Correction," said Fields. "We find lodging, change our clothes, locate the bank president, and convince him that this is an emergency and I must make a major withdrawal tonight."

"He won't do it," I said.

Fields poured himself a drink, downed it in a single gulp, and said, "I can be persuasive where my hard-earned money is involved. There, a motel." Our single headlight shone over the sign that read: Ogallala Redskin Motel, Vacancy.

Gunther turned the Cadillac into the driveway and parked in front of the motel's office. There were two other cars in the lot, before the one-story line of rooms.

The clerk behind the counter sat in a chair, asleep. The voice of Raymond on "Inner Sanctum" came over the radio in front of the sleeping clerk. Raymond said tonight's guest would be Lon Chaney, Jr. That didn't wake the clerk so I hit the bell on his desk. He jumped up and looked around. He was somewhere in his sixties, losing his hair and gaining a belly. His shirt was flannel and not tucked in.

Gunther and Fields had waited in the car. We figured I was least conspicuous of the three of us.

"Three rooms," I said.

"Many as you want," the clerk said. "Two dollars a night each.

Radio in every room and a shower. A couple of the rooms have tubs."

"Three in a row," I said, taking out six dollars and putting it on the counter.

"How many banks are there in Ogallala?" I said.

He looked at me with new interest now. I looked like a man who might rob a bank.

"One, right now," he said cautiously.

"The president's name?" I said.

"Saunders, Mr. Jeffrey Saunders," he said.

I smiled. It didn't work. The clerk still looked suspicious.

"I am traveling with a man who wants to build a large hardware store in town," I whispered, though there was no one around. "We want to set up an account as quietly as possible and get right to work on acquiring land and beginning construction."

"We've already got a hardware store," the man said. "Bainbridge's."

"We know all about Bainbridge's," I said. "We are in the process of buying out Bainbridge's. This is all hush-hush."

The man looked perplexed. I took out a five-dollar bill and handed it to him.

"People find out about what we're doing and prices are going to go up," I said. "Be best if no one knows we're in town."

"Gotcha," said the man with a wink, pulling in the five spot.

I registered as Ronald, Richard, and Ryan North, took the keys, and reminded the clerk that our business was of the greatest secrecy and that we would be needing a man who could keep a secret as manager of the store.

"Name's Floyd Simpson," he said, tucking in his shirt.

"I won't forget it, Floyd," I said, taking the keys.

Gunther parked the battle-scarred car around the end of the last room, where it wouldn't be seen by anyone coming down the highway.

"Everyone freshen up," Fields said, taking his key for room 3.

"We congregate in twenty minutes for our meeting with the president of the bank, whose name is . . ."

"Jeffrey Saunders," I said.

"I'm sure he's in the phone book," said Fields, looking back at the car and patting its dented and bruised left fender. "Stout warriors, these Cadillacs."

Gunther looked exhausted. He went into room 4 with his bag and I went into room 2 with mine.

I washed, shaved, wiped my dirty shoes with a frayed wash-cloth, and sat in a chair with my .38 in my lap, waiting for what was left of the twenty minutes to pass. They passed quickly.

There was a knock on the door and Fields's voice said, "It is I."

I opened the door and there he stood. The whole dangerous adventure had brought him to life. He looked fresh, clean, and alert.

"We have a rendezvous with Mr. Saunders at the bank in fifteen minutes," he said. "I did not speak directly with Mr. Saunders, who was occupied, but with his wife, who relayed my plight with great success and the requisite show of emergency. Shall we repack so that we can make a hasty departure from our possible pursuers after I collect my cash?"

I agreed and we had everything back in the car within five minutes.

I wasn't too happy about driving into town in the Caddy. One of the Klansmen might recognize it, but it was Sunday night and the town was quiet. Gunther found the small bank. A man in a dark suit stood on the steps. He was about fifty, magnificent mane of dark hair, and a ruddy face that suggested a fondness for a beer or two, or something even stronger.

Gunther let us out and pulled around the corner onto a dark street.

Fields moved in front of me to the waiting man, who smiled and held out his hand.

"Mr. Saunders, I presume?" said Fields. "This is my associate, Mr. Peters. Another associate, Mr. Wherthman, is parking our vehicle and will join us."

"Pleasure to meet you all," Saunders said, taking my hand after he shook Fields's.

I nodded. It was no pleasure. The voice of Mr. Jeffrey Saunders was definitely the voice of the head Klansman with the chain around his neck.

Chapter Nine

Whenever a lion starts chasing you, don't stop to change your clothes.

Gunther came hurrying to the front of the bank and I watched Saunders's face. The small benevolent smile he had perfected over many years, the bank official's smile, remained.

"Sorry to get you out on a Sunday night," I said.

Saunders took out his keys and opened the front door of the bank. We stepped in.

"For a man of Mr. Fields's stature, and on the basis of this being an emergency, I am most willing to be of service," said Saunders, closing the door and switching on the light. "I have already informed the police that we are here so that no officer will come running in when he sees the lights."

"I thought of everything," said Fields.

"Not everything," said Saunders, still smiling, "but it is almost always possible to rectify errors or learn to live with them and go on to other endeavors."

The bank was small, the smallest we had been in yet. Two tellers' cages, a wooden table around arm height where people could make out their checks or calculate their wins and losses, a pair of doors to our left, both to offices with clear glass windows so the occupant could look out at the bank and directly at customers and the tellers.

Saunders opened his office door and stepped back, after turning on the light, to let the three of us in. The office wasn't large, but it would do. An oak desk and chair with a barred window behind them, a small round table, also oak, with three plain chairs.

"Humble, but adequate for a town this size," he said. "We get a substantial business from the farm community. Shall we sit?"

He pointed to the table. We sat and he went behind his desk to a solid-looking swivel chair. With my hand under the table, I pulled out my .38 and aimed it across at Saunders.

"A quaint establishment," Fields said, looking around as he had in the lobby. "Character. Small and neighborly."

"That's what we strive for," said Saunders, his smile growing a bit larger. "Now, what can I do for you?"

"I wish to make a withdrawal," Fields said. "Many years ago, under the name of Oscar Treadmill, I opened an account when I passed through your delightful community while on tour. I should now like to liquidate that account of six thousand dollars, plus all interest incurred." -

Saunders stopped smiling.

"I have been president of this bank for twenty-two years," he said. "Only once before have I been called upon to come in on a Sunday to conduct a transaction. Today I have been called in twice."

"He's been here," I said with a sigh.

"Someone calling himself Oscar Treadmill appeared here today and made a withdrawal?" asked Fields.

"Called this morning," Saunders said. "Said it was a matter of life and death, could only stay in town a few hours and then had to get back to New Orleans to pay for an operation for one of his children. Said he planned to drive all night to get the money in the doctor's hands by sometime tomorrow. I pointed out that it was highly irregular, but he was almost in tears. I met him late in the morning. He produced the bankbook and signed for the withdrawal."

"You gave him my money," said Fields.

Saunders reached into his desk and produced a sheet of paper. He passed it to Fields, who sat to his left. Fields examined the sheet.

"Withdrawal statement," said Saunders. "I plan to file it in the morning."

"Signature's nothing like mine, like mine when I signed 'Oscar Treadmill.' "

"Mr. Treadmill had suffered an accident in his hurry to get here," said Saunders, folding his hands on the table as he watched Fields. "His left arm was in a cast, right down to his fingers."

"How did he expect to drive to New Orleans like that?" said Fields. "The cast was a fake. I've used dozens of them for all appendages—well, almost all appendages."

"Mr. Treadmill signed with his left hand," said Saunders. "There is a similarity."

"Yes," said Fields, looking at the sheet before him. "Not incomparable to the remarkable resemblance between Dolores Del Rio and Franklin Delano Roosevelt."

"He had the bankbook," said Saunders. "And the arm in a cast."

"Did he show some identification?" I asked.

"Indeed," said Saunders. "As I recall, a ration book, a driver's license, a draft card."

"All reading Oscar Treadmill," I said.

"Indeed," Saunders replied.

"All with the same signature on this withdrawal sheet?" I asked.

"The same," said Saunders.

"So," I went on, "he got them all after he injured his hand, which he told you he had done on the way here."

"Point well taken," said Saunders. "I should have been more observant, but it was an emergency and . . ."

"Every one of those cards can be erased and new names put in," I said.

"You know quite a bit about such things," said Saunders.

"I'm a private investigator," I said.

"I see," said Saunders, shaking his head. "I neglected to tell you that he had one piece of identification, a membership card for a social organization to which I belong."

I let that pass for a moment. Gunther and Fields watched the verbal Ping-Pong game going on between me and Saunders.

"What did this guy look like?"

"I'm afraid I rather concentrated on his broken arm and hand," said Saunders, "but he had dark hair, about your height and age, possibly a few pounds heavier than you are."

"Did he look like a primate?" asked Fields.

"Now that you mention it," said Saunders, "there was a resemblance to some kind of simian."

"He didn't really tell you he needed the money for a doctor," I said, guessing.

Saunders sat silently, hands folded, head slightly cocked to the left with an air of curiosity. "He didn't?"

"You were a busy man today," I said. "It would take more than a man who didn't want to wait a day to get you in here for the first time in over twenty years. You want my guess?"

"Please," said Saunders amiably.

"He said he needed it for the Klan," I obliged. "Probably didn't have any of that identification except a Klan membership card with a name other than Oscar Treadmill. And the name on the Klan card was?"

"There was no Klan card," Saunders said. "But the name on the organization card to which I referred was written some time ago and was an almost illegible scrawl, a common phenomenon in the banking business. As far as I, and this bank, are concerned, the simian gentleman with the bad arm made a valid withdrawal this morning. I'm sorry. As much respect as I have for Mr. Fields, the name on the account was not his, he has no bankbook, and the account holder presented the book and more than sufficient identification. Mr. Fields's claim may be quite valid, but he is, in fact, without evidence of his claim to this account."

"Do you suppose," said Fields, "that my cohorts and I are gamboling across the nation, gleefully rousing bank presidents with false claims to accounts?"

"I really don't know," said Saunders. "It sounds rather far-fetched, but . . ."

Gunther leaned over to whisper in my ear. I nodded as he sat back. Saunders's hands were no longer folded in front of him. They were out of sight beneath the desk. Gunther's height had allowed him a partial view of something metallic in the banker's hand.

"Guess what I've got in my hand?" I said.

"Let's not get obscene," Fields said.

Saunders didn't answer.

"I'm holding the same thing you are," I said.

"Godfrey Daniel," said Fields. "I've stumbled into a den of covert Victorian depravity."

I took my hand from under the table and showed the .38, which I leveled at him.

"A bank robbery," Saunders said as he rose, showing no weapon. "Who would believe that W. C. Fields . . . or are you an impostor? . . . that's it. You *look* like an impostor."

Gunther got up and moved to Saunders's side. He reached out of sight toward the swivel chair and came up with a fair-sized Colt six-shooter. Saunders looked at it.

"Protection for just such an incident as this," Saunders said, showing not the smallest sign of fear.

Fields and I rose from our chairs and moved toward Saunders.

"And when we leave," I said. "You plan to call the police and say you stopped a bank robbery?"

"I believe that is what is taking place," said Saunders.

"And if Gunther didn't find your gun and I didn't have one, you would have shot the robbers and claimed you really believed Fields was an impostor."

Before either of us could say anything more, Fields leaned over the desk and took a short jab at Saunders's face. The punch landed square on the nose. Saunders's hands went to his nose and he began to gulp.

"Blood," he said.

Gunther took out a handkerchief and handed it to the banker, who put it to his nose in an attempt to stop the bleeding.

"You've broken my nose," he said.

"That was the intention," said Fields, sitting back. "Short, hard jab to the nose with your shoulder behind it. Boxer turned strong man named Babe Washington taught me that. He was, by the way, a Negro gentleman."

"This," said Saunders, looking at the bloody handkerchief and touching his swollen nose, "is evidence of your intent to rob the bank."

"It's evidence of my popping you in an attempt to extract some small modicum of solace from this sham," said Fields.

"Chief of police," I said, "is he a Klan member?"

"He's half Sioux," said Saunders with contempt, handkerchief now red.

"Hold your head back," said Fields. "Any Boy Scout could tell you that."

Saunders held back his head.

"When we leave here," I said, "you're not calling the police. If you do, we establish Mr. Fields's identity and tell them and whatever reporters and radio stations around here that you're the head of the local KKK."

"They won't believe you," said Saunders, his head back, blood still coming, but now in a trickle, onto his shirt. "You can't prove it."

"They'll believe W. C. Fields," I said.

"I shall positively identify you," said Fields. "I am a master at voices and will gladly allow the constabulary to test my ability to recognize voices, even with a curtain between me and the speaker."

"You will lose a great many customers," Gunther said. "Judging from the relatively small turnout at your obscene—may I borrow the word?"

"Be my guest," said Fields with a bow of his head.

"Your obscene gathering tonight," Gunther went on, "I would guess that your group has far less than significant support in the community."

"That will change," said Saunders, sitting up. The bleeding had stopped. The nose was large and discolored. "We'll grow."

"Perhaps," said Gunther, showing more emotion than I had seen from him on the trip or, for that matter, in the more than three years I'd known him. "I witnessed rallies like yours, rallies of Nazis in brown uniforms instead of white ones. Hamburg, Landstuhl, Bremen, Berlin. The same hate from foul mouths. The foul mouth in Berlin was that of Hitler himself. I heard it and I left Germany. I left Europe. I left the spreading hate mongers."

"Freaks like you will be the first to go," said Saunders in the voice that was now clearly that of the Klan leader with the chain, the angry voice, altered slightly by now having to breathe through his mouth.

"There is no end," said Gunther, looking at Saunders with contempt.

"Little fella's got the goods," said Fields. "I think my compatriot, Mr. Peters, is absolutely correct. You're not calling the police when we leave."

Saunders, his face a bloody disaster, said, "I can call other people."

"It'll take these other people time to put on their shoes and pants, get in their cars, and get here," I said. "By that time, we'll be long gone on our way back to Philadelphia."

Saunders said nothing.

"Besides," I said, "while Gunther sits here willing to put a bullet in your face with your own gun, I'm going to pull out every phone in the bank and then we're going to put holes in all four of your tires. I'll tie you in your chair just tightly enough that it'll take you a few minutes to get loose and a few more minutes on a Sunday night to find a phone."

We were back in the battle-scarred Caddy about five minutes

later. Gunther made a U-turn and headed down the street in the direction of the motel. When we had traveled about two blocks he turned left, drove another street over, and then turned left again, heading west.

"It was almost worth six thousand plus interest to break that son of a bitch's nose."

"Can you really recognize voices that well?" I asked as Gunther speeded down the highway.

Fields had already finished a cocktail he had mixed hastily as we fled Ogallala. "My gallant knight," he said, reaching into his pocket. "I did not have the vaguest idea that Saunders was the Klan leader till you exposed him. Clark Gable himself could call me on the phone and I'd assume he was an insurance salesman. Here."

He handed me some bills.

"Today's pay," he said, lying back and closing his eyes. "You've earned it. Onward to Rifle, Colorado, ominously named, considering our adventures of the last several days. I am determined to thwart and catch that damned Chimp and get every penny of my money back."

We could see that Rifle, Colorado, when we drove down the main street the next morning, was even smaller than Ogallala. It was a Monday and not much should have been going on, but it looked like almost everyone in town was on the sidewalk—and a few with noses touching store windows from inside—watching our wreck wobble down the street.

Somewhere on the way, when Fields and I were asleep, Gunther had found a place to get gas. He told me he and the attendant had a hard time getting the dented gas-tank door open. But they had succeeded, and with the wind whistling through the broken windows, Fields and I had slept soundly. And now, fully rested and having satisfied his morning thirst, Fields was prepared for the adoration which he assumed was responsible for the throng. Somehow, he said, word of his arrival had reached the hamlet.

Fields, unable to resist a crowd, opened his window and leaned out to doff his hat to the ladies. It was a one-car clown parade.

"Stop the vehicle," Fields said, and Gunther pulled over.

Four women in summer dresses were watching us. They ranged in age from about twenty-five to fifty.

"Pardon me," said Fields. "Can one of you fine examples of Colorado pulchritude direct us to the bank?"

"Next street over, turn right," said the oldest woman with a shy smile. "Can't miss it. You're W. C. Fields."

"You have extracted a confession," he said. "And though my band of weary travelers and I will be in your fair city but an hour or so, I shall always remember the kind reception of your small but character-steeped town."

"Quite a day for us already and it's still morning," said another woman. "Normally we wouldn't all be out and catch you coming down the street if it weren't for the shooting."

"Shooting?"

"About an hour ago," said the oldest woman. "Some crazy fool, not from town or an Indian, stood right out in the middle of the street shooting a pistol. Shot the window right out of a car just driving a few yards farther than you are now. Driver just sped up. The man in the street kept shooting. Before the state police could get here he was gone, went running to a parked car."

"What did he look like?" asked Fields.

"Sort of like a . . . I don't know . . . a monkey face, sort of," said the youngest one.

"Jessie was closest," said the eldest woman. "She saw best."

"Had a crazy look in his eyes," said Jessie. "Looked right in my face and then ran for his car."

"What kind of car?" asked Fields.

"Don't know," said Jesse. "Dark, kind of regular size. I'm not so sure about cars."

"I think it was a Ford," said the woman who hadn't spoken.

"Thank you, ladies," Fields said, pulling his head back into the car and turning to Gunther. "Drive on, and step on it."

When we were out of earshot of the ladies, Fields said, "The Chimp's lost what little was left of his mind. I knew I should have brought my shotgun."

Gunther drove to the corner, turned right, and found the bank without any trouble, a small white adobe building nestled between a two-story office building with a bakery on the ground floor, and a radio store, in whose small window on a white carpet stood a full-speaker, stand-up, parlor model brown wooden Philco. The sign next to it, in big letters, a different color for each line, read: "The latest in sound technology, pick up short-wave and hear what our boys overseas are listening to, a smart and beautiful addition to any living room." Next to the magnificent Philco was a shelf of small plastic, wood, and cardboard-covered table models and portables.

Fields was out of the car and through the front door of the bank, with Gunther and myself right behind him. It was one hell of a small bank, the smallest yet. I wondered what had brought Fields through Rifle, Colorado, to make his deposit in the first place.

There was a single teller's window and a single desk across from it with two chairs in front of it. Behind the teller's cage stood a woman. At the desk sat another, older woman. There were no customers. There were no offices, though there was a rest room in the rear of the bank next to a barred window. The walls were white and could use another coat, but the place was neat and clean. Behind the woman at the desk hung a portrait of Franklin and Eleanor Roosevelt.

Fields walked quickly to the woman at the desk, who took off her glasses and looked up at us calmly. She was no more than forty, dark and pretty with a slight hook to her nose. She was wearing a white blouse under a gray jacket and matching skirt.

"Yes?" she said.

"The president," Fields replied.

"I'm the president," she answered. "Belle Starr."

"Belle . . . are you any relation to the original bearer of that name?"

"None," she said. "My father, president of this bank before me, who fancied that he had a sense of humor, thought it would be funny to name me Belle, after the notorious thief."

"Asked about your name frequently, are you?"

"At least by every stranger whom I have the pleasure of talking to," she said.

Fields sat across from her. I motioned to Gunther to sit in the other chair and drew one up from the corner of the room. Belle Starr was a pro. We were all unshaven. Gunther was three feet tall and I looked more than ever like a desperate man aiming for the FBI's most-wanted list.

"Has a stranger been in here today to make a withdrawal?" asked Fields.

"No," she said.

Fields smiled. I wondered why Albert Woloski had skipped the bank and chosen to go nuts in the street.

"And yesterday was Sunday. You weren't open, didn't open?" Fields went on.

"Right," she said, showing no open curiosity.

"I want to make a withdrawal on an old account," Fields said.

"I know our depositors' names, even those going back many years," she said. "I worked here when I was twelve. My father was president of the bank, as was his father. We have no account in the name of W. C. Fields."

"Used a pseudonym," Fields whispered, holding a finger to his lips and looking across at the teller, who was pretending to write something. "Incognito."

"Fine," said Miss Starr. "If you'll just give me your bank-book . . ."

"Lost," said Fields.

"That shouldn't be a problem," Belle Starr, bank president, said. "What name did you have the account under and how much did you deposit?"

Fields was smiling as he reached his hand into his pocket for his sheet of paper, and then the smile departed.

"Gone," he said. "Lost it last night during the . . . lost it."

"I've got to have a name so I can locate the account and we can check your signature before I can approve the withdrawal," Belle Starr said sympathetically.

"You can see I'm W. C. Fields," he said, searching all of his pockets and coming up with cash, some of it in rolls, some of it loose.

He piled objects from his pockets onto Belle Starr's desk: cash, a wallet, a Ping-Pong ball, a small box of Smith Brothers cough drops, but no note.

"Let me think," he said, looking up at the ceiling. "Clarence Barnacle."

Miss Starr shook her head.

"Silas Jones Jorgan?"

"No," she replied.

In ten minutes of thinking, he came up with Thomas Blad-derstone, Uriah Heep, Horatio Fizkin, Samuel Slumkey, Eustace McGargle, Augustus Winterbottom, Harold Bissonette, Am-brose Wolfinger—

"That sounds familiar," she said.

"Want to hear more?" he asked.

"That might be quite enough," she said, rising and going to the door next to the teller's window.

The teller opened the door next to her cage, let President Belle Starr in, and closed the door immediately.

"Progress," said Fields. "We've beaten the scoundrel."

Miss Starr, glasses firmly perched on her nose, came out of

the teller's door about two minutes later with a large book in her arms. She brought it to her desk as the teller closed the door behind her. Book in front of her, Miss Starr said, "We cross-reference alphabetically every year." She went down a line of names and numbers. "Here, Ambrose Wolfinger."

"I'll take it in cash. Large denominations," said Fields.

"We've got to check the signature now," she said, returning the book to wherever it had come from behind the teller's door.

It took her about five minutes this time and she came out with a sheet of paper. She sat and said, "This was in the file for 1919."

"Bad year for the Germans," said Fields. "Pretty good year for me."

She took a form out of her desk and made an X on it.

"Sign there," she said. "Ambrose Wolfinger."

Fields signed. She examined the signature carefully and said, "Some slight differences, but I've seen thousands of signatures. These match."

"Splendid," said Fields, rubbing his hands together and looking at me in triumph. "Close the account."

Miss Starr nodded and took the sheets to the teller, who looked over at our trio. A look of something like disbelief crossed her face and disappeared quickly.

Belle Starr was back in less than a minute with a white envelope which she handed to Fields, who opened it. It was full of bills. We sat quietly while he counted.

"One thousand and forty dollars?" he said, looking up.

"Most of that is interest," she said. "There's a statement inside."

Fields took out the statement, looked at it, put it back, and stuffed the envelope and his belongings into his pockets. "Must have been short of cash at the time," he mumbled.

Miss Starr said nothing. She folded her hands in front of her. I was learning that that was what bankers do to show they were being polite and not going on with the job of running the bank till we left. Fields rose and began to do just that.

Gunther said thank you. Miss Starr smiled after him.

"A little over a thousand dollars," said Fields, standing in the street. "We beat the Chimp for a thousand dollars. He's got a bagful, close to half a million, but, by Godfrey, we beat him this time. On to . . ."

"Panguitch, Utah," Gunther said. "But I must bathe, shave, and change my clothing." Gunther looked more than half asleep.

"Quite right, a quick stop at the nearest hostelry," said Fields.

"And we should have a mechanic examine the automobile," Gunther said.

"Minor technicalities," said Fields with a wave of his hand. "We have had one small victory. We shall have another and recover my lucre. And we shall point a finger at that murderous knave the Chimp . . ."

"Albert Woloski," I corrected.

"Point a finger at Albert Woloski, who is not worthy of the normal Homo sapiens name, and say, 'Thou art the man.' I'll drive to Utah. Our intrepid Mr. Wherthman will sleep."

I'd seen enough of Fields's driving. "I'll drive," I said. "After we clean up and have a garage look at the car."

Fields reluctantly agreed. We found a gas station with a mechanic, who marveled at the car and said he'd look at it while we freshened up. He was thin, not too old, and wore a baseball cap. He was a mass of grease and oil. He recommended the Sundance Hotel half a block away. We each carried a suitcase and headed for the Sundance. An hour later, after sharing a single room with a single bath and changing, we were back at the gas station.

"Did what I could," he said. "Good car. Should run all right and I can get you windows and do some body work if you give me two, maybe three days."

"Don't have the time, my man," said Fields. "We are on the trail of a fiend."

The garage man wiped his hands and nodded. Fields paid him a reasonable fee, with every repair listed in clear print. And then we were on our way again, with me driving, Gunther asleep in the backseat in his three-piece suit, and Fields sipping his way across the state line. I followed the map and headed for Pan-guitch, Utah.

Chapter Ten

The time has come to take the bull by the tail and face the situation.

We had to stop three times on the way to Panguitch, all three times for water and oil for the car. Both were leaking at a slow but steady rate. There were other things wrong with the Caddy, but Fields didn't want to think about them now. His icebox was safe and he had plenty of time to refill it while Gunther and I grabbed a bite at one of the combination diner/gas stations where we were invariably told by the man who looked under the hood that the car needed some serious attention.

"When we reach Los Angeles," said Fields. "We've no time to dawdle."

When we had left our third gas station in Utah, Fields said, "You notice how every garage establishment with which we have dealt in this state has an attendant who looks exactly like the previous garage attendant? It's like that Bugs Bunny cartoon with the turtles who all look alike and plant themselves along the race route to beat out the rabbit. Always admired that family. The turtles. Clever con man using triplets could conjure up some sort of real scam not dissimilar to the rabbit's plight. I shall ponder the issue."

Panguitch is located on Route 89 between Capitol Reef National Park and Bryce Canyon National Park. We made it without anyone taking a shot at us, but we had not made good time in spite of Fields's urging through the speaker in the backseat. He had taken to closing the sliding window between us to cut down on the wind blowing in through the windshield. For most of the trip he had settled into almost a running commentary to me.

He warned me about turns in the road, oncoming traffic, impending lights, speed limits, and the dangers of drinking water. Gunther did not wake up. I drove, slowly, steadily. At one point Fields shouted, "Hurry up. We've got a crazy chimpanzee somewhere behind or ahead of us and another bank to get to."

I tried to pick up speed. Instead I picked up a metallic knocking which sounded as if it would be happy to get far worse. After ten miles, Fields relented and allowed me to slow down.

"Should be driving myself," said Fields.

It was twilight in Panguitch when we clanked into the town, another small town like the ones we had been in before. The main difference was that this one, located between two national parks, was designed for tourists. There were people in the streets, and the stores, restaurants, and bars—called "saloons" now that we were officially in the West—were open. Almost everything looked open but the bank which, according to the sign on the door, closed down at four in the afternoon and opened in the morning at nine.

We checked into a hotel that was supposed to remind its customers of the wild days of the past. The walls were wood. The beams on the ceiling were exposed. The chairs in the lobby were dark, gnarled wood with cushions. But it was the walls that got to Fields. They were filled with the mounted heads of animals.

"Jack Barrymore had hideous things like that in his house," said Fields. "Don't think he shot one of them. They always gave me the heebie-jeebies. What is that thing, a skunk?"

"That's a wolverine," the dour woman behind the desk said, looking over our odd trio and turning the book for us to sign in.

"Any of those things in the bedrooms?" he asked as he signed the register with a flourish.

"No," she said. "Payment in advance. Three dollars for each room."

Fields dug in his pocket, came up with a handful of bills, found a ten, and handed it to her.

"Keep fifty cents for yourself," he said. "A small gratuity in exchange for your assurance that my room will not look like Buffalo Bill's slaughterhouse."

She was thin, dark, probably some Indian in her and lacking in a sense of humor or a sense of anger, at least any she showed. She handed us the keys.

"You wouldn't happen to know the name of your bank president," Fields asked.

"Douglas Mutter," she said.

"Could you get him on the phone for me?" asked Fields with a smile.

"Nope," she said.

"The reason?" asked Fields.

"Off hunting, be gone most of the night," she said.

"You're sure," said Fields.

"Went with my husband," she said. "No business of yours, but my guess is they'll be doing more drinking than hunting."

"Drinking is a much more humane endeavor," said Fields.

"Yeah," she said. "You kill yourself slow instead of killing the animal fast. My Alex didn't start drinking much till they told us our boy, Robby, was missing on one of those islands in the Pacific."

"And you?" Fields asked. "Do you take solace in the occasional drink or two?"

"I have the Lord," she said.

I expected a quip from Fields. There was none.

"I'm sorry," he said. "I hope the lad turns up safe and sound. Is there a vice-president of the bank?"

"Alex," she said. "I run the hotel pretty much, and he works at the bank."

"Then we'll simply have to wait till the gates of gold open in the morning," said Fields.

"Bank opens at nine," she said. "Providing Doug Mutter and Alex or either one of them is sober enough. A good dose of Fletcher's Castoria and fifteen or twenty minutes in the bathroom with the newspaper usually sets Alex right. Either way, one of them always manages to be here on time with a pressed suit and smile. They always manage."

"Pardon me," said Gunther. "Could you direct me to a reliable garage that might still be open?"

"Andy Swerling's place is down to the left two blocks, turn right," she said.

"I'll take the car there as soon as I get my things in my room," he said.

"And I shall freshen up and visit yon saloon," said Fields, pointing through the hotel window at a place across the street. "Do they, perchance, have a pool table?"

"They got a pool table," the clerk said, looking at the names Fields had signed in the book. "You're W. C. Fields?"

"I am," Fields admitted with a humble smile.

"The gospel singer?"

"No, madam," he said, holding his hat and his temper. "You are thinking of Raymond W. Fields of Wichita, Kansas, who engages not only in the hideous profession of gargling, which he calls music, but insists on spewing forth ditties suggesting such unnatural things as temperance and abstinence from worldly pleasures and satisfying dysfunctions."

The woman simply stared at Fields till he gave up.

"Meet me at the saloon," he said to us as we moved across the lobby to the stairway. "We'll have a drink or two and some petit fours of Ritz crackers topped with patriotic squares of Prem."

"Woloski," I reminded him as we walked down a corridor, searching for our rooms.

"The Chimp? Crazy son of a bitch is probably somewhere in the desert in Nevada, shooting at prairie dogs in the moonlight."

"Or he could have gotten here before us and worked his broken-finger scam at the bank," I said. "Or he could be sitting outside somewhere waiting to take a shot at you."

"Let him try," said Fields. "The blood of generations of my ancestors rises within me, liberally mixed with more than half a century of alcoholic refreshment. My dander is up—whatever that means," he said, looking at Gunther, who was too exhausted to even listen.

"I'll shave, change my underwear, make a few calls, and meet you at the saloon," I said.

"I shall find Andy Swerling's service establishment," said Gunther, "and then, if you will excuse me, I shall find a nearby restaurant, have a quiet meal, and go to bed."

"The night is young," said Fields as we paused before Gunther's room.

"I have aged greatly over the past several days," said Gunther, solemnly entering his room. "Good night."

"Odd little fellow," said Fields as we moved down one door to his room. "Knew a midget once, even smaller than Gunther, acrobat, wouldn't go out with women who didn't outweigh him at least four to one. Had no trouble with this precondition, as I recall."

Fields opened his door and stepped in with his picnic basket and large suitcase. He flicked on the wall switch and looked around at the wood-paneled walls. The room had the same Western motif as the lobby but without the mounted heads. There were a pair of paintings on the wall, one of an Indian with a colorful feather headdress, his arms folded; the other of a cowboy, his hat in his hand as he sat astride his racing horse, a few feet behind a trio of cows.

"Vincent van Gogh must have slept here," Fields said, examining the paintings.

"I'll go to the saloon with you," I said. "Just stay in here. I'll clean up, make my calls, and come back."

"Let's have a new code," said Fields.

"New code?"

"You know, two short knocks and a pause, and then another knock," Fields whispered. "Chimp may have figured out the last one."

"All right," I said. "But by now you know my voice."

"But what if the Chimp captures you and forces you at gun-point to knock at my door and call out, 'It is I'?"

"Two short, pause, and then another knock," I agreed.

"Should have thought of that back in Ogallala," he said, closing the door behind me as I moved to my room and went in.

The room looked exactly like Fields's except my paintings were a pair of cowboys coming toward me with a few dozen Indians in pursuit. The other painting was a man in a cowboy hat. He had a neatly trimmed beard and mustache and he held a rifle cradled in his arms like a baby.

I moved to the phone, went through the clerk, told her I'd pay my phone bills before I went out for dinner, and got through to the police precinct in Philadelphia, where I asked the desk officer for Gus Belcher.

"You've got it," said the officer wearily.

I got Belcher's partner. He said Belcher was on his way in and could call me back in a few minutes. I hung up, took a quick shower while listening for the phone, shaved, dried myself, and had just gotten my undershorts on when the phone rang.

"Belcher?"

"Right," he said wearily. "I talked to the FBI again. They'll talk to Fields when he gets back to Los Angeles. FBI says the dead guy checks out, knew Barrymore. About the rest, who knows? Woloski, the Chimp, is another tale." Belcher yawned. "A few new items. Nothing on his record for the last eight years. Before that, he was even busier than we thought. Armed robbery. Disorderly conduct. Assault with a deadly weapon. Picked up on suspicion of driving a getaway vehicle in a bank robbery in New Mexico."

"He shot up a street in Rifle, Colorado, yesterday," I said. "Or was that this morning?"

"I'll pass it on to the FBI. How's Fields coming on getting his money?"

"Could be better," I said. "We're on the last one of the stolen bankbooks, in Panguitch, Utah."

"Hold on a second," he said. I held on, heard voices, and he came back with, "My partner says, did they get all his bank account books?"

"No," I said.

"Mickey thinks he should put them in a safe place," said Belcher. "Fast. If Woloski is starting to shoot up towns, he's liable to be crazy enough to go for the books Lester Burton left behind."

"Good thought," I said.

"Had a long day," Belcher said. "I'll give the L.A. police a call and tell them what's going on. From then on, it's up to the FBI and the Los Angeles police. You're way out of our territory and we've got two murders, an armed robbery with the victim in a hospital, and a jewelry store robbery. Assault victim's a sailor. Can you imagine that? We're at war and some piece of crap beats up a sailor?"

I could imagine it. I had seen worse.

"Thanks for the help," I said.

"Okay, just keep Fields safe so he can start making pictures again," said Belcher, hanging up.

I called Anita in Los Angeles. No answer at her apartment. I tried the diner. She was still there. I told her I would be back in the city in a few days. She told me to call her as soon as I got in. I almost told her I loved her, but I wasn't sure about that yet. I was sure I missed her and told her so.

"Same goes for me," she said.

We hung up. I got the operator and asked for Information in Los Angeles, Gonsenelli, probably V. The operator said there was a V. Gonsenelli. I got another operator and rang the number. After two rings, Violet answered.

"Violet? It's me, Toby," I said.

"Beau Jack won," she said.

"I know," I said. "I'll pay you when I get back tomorrow or the day after."

"I don't know if I'll be there," she said softly. "Mrs. Minck came in, saw me, and burst right in on Dr. Minck, who had a patient in the chair in the middle of a very delicate procedure. I could hear her yelling. She wanted me fired. Dr. Minck said I worked for you, not him, and she said that if that was the truth why was I sitting in the reception room. She demanded that he fire me and then she left without looking at me again. She's not a nice person."

"She doesn't care for me either," I said. "And you're not fired. I have a deal with Shelly. Worst case, we move out into another office in the Faraday and I pay you. Okay?"

She didn't sound so sure.

"I like meeting all the patients," she said. "And Dr. Minck is funny."

"A convulsive riot," I said.

"But . . ." she went on, "if it has to be . . . and you know a lot about boxing."

"I thought I did till I met you. We'll see," I said. "I'll talk to Shelly. Do I have any messages, mail?"

"Lots," she said, "but they're back at the office. I know your brother called. Someone named Anne called. Said you'd know who she was. And there was a crazy-sounding guy named Albert something."

"Woloski?" I said.

"That sounds like it," said Violet. "Said you'd better be careful. Things like that. Sounded crazy. Say, listen, I'm sorry, Mr. Peters, but my sister's here and we want to catch *Hello Frisco, Hello* at the movies at eight. My sister thinks she looks like Alice Faye. Even dyed her hair blond. I told her I think Dr. Minck looks a little like Jack Oakie."

"Enjoy your movie," I said.

We hung up. I asked the hotel operator to get me my brother's number. She reminded me that I had to pay the bill when I came down for dinner. I told her I remembered.

"Hello," a boy answered.

"Nate?" I asked.

"David," my other nephew answered.

"This is Uncle Toby," I said.

"Did you shoot anybody today?" he asked.

"Not today, but a man who looks like a big ape has been try-ing to kill me for the past few days," I said.

"Are you going to plug him?"

"I don't think so," I said. "But I'll let you know if I do. You ever ask your father if he shoots people?"

"He won't talk to any of us about his work, not even mom."

"Is your father home?"

"No," he said. "He has to work late tonight again. Mom's home."

"Put her on," I said.

"Uncle Toby," he said. "Call us Nathaniel and David from now on."

"I'll do that," I said. "Do I call Lucy Lucille?"

"She's too little to care," he said. "I'll get mom. We're listen-ing to 'The Man Called X' on the radio. The bad guys have Thurston. Paggon Zelschmidt went for help. I think I hear shots."

"Toby?" Ruth said, coming on the line and sounding a lot stronger than she had in months.

Ruth had come close to dying. The doctors had never quite figured out what was wrong with her but she had lost weight she couldn't afford to lose and was running a fever of 104 for a cou-ple of days. It had come on gradually. Specialists had been called in. I had been working for Bette Davis at the time, and Davis, who was Ruth's favorite actress, had visited her in the hospital. Whatever it was that had been killing Ruth started slowly to go away, and whether what kept her alive was one of the treatments the specialists gave her, or Davis's visit, or her will not to leave her family, no one knew. She was better. Not perfect, but a lot better. The cost of Ruth's sickness had put my brother deep into a second mortgage and loans. I had contributed when I was flush with a solid client. There was a way to go before they were out of debt. But they were all alive and well.

"How you doing, Ruth?"

"Much better," she said. "Where are you?"

"Panguitch, Utah," I said.

"You're joking?"

"No," I said. "I'm with a client. Phil's been trying to reach me."

"He's working late."

"I know. Dave . . . David told me."

"I don't know what it's about, Toby. I asked him to call you and invite you for dinner next Sunday. Will you be back?"

"Can I bring a friend?" I said.

"Friend?"

"A lady," I said.

"Sure," said Ruth.

"Sure you're up to it?"

"Positive," she said. "My mom will be here to help."

"We'll be there," I said. "If Phil was trying to reach me about something else, I should be back home by tomorrow night."

"Excuse me if this hurts," she said. "But I read in the *Times* that Anne is getting married to Preston Stewart. Are you all right?"

"I'm all right," I said. "Lady who's coming to dinner with me is making a big difference."

"That's good. Take care, Toby," she said.

We hung up. I zipped up my waterproof gabardine jacket after putting on my gun and holster and went out in the hall, locking my room.

When I got to Fields's room, I had forgotten the knock I was supposed to give. I tried two, pause, and knock. No answer. I tried three, pause, knock. No answer. Finally, I just knocked and said, "It's me."

No answer. I tried the door. It was locked. I hurried down the stairs and went to the desk, where the same woman stood.

"The man I checked in with," I said. "Did he go out?"

"Little one or the fat one?" she asked.

"Fat one. Do you know where?"

"Saloon," she said. "Two dollars and eighteen cents. Phone calls."

I dug out my ragged wallet, handed over two dollars, and found a quarter in my jacket pocket.

"Keep the change," I said and ran out the front door and across the street.

There were voices coming from inside, but no music. For some reason I expected a jukebox blasting in the saloon. And then I remembered Fields's hatred of all singing. I went inside. It was small, four tables in front, a bar against the far wall with a mirror. There was a big painting of a snow-covered mountain on the wall to the left, and on the wall to my right a painting of a broad, green field full of grazing cows. Under the picture, distracting from the movie-version image of a Western bar, was a darkened jukebox. One old man, who looked like he'd had more than enough a decade earlier, sat alone at one of the tables, staring at nothing. A group of maybe fifteen people were huddled in an alcove off the bar to the right.

I moved to the group and pushed my way through, half expecting to see Fields's body on the floor and the Chimp standing over him with a gun. Since I was dealing with tourists and not cowboys, I didn't have much trouble getting through the crowd.

There was Fields at a pool table, a martini in one hand, a cue in the other. He was circling the table, examining the scattered balls critically. He leaned over, squinted, took a drink, and stood up.

"Hold this for me, my good man," he said, handing his glass to a bespectacled, bald tourist in a plaid winter jacket. "Are you a drinking man?" Fields asked.

"A beer or two, sometimes," he said.

"Well, what you are holding is a martini," said Fields. "You are to guard it with your life and resist the temptation to take even the smallest of sips."

"I won't," said the man.

"Won't what? Take a drink or resist temptation?"

"Take a drink."

"Good—always give in to temptation," he said. "It may cut down on your life, but what there is of it, if you can banish guilt from your mind, will be filled with contentment and bliss."

I looked around the small crowd. They were smiling, enjoying the free and unexpected performance by W. C. Fields.

"I shall endeavor," he said, addressing the assemblage and nodding to me, "to propel the cue ball over the six and into the twelve, which will roll gently but decisively into yon side pocket. I shall do so with the cue behind my back and either right- or left-handed."

"I'll bet he's left-handed," someone said.

"No, I remember from the movies. He's right-handed. I think."

"Come, gentlemen and ladies," said Fields. "There are but eleven hours till the bank opens and I transact my business. A decisive majority of voices in a mockery of Greek chorus is called for."

"Left," came the majority.

Fields nodded, half sat on the edge of the table, chalked his cue, and looked at the man holding the martini. "I'll accept no claims of evaporation," said Fields. Then he returned to his shot, paused, and did exactly what he said he would do. The cue ball jumped over the six and into the twelve, which rolled smoothly into the side pocket.

"Game's a little off," said Fields, retrieving his drink. "Not used to playing with unwarped cues."

I went back through the crowd, moved to the bar, ordered a beer and some sandwiches. I drank some of my beer while I waited and listened to the pool balls clicking, the crowd applauding, and Fields's voice speaking, though I couldn't make out the words.

The bartender, a short, heavy man with white hair, wearing boots, black pants, a white shirt, and a black vest that made him look like a down-on-his-luck riverboat gambler, came back with sandwiches and said, "Had one tuna left, one straight cheese with lettuce and mayo, and Spam and cheese with mayo, and a chopped liver on rye."

"Chopped liver?"

"Short-order cook just moved here from New York City," he said. "Sometimes we have corned beef a friend of his ships in. Cook used to be a stockbroker. Gave it up. Ulcers, headaches."

I took the plate of sandwiches and paid the bill. Juggling the beer and sandwich plate through the crowd I approached Fields, who was lining up another shot. He paused to examine the plate, looked at each sandwich with distaste, and settled on the straight cheese with lettuce and mayo.

"Did I pay you today?" he asked while the crowd waited.

"No," I said.

He pulled bills out of his pocket and handed the right amount to me.

"Expenses?"

"Phone calls, sandwiches—four dollars, rounding it out."

He handed me a five and I gave him a dollar change. I moved back to the edge of the crowd with my beer and sandwiches and kept on guard against the sudden appearance of the Chimp. I imagined him madly firing his gun in the general direction of Fields or me, bullets thudding into surprised spectators and ricocheting from billiard balls. My plan, to the extent that I had one, was to drop the beer and sandwiches and go for the .38 under my zipper jacket.

But the Chimp didn't appear, and Fields continued his show and his consumption of martinis for almost two hours more, when the bartender in black shouted, "Closing."

"I'll pay twenty dollars to keep the establishment open another half hour," said Fields.

"Sorry," said the barkeep. "Curfew. Police'll be driving by in a few minutes to be sure we're obeying the city law."

Reluctantly, Fields hung up his cue and bowed slightly to the small though enthusiastic crowd, which burst into applause.

"That'll give them something to tell the kids when they get back to Cleveland," said Fields after he settled his bar bill.

I looked back at the pool table, which I could see, now that people were paying their tabs and heading for the door. Fields had eaten less than half his sandwich.

No one tried to kill us in the street. No longer giving a show, Fields went silent and said nothing all the way to his room. I watched him go in, turn on the lights, and check to be sure the windows were locked and there were no intruders.

"I think I'll read a little *Bleak House* before turning in," he said. "Wish the damn place had a barber chair."

I waited till he locked the door behind me and I went to my room. I opened the door, turned on the light, and found myself looking at Albert Woloski, the Chimp, who sat in a chair facing the door. He had a large gun in his hand.

Chapter Eleven

Nurse, don't forget the olive in my sedative.

"Close it," he said.

I closed the door.

"Sit," he said, pointing to a wooden chair.

I sat.

"You're gonna listen to me," he said.

"Damn right," I said.

Since my .38 was under the left arm of my zipper jacket, I had no plans for a shootout unless I had no choice. In the first place, I'm a lousy shot. In the second place, there was a chance I could survive and find out what he'd done with W. C. Fields's money.

"You listening?" he said nervously.

"Try me," I said, hands on my knees.

He looked at the paintings on my walls as if they were particularly fascinating. I waited. I was a good waiter and a good listener. Even my ex-wife, Anne, who was about to marry the movie star, acknowledged that. Her primary complaints were about my "childish attitude," "irresponsibility," "lack of ambition," "the danger of my job," and my "frequent, sudden absences."

She was right about all of that, but I was a pretty good listener, especially with a gun in the hands of a possible murderer aimed at my stomach.

"It wasn't right when you and Mr. Fields took the dwarf with you to drive," he began.

"Gunther's a midget, or a little person," I corrected. "He is anatomically perfectly proportioned."

"What the hell do I care?" said the Chimp. "You listening or you telling?"

"Keeping things straight," I said.

"I've been keeping loonies and tough guys away from Mr. Fields for three years and I didn't even tell him," said the Chimp. "I'm a good driver."

"The best," I agreed.

"Don't do that," he said

"What?"

"What do you call it . . . humor me."

He raised the gun to the general area of my chest.

"I won't," I said. "I'll just listen."

"I like Mr. Fields," the Chimp went on. "He didn't care about my record. Didn't even check. Pays me well. And he's funny. I'm not a laugher, but he's funny. I don't even mind him calling me Chimp. I know what I look like, and Chimp is better than Albert Woloski."

I didn't argue with him.

"Mr. Fields needs protection," he went on. "I took all my money, two hundred and twenty-four dollars, and followed you to Philadelphia. I was on the same planes as you, got on first, kept my head down and a magazine in front of me. Waited till you got off, and followed in a cab. Airplane took a big chunk of my cash. Now I was taking cabs. I know some guys there, in Philly, I did time with. When I knew where you were staying, I looked up one of the guys. He came up with a car for me, cheap, but it didn't leave me with much, enough for food, a little backup for gas. I borrowed some tools in case I had to fix the car. I'm good with cars."

He was waiting for an answer.

"I've noticed," I said.

He nodded and continued. "Started following you way back when you headed for Lancaster. Then I saw the blue Ford. He was trailing you, only not so far back. I saw it all. Saw him shoot at you. When you stopped at night, I slept in my car or on a fire escape, watched Mr. Fields's room. Days when you didn't stop, I didn't stop. That time you caught me, I was sitting on the fire escape at the end of the hall. I heard the two shots and ran to Mr. Fields's room. There was a guy there standing over the bed. I shot at him. He went out the window. I checked the bed. Mr. Fields wasn't there. Then you came in. I didn't want to shoot you."

"Thanks," I said, remembering the death threats to me and to Fields.

"So, I went out the window. The next day I started following *him*. He didn't go into any of the banks. But I did see this tall, skinny guy everyplace we went. He never talked to the guy I was following, had his own car."

"Burton," I said. "The tall guy's name was Lester Burton. He was a forger. He stole the bankbooks. He was getting Mr. Fields's money out of the banks. He was going to give it back. John Barrymore had hired him to get the money, part April Fools' joke, part an attempt to protect Fields's money."

The Chimp didn't quite understand, but he nodded at what he could make of it.

"The other guy who tried to shoot Mr. Fields, I followed him to the park the night he killed the tall guy," the Chimp said. "I saw him shoot. I thought he was shooting at you. I couldn't figure. Then he ran. I thought he might be running to shoot Mr. Fields. So I went to the hotel."

"You recognize this killer?" I asked.

"I would now. Never saw him before Lancaster. After he killed the tall man, Burton?"

"Burton," I confirmed.

"I lost him. Don't know what he did."

"He ran to Burton's room and took all of Mr. Fields's money."

The Chimp nodded. It looked like fresh news to him.

"I saw him shoot out your windows when you went to that Klan rally," he said, getting back to simpler ground. "He followed you, stayed hidden. I looked for him."

"I saw you," I said.

"Then I saw him behind some trees," said the Chimp. "He had a rifle. Aimed it at Mr. Fields. Then, just when I was going to get him, Mr. Fields sent the crowd after me. I can't blame him. He didn't know. I had to hide, go back for the car later. I knew the killer was after both of you."

"What did he look like?"

"About as tall as you, as old as you, darker hair, good build, face like . . ." Albert looked around, scrunching up his face in an attempt to find the words to describe the man who had Fields's money and had murdered Burton. "He's more like me than you that way," he said.

I'm no prize with my smashed nose and battle scars—the face of an ex-pug who's been through a few dozen bouts more than he should have. But on a reasonably fair scale, between me and the Chimp were all the homely men in the world. On the other side of the scale were the truly ugly.

"Yesterday, at least I think it was yesterday," he said. "In Rifle, I saw him drive down the street and park. It was my best chance. I'm running out of money and the car is making noises. I got out and took some shots at him. Lots of shots. I missed. I need to be up close."

"I know the feeling," I said.

"He jumped back in his car and drove away," said the Chimp.

"Which is why he didn't go to the bank," I said.

"I don't know about that," said the Chimp, "but I'm low on food money, gas money, car-repair money. I'm low on money. I can keep following, but I'm gonna run out soon."

"And you want me to give you money so you can keep following us?" I asked.

"A loan," he said. "I can't leave Mr. Fields alone. That guy'll get him and you and the little guy. If I don't get money, I'll have to steal a car to keep watching your back. You believe me?"

"I've been fooled by a lot of liars," I said, "but I believe you."

I didn't add that part of the reason I believed him was that he didn't seem bright enough to make up the whole thing. Besides that, he had the gun.

I pulled out my wallet. There were a couple hundred dollars in it from Fields's daily payments and what I had left of my own. I put five twenties on the table next to me.

"Up," he said.

I stood up.

"Over by the bathroom," he said.

I moved over to the bathroom.

"Inside," he said.

I went in.

"I'm tellin' the truth," he said, picking up the twenties from the table. "I'll be watching your back, looking for the guy. I'll do better. Close the door."

I closed the bathroom door and heard him moving something. I could hear him coming toward the bathroom door. When I could sense him right outside, I knew I could pull out my .38 and fire through the door four or five times and probably get him, but I believed his story.

I heard my hotel-room door open and close and I pushed at the bathroom door. It opened out. The Chimp had propped a chair under the handle. It didn't take much to slide the chair back till it fell on the floor. There was no point in chasing the Chimp.

I unzipped my jacket, ready to go for my gun, knowing now there was a man after us or in front of us with a bagful of money and a willingness to kill. I put my ear to Fields's door and heard something between a snort and a snore. Back in my own room, I took off my jacket, gun, and holster, pulled the blanket from the bed along with the pillows, and placed the gun and holster next to the makeshift bed on the floor. I had learned to gauge mattresses. This one was definitely too soft and I knew that if I tried to sleep on it I probably wouldn't be able to stand in the morning.

I brushed my teeth, shaved so I would be relatively ready at dawn, packed my things, left the bathroom light on, turned off the other lights after locking my door and putting the same chair under the doorknob that the Chimp had put under the bathroom door. It wouldn't stop a killer, but it should slow him down long enough to wake me and give me time to reach my weapon.

My plan was to stay nearly awake all night. I lay there trying to figure it all out and failed. In fact, I had successfully failed at everything during this dash across America. The only thing I could point to in my favor was that Fields was still alive, but I wasn't sure how much of that was due to anything I had done.

I dreamed. I knew Koko the Clown was going to show up, with or without Betty Boop and Bimbo. Even Popeye and Wimpy might make an occasional appearance in my Koko dreams. I get the feeling that the dreams are trying to tell me something, but, like Juanita the fortune-teller's warnings, I can never figure out what it is. Anne said the cartoon dreams were manifestations of arrested development. Her vocabulary is a lot better than mine.

Cab Calloway was in this one, dressed in white, singing "Minnie the Moocher" while Betty Boop danced. I was the audience, alone except for one dark figure about five tables back. Since Calloway and Betty were looking directly at me, I couldn't turn and get a good look at the shadow man.

Then, suddenly, Koko was standing on my table, mimicking the movements of Calloway and Betty. Calloway and Betty suddenly disappeared and Russ Columbo was on the small stage, gazing soulfully at me and singing "Juanita." The shadow man had moved a few tables closer and I was afraid to turn and look. Koko was sitting on the table now, his head spinning around while Columbo continued to sing.

"Listen," said Koko, his head suddenly stopping. "Listen to the song."

I did listen and I suddenly remembered, Juanita the fortune-teller in the Faraday Building had said something about two dead men.

Something hard jabbed into the center of my back. Koko said, "Uh-oh," and disappeared. I woke up.

The sun was coming through the windows and I reached under my back. I had rolled over onto my own gun. I was lucky it hadn't gone off. My first thought was to check my watch. Habit. It said it was 11:43. I knew it wasn't close to that. I got up, an ache in my upper back, wondering who the shadow man was and who the second dead man was or was going to be.

Before I did anything else, I called the desk and found out it was a little after eight in the morning. I threw some water on my face, tried to straighten the wrinkles in my clothes, went back in the other room, put on my holster, gun, and jacket, and threw the blankets and pillows back on the bed. A brush of my fingers through my hair and I was ready to go. I had never really unpacked except to get out clean underwear and a shirt.

I pushed the chair out from under my doorknob and went to Fields's room, where I knocked.

"It is open," he said. "And you are a tad tardy."

I went in. Fields was packed and ready. He wore a fresh, seemingly pressed cream-colored suit and an even whiter shirt with a large black bow tie.

"Used to do a gag on stage at this point," he said. "Drink in my hand, as you see me thus, I looked down at my watch to check the time. Drink, of course, tips into my lap. In fact, I had so mastered the trick that I could spill all of the drink onto the floor between my legs without getting a drop on me. Never used real alcohol. Waste. I'd get up. Dance around. Knock at the door on stage and in would come a lovely, scantily clad maiden who supposedly saw the wet spot in my crotch and said, 'Mr. Fields, what happened?'

" 'Anticipation,' I would reply. The audience would go wild. Never failed. Except for the prudes. Then the gag started to show up all over the place. I anticipate this morning."

I decided to wait till we were comfortably settled in the car and headed back to Los Angeles before I told him about my visit from Albert Woloski.

Fields finished his drink and rose, cane in hand. I noticed he was wearing spats. His hair was slightly moist and brushed back. This was our last chance, the final stop of the line on Burton's list.

"Then let's go," I said, taking his heavy suitcase in addition to mine while he picked up the picnic basket.

I was about to knock at Gunther's door when Fields stopped my hand.

"Little fellow's been up and about for hours. All packed. Car's in front of the hotel. I'd say he's in the lobby waiting."

I knocked. No answer. Fields was right. Gunther was in the lobby, fully suited, seated in a wooden-armed chair, his feet about eight inches from the floor. He was reading a magazine.

When we approached him, he looked up at us and then back down, reading aloud.

> *The pulse that stirs in the mind,*
> *The mind that urges bone,*
> *Move to the same wind*
> *That blows over stone.*

He put down the magazine, April's *Atlantic Monthly*, and said, "By Theodore Spencer. Bought it this morning to bring to Jeremy Butler on the chance that he might miss it."

I doubted if Jeremy had missed a single issue of the magazine since he was twelve, but I just nodded.

"Might buy me a copy of that," said Fields, turning to lead us out the hotel's front door and into the sunlight. "By gad, you've got windows back in."

Gunther, suitcase in hand, stood straight and nodded. "The radiator is also repaired with welding, as is the oil line. The knocking sound at high speed was a transmission problem which has been repaired by simply tightening screws and bolts by the garage man. About the body . . . again, there was no time."

"How much you out of pocket?" asked Fields.

"Twenty-seven dollars," said Gunther.

Fields extracted three tens, as if by feel, and handed them to Gunther.

"Use the difference for gas," he said. "You deserve a battle-field commission and I hereby give you one. Captain Gunther Wherthman of the W. C. Fields coast-to-coast monetary expedition."

Fields tapped the amused Gunther gently on each shoulder with his cane and then, picnic basket in hand, climbed into the rear of the car, leaving Gunther and me to pack his bag and ours into the trunk.

We were at the bank in three minutes. The street was just coming alive and not much at that. Gunther parked directly in front of the bank in a space specifically marked No Parking. "Park here, Captain," Fields had ordered, and Gunther had obeyed.

"We're forty-five minutes early," I said, looking at the clock on the dashboard.

"Perfect," said Fields with a smile.

"Time for Gunther and me to run over to that restaurant across the street for a fast coffee and breakfast," I said.

"I have already eaten," said Gunther.

"Up at the crack of dawn, well fed, ready for battle," said Fields. "He'll make major before this excursion has run its course."

"I'm getting breakfast," I said and got out of the car.

Less than fifteen minutes later, since I was the first customer of the morning, I had finished toast, eggs over easy, hash browns, and two cups of coffee. I sat at the counter where I could see the car and the bank. The Caddy didn't move and the bank didn't open.

I was just crossing the street when a man somewhere around

fifty, wearing overalls, a red-flannel shirt, and a hunter's cap, walked up to the bank door and started to open it.

Fields, Gunther, and I were at his side before the door was halfway open. The man looked more than tired and more than slightly hung over. "You're Fields," he said.

"Correct," said Fields, offering his hand.

"I'm Doug Mutter," he said. "Alex'll be along later. His missus left a message with my missus that you were looking for us. Haven't had time to change."

He went to his left inside the bank and pulled open the curtains. The small bank needed no electric lights this morning.

"This way," said Mutter, waving for us to follow him past teller cages, beyond a quartet of desks, and into an office with his name on the door. He motioned for each of us to take a seat while he opened blinds, revealing barred windows.

President Mutter sat down in his wooden swivel chair, closed his eyes, rubbed his forehead, and felt the gray stubble of his face before turning to us.

"The situation—" Fields began.

"No situation," said Mutter, taking off his cap and placing it on the desk. His hair was a wild tangle of yellow with perhaps the first tinges of gray mixed in.

"Used to call you Whitey?" asked Fields.

"Some still do," said Mutter.

"Me too," said Fields.

Mutter pushed two sheets of paper across his desk toward Fields.

"The problem is this," said Fields. "I seem to have forgotten what name . . ."

"Your own," said Doug Mutter, rubbing the bridge of his nose. "You opened the account as W. C. Fields. Just sign. Show some identification."

Fields raised an eyebrow, and pulled out his billfold. Mutter gave it a quick glance and waved it away, looked at Fields's signature, and opened his desk drawer. There was a neatly wrapped pile of bills.

"Six thousand seven hundred and fifty, including interest," said Mutter. "Alex and I stopped by just before sunup. Count it."

"No need," said Fields with a smile. "It is a pleasure and a surprise to meet such an honest and trusting bank official."

Mutter put his head in his hand and gave us a gesture of dismissal.

"Occasional drinking has killed more than one honest man," said Fields. "I suggest working your way up to a habit or never getting beyond the slight social tipple. What you and Alex have done is disastrous."

Mutter didn't move. We got up, left him alone, went out the door, and made our way back to the car.

"That's it," I said as Fields tucked the new stack of bills in his picnic basket alongside his thermos, his olive jar, and his bottles of gin and vermouth.

"Not by a long shot," he said, sitting back. "Not by a ten under par with a couple of holes in one. We get back my money and we put the Chimp behind bars."

"He didn't do it," I said as Gunther put the car in gear. The transmission sounded fine.

Fields, in the act of mixing a drink, looked over at me. "Not alone," he said. "I figured that out. Whoever shot Jack's prankster and pulled off the finger-in-the-cast routine required more gray matter than the Chimp possesses."

"No," I said. "He was in my room last night." I told Fields what Albert Woloski had told me. He listened carefully and nodded his head.

"Then," he said, "it will make the pursuit of my missing savings a bit more difficult, though the Chimp has, if his story is true, seen the thief and killer and can identify him."

"I think it's true," I said.

We were on the open road now, just a mile or so outside of town, heading for Los Angeles, when Gunther slid back the window and said, "There is a car in the ditch ahead."

I looked out the window. The car was on its side and a figure was in the front passenger seat. The figure didn't seem to be moving. The car looked as if it had tumbled over at least once.

"Pull over," I said.

"It may be a trap," said Fields.

"How could the killer know we'd be the ones to find the car?" I asked.

"A hunch, the knowledge that we'd leave when we got the money, the . . . stop the car."

Gunther pulled over in front of the downed automobile. It was a prewar Oldsmobile. Through the cracked windshield we could see someone crunched against the passenger door. As we moved forward, I unzipped my jacket so I could reach my .38 and probably manage to shoot all of us if anything happened.

At first we couldn't tell who the man was. His face was covered with blood, but his body was the first giveaway and then his voice, soft, tired, through the open driver's-side window.

"It's the Chimp," said Fields.

"Shot me," said Albert Woloski. "Through the window."

"We can see," I said.

"Hurts," he said.

"I'll get help," said Gunther, turning to hurry back to the car.

"No," said the Chimp as loud as he could. "Lots of shots. Broken. Get the police."

I was leaning close to Woloski now. "First we'll get you to a hospital, and then we'll get the police," I said.

He reached up and grabbed my jacket with his bloody hand. Even with at least four bullet holes in him and who knows how many broken bones and punctured organs, he was strong enough to pull me toward him and barely gasp, "Get the police. The police."

"Fear not," said Fields. "We'll get medical and constabulary assistance. I was wrong about you, Albert. I should have nicknamed you Gunga Din."

I don't know if it was a smile or a grimace of pain, but it appeared on Woloski's bloody face and he released my jacket and slumped back. I pushed broken glass out of the way and reached in to touch his bloody neck. No pulse. His heavy breathing had stopped. I forced myself to lift one of his eyelids. There was nothing but death in them.

"Gone," I said.

The three of us looked down at the corpse.

"What now?" asked Fields.

"We can go home, call it a loss, and whoever did this will stop killing people and live a life of ease off your money," I said.

"Are you quitting?" he asked.

"I'm considering it," I said and then looked down at the body and the blood on my jacket. "I've considered. If you want me, I'm still on."

"Good," said Fields. "To Los Angeles to pursue a strategy to recover my money and put the culprit in jail for the rest of his life. He has now murdered two of the few apparently honorable men on this spinning orb."

We got back in the car and headed for Los Angeles. Gunther stopped at the next town, and I called in the murder and its location to the Utah State Police without giving my name.

Chapter Twelve

I advocate extreme self-control. Never drink anything stronger than gin before breakfast.

"Where's the butler?" asked Fields as the door to his house opened. He had been unable to find his keys and was showing definite signs of irritation toward the woman who opened the door.

"Quit," said Fields's secretary, Miss Michaels, dressed for business and awaiting the return of her boss, who had called her from a dusty phone booth just across the California border.

The Cadillac grumbled away with Gunther behind the wheel. Miss Michaels barely gave the battered, disappearing car a look. She was used to such things, I suppose. I was carrying Fields's two suitcases and my own. Gunther was going to drive the Caddy to No-Neck Arnie's garage for a body job, and then get back to work. Gunther had told me at one of our rest stops that if I required his services for another odyssey with Mr. Fields he would prefer not to be a part of it, though he would do so if I asked him. I promised not to ask him.

"Is he here?" asked Fields, bustling past her.

"He is," she said. "In your office. I reached him immediately after you called."

"My office?" said Fields. "I don't want that chiseler going through my personal effects."

I put Fields's suitcases down inside the door and kept my own in hand.

"He's checking the remaining bankbooks," said Miss Michaels, now behind Fields as he examined each room and noted, with some satisfaction, that the ceiling in the living room seemed to be sagging a bit more. There was a low balcony overlooking the living room, where a maid was working.

"What the hell is she cleaning?" Fields demanded.

"It gets dusty," said Miss Michaels calmly as he moved through the room and up the stairs.

Fields, Miss Michaels, and I entered his office. Seated at the table near Fields's desk was an overweight, white-haired man in a pair of brown slacks, a tan shirt, and an open sports jacket that matched his slacks. The man had a long pad of paper and a pile of different-color and different-size bankbooks in front of him. He did not look up when Fields entered the room.

"Miss Michaels," Fields announced. "I am going to shower, shave, put on comfortable accoutrement, deal with that thief who claims to be an accountant and is going through my private financial papers sans permission, dictate several letters to you, and then meet with Mr. Peters here to plan our future strategy. I'll inform you when I am ready for you. Meanwhile, Mr. Peters may want to freshen up."

The accountant, who was introduced to me as John Neuenfeldt by Miss Michaels, lifted a hand—the one without the Parker pen in it—to acknowledge the introduction.

"I'll be charming later," Neuenfeldt said.

Miss Michaels led me to a bathroom on the first floor, showed me where the towels were, and disappeared. I put my suitcase down on a laundry hamper, surprised that the room was pink, the towels white, and the shower curtains pink with white polka dots. There was a fresh bar of green Palmolive soap and even an unopened bottle of Prell shampoo. The room didn't have a touch of the Fields eccentricity. Even the oil painting on the wall—of a seaside picnic—was out of keeping with the lunacy of Fields's house.

I got out the last of my fresh underwear and socks and a clean blue short-sleeved cotton shirt that didn't go too badly with my dark slacks. I got undressed, looked at myself in the mirror, and wondered how that man could be me. In almost half a century of life, I was still a little surprised by the tough, broken-nosed, ruffle-haired man in front of me. Part of it was the stubble on my chin, neck, and cheeks, but most of it was me.

I turned on the hot water in the shower, ignored the pink scale in the corner that would tell me what I already knew. I had eaten too much, exercised not at all, and put on a few pounds in the last week.

The water felt good, hot, and relaxing while I washed, shaved, and shampooed. I let the hot water beat down on my aching lower back three or four minutes. I just stood there with my eyes closed and began to sing my usual medley of shower jingles:

"Don't despair, use your head, save your hair with Fitch shampoo. . . . Rinso white, Rinso white, happy little washday song. . . . Oh, the big red letters stand for the Jell-O family. . . . Buy Eversharp, try Eversharp for writing pleasure . . ."

A voice crackled into the room.

"No singing in my abode," came Fields's voice. "I consider it a far greater sin than blasphemy in a Catholic church. Peters, get dressed and get back up here."

The crackling stopped. I got out, dried myself, found the hidden speaker and microphone in a vent in the ceiling, and got dressed, taking an extra few seconds to comb my hair. With my bag repacked and my zipper jacket back on, my .38 under it tucked neatly in my holster, I made my way back up to Fields's office and knocked.

"It's open," Fields shouted.

I went in. Fields was behind his desk, wearing an ornate dark kimono with dragons on it. It looked to be silk. So did the sash around his ample middle. He held a drink in his hand and his nose was covered with white cream. Miss Michaels was seated across the desk from him. His chair was decidedly higher than hers. In fact, her chair looked like one Gunther might be comfortable in. She had a pad out and a pencil in hand.

John Neuenfeldt, the accountant, was still hunched over his pad and the bankbooks.

"Have a seat, Peters," Fields said, swiveling so he could take a look at his war map on the wall. "I'm just concluding a few essential missives."

I put my bag down and took a seat, a solid walnut chair with curved arms.

"Read that back to me, my dear," he said. "I've momentarily lost myself in the solar system of my unconscious."

"Dear Chinaman," Miss Michaels read. "All is well here except for the nightly attacks by the Kickapoos. I too was under the impression that they were a peaceful tribe and had all been slaughtered by land-grabbing Comanches, but history as written is a sham."

"Ah, yes," said Fields, taking a sip. "Let us continue. 'We are having no trouble fighting off the attacks with my shotgun. I'm down to two drinks before breakfast, am exercising regularly, and weighing movie offers which keep coming in as I endeavor to finish my script about the man who inherits a zoo. I'll see you next week. Don't bring me a new tie. I miss you.'"

"Signed?" Miss Michaels asked.

"Woody," Fields said, looking at me and Neuenfeldt to see if we were going to react. We didn't. He went on. "Letters to the presidents of all the banks on the list you prepared, the ones we went to, with the exception of the last two. 'Dear Sir or Madam, a lawsuit will be forthcoming and you know why.' Sign it 'W. C. Fields, unwitting dupe who should have been protected by an institution that should have shown greater perspicacity.'"

Miss Michaels looked up as John Neuenfeldt let out a small sigh and straightened, no longer writing, his eyes on the notes he had made on the pad in front of him.

"To the president of the Borden Dairy Company," Fields went on as Miss Michaels began to transcribe. "'A traitor on my staff, who has yet to be identified with certainty, put several spoons of your Hemo concoction in a medicinal beverage in the hope, I expect, of sneaking some of the vitamins and claimed nutrients into my finely tuned internal organs. I have my suspicions about who it was, but I'll keep them to myself until I have compiled sufficient evidence.' "

He paused to glance at Miss Michaels, who sat placidly waiting for him to continue.

" 'However,' " he went on, " 'it may delight you to know that the resultant liquid concoction was surprisingly palatable. So, here is my recipe, which I offer to you for use in your advertisements featuring the grinning cow, providing I am given appropriate credit, a letter of gratitude, and a gratuity of no less than five thousand dollars. Mix a martini and add three teaspoons of Hemo. Stir thoroughly. Drink quickly and follow up with a Hemo-less martini. I hope you fully appreciate this suggestion, which should net you at least half a million new buyers of your product. Yours cordially, W. C. Fields.' Another letter to Ken Murray . . .' "

"I'm finished," Neuenfeldt interrupted in a weary tenor.

Fields turned to face the accountant as if he had forgotten the man existed. "The result?"

"I'll recheck my figures," Neuenfeldt said, "but I'd say, within two thousand dollars, that a total of over three hundred thousand, seven hundred and forty dollars was stolen from your accounts. The two-thousand-dollar leeway is necessary only because the rate of interest may have varied since the time you made your deposits."

Fields waved Miss Michaels from the room, saying, "We'll continue our epistolary ventures later. I'll call."

She got up and left, closing the door quietly behind her.

"If you called me in before the bankbooks were taken," said Neuenfeldt, rubbing the bridge of his nose, "we could have saved it all with phone calls. Told each bank you were withdrawing your money and that we were sending appropriate documentation, which I could have prepared. Checks would have come right back to you."

"How much didn't they get?" Fields said, pointing to the remaining bankbooks.

"Whoever took your bankbooks," said Neuenfeldt, pad in his lap, turning now to fully face Fields, "just grabbed a big pile, didn't check the balances, which wouldn't have been accurate anyway, since they didn't include interest."

"How much do I have left in those accounts?" Fields said, waving at the pile of books.

"Again," said Neuenfeldt, "I'm within a few thousand dollars, but I'd say somewhere over five hundred and fifty-six thousand dollars."

"Plan," said Fields, turning to me, apparently having no idea, or not caring, how bizarre he looked in his silk kimono and his white nose. "I hide those savings-account books. Big John prepares the documentation and I sign the right letters after Miss Michaels prepares them."

Neuenfeldt got up slowly, tucked his pad into his briefcase on the desk, and said, "I'll prepare a report this afternoon on how we can quickly put a hold on the untouched accounts and on how to get your money out of each account. I'll bill you for my services later."

"How much?" said Fields when Neuenfeldt, moving lightly on his feet for a heavy man, had almost reached the door.

"Five hundred dollars," said the accountant.

"Five hund—" Fields began. "I'll take you to court. You don't get a penny over one hundred. Any judge will be in tears once he hears I've lost more than a quarter of a million smackers."

Neuenfeldt was unshaken. He sighed deeply and turned to Fields. "Five hundred or no report, no instructions on how to proceed. Just fifty dollars for my visit today and a recommendation, if you want it, on several other accountants you can call in. I doubt if they'll charge you less, and it'll take them valuable time to figure out this whole mess."

"Five hundred dollars," Fields said after a brief hesitation. "Send your bill."

Neuenfeldt nodded and left the room. I was alone with Fields.

"I'll hide the bankbooks," said Fields, looking at me. "You start working on finding my stolen lucre and who killed Burton and the Chimp."

"Same pay," I said.

"Same pay," he said.

"If I don't come up with leads in a week," I said, "the deal's off and we let the police follow up. Beyond that, you'd be wasting your money."

There was a knock on the door as I reached for my suitcase and prepared to leave.

"Come in," shouted Fields. "Man can't get a moment's solitude to compose himself in this Gothic manse."

Miss Michaels appeared at the door. There was a man behind her. She left him standing, hat in hand, as she crossed the room and handed Fields a card. Fields looked at it and indicated that she should give it to me. The card was white with a black seal in the middle. It had the name Walter McEvoy in the left-hand corner in dark ink. Under his name was simply the word "Agent," and in the lower right-hand corner was inscribed, "Federal Bureau of Investigation."

I put the card in my jacket pocket as McEvoy stepped in. Miss Michaels closed the door as she left and we looked at the FBI agent. Around forty, well built, neatly pressed dark suit, white shirt, and dark tie. He had a good-looking round face and neatly barbered yellow curly hair.

"And what service can I perform for the Federal Bureau of Investigation," said Fields. "My discord with the Internal Revenue Service is between me and them. I will continue to deduct the cost of billiard balls, regardless of whether armed federal officers attempt to intimidate me."

"Mr. Fields," said McEvoy calmly, hat in hand, almost at attention. "The Philadelphia police informed us of the murders and the thefts. Had you come to us before you—"

"I don't need any more advice on what I should have done,"

said Fields, taking another sip. "What are you going to do now?"

"Get a complete statement from you," he said. "And the men who accompanied you. We've already checked on Lester Burton's story. It appears to be true. Since Albert Woloski was an ex-convict, we're checking out known criminals with whom he might have been affiliated. We'll get descriptions. We're already trying to find fingerprints and any other evidence we can work from."

"This is the famed criminologist, Toby Peters," Fields said, pointing to me.

McEvoy nodded in my direction.

"Mr. Peters and a Swiss midget accompanied me on my failed voyage," said Fields.

"May I sit?" asked McEvoy.

Fields pointed to Miss Michael's small chair. McEvoy took the one Neuenfeldt had vacated instead and turned it to face us.

"I'd like your statements individually," he said, placing his hat on the desk next to the pile of bankbooks. "And without the other person present."

It was reasonable police procedure. I nodded to Fields, who said to me, "Peters, why don't you go dally at the billiard table? I'll call you when we're done here."

I picked up my bag, went out, closed the door, and did as Fields suggested. I can play pool better than I can shoot a gun, but not much better. My brother once suggested that I have my eyes examined. Maybe he was right. I found a cue and fooled around. It wasn't more than fifteen minutes before I heard Fields's voice from somewhere in the room.

"Remain where you are, Peters," he said. "Agent McEvoy will be down forthwith. I will retire to my boudoir for more episto-lary missives and contemplation."

Instead of the speaker clicking off, I heard Agent McEvoy say, "Thanks for your time and I'd appreciate having that list of banks where you still have money, as soon as possible. We can put a stop on any attempts at withdrawal. I'd also strongly suggest that you put these remaining bankbooks someplace safe and very soon. Whoever this person is, he's a double-murderer now."

Then the speaker clicked off.

Fields had not told the FBI agent of Accountant Neuenfeldt's plan to do just about what the FBI was planning.

I stood at the billiard table, waiting for McEvoy, who appeared in less than a minute, walking tall. I went to one of the high stools against the wall and sat down while he flipped pages in his notebook, went over his Fields notes, and looked at me.

"Shouldn't take too long," he said with a sympathetic smile, glancing around for a normal chair. There were none.

He placed his hat on the pool table and sat on the stool next to mine. He asked questions. I answered. He knew what he was doing. He closed the notebook, got down, shook my hand, and said, "We're spread pretty thin now. Most of our manpower is concentrating on espionage, sabotage, infiltration. But I've assured Mr. Fields that we won't neglect this case and that we hope to recover his money."

"In short," I said, "you can take over for me."

"That's between you and Mr. Fields," he said, picking up his hat and moving toward the hallway and the door. "I can let myself out."

When I heard the front door close, I said, "You get all that?" I heard the low hum of the hidden microphone when Fields had turned it on.

"Every utterance," came Fields's voice.

"You still want me on the case?" I asked.

"The man who leaves his fate to the federal bureaucracy is the man who has a faith which is unthinkable to even a moderately trained orangutan. Go forth and find the bastards who killed the Chimp and Jack Barrymore's man. And finding the money they've already taken wouldn't be a bad idea either."

"McEvoy's right," I said. "Put the rest of the bankbooks someplace safe. I'll keep you posted."

"The criminal has broken two commandments," came Fields's

voice, godlike, though surrounded by static. "First, thou shalt not kill more than a fifth. Second, thou shalt not steal except from other comedians."

I found a phone in the hallway and called a Black Top cab. I was tired. I didn't know where I was going to start my search. I was scrubbed, shaved, and ready for a few days of sleep.

When I got to Mrs. Plaut's Boardinghouse on Heliotrope, the good woman was standing on the front porch, aproned, as straight as the broom she carried, and apparently waiting for me.

"Saw the cab pull up," she explained. "Doubler began to chirp."

Doubler, I assumed, was the latest name for her bird. I had no intention of asking why she had given it the odd name.

"He is a bird of wondrous powers as yet not fully explored," I said, lugging my suitcase up the steps and pausing before the front door. She blocked me with her small, thin, and not at all frail body.

"You are being sarcastic," she said.

"I am being tired," I answered. "Now, if I could just . . ."

Her hand was out, expecting something. Then I realized what she was expecting. I put my bag down on the porch swing and took out her manuscript.

"W. C. Fields loved it," I said. "He thinks it might be movie material. Wants to see you about it. He'll call."

"I'll consider it," she said seriously. "Did you comment?"

"In the margins," I said. "I love it."

She clutched broom and manuscript to her bosom and stepped out of the way to let me through. The photograph of Eleanor Roosevelt that hung on the porch wall was tilted. I adjusted it. Eleanor Roosevelt had signed it and given it to me. I had turned it over as a token of peace to Mrs. Plaut who, thinking it was Marie Dressler, proudly displayed it on the porch.

"Mr. Wherthman returned this morning," she said, following me into the house.

"I know," I said, heading for the stairs.

"I put a bowl of Aunt Ellendorf's peanut-butter rice pudding on your table," she said as I trudged up the stairs.

"Sounds like what I need," I said.

I was at the top of the stairs now. The phone was ringing.

"Someone's been calling for you all morning," she said from below, shifting the manuscript under her right arm.

"Who?"

The phone kept ringing.

"Man. Didn't leave a name. Mr. Hill took one of the calls before he went off to deliver his letters."

I paused, looking at the phone on the wall.

"I plan to let it ring next time," she said. "It is not unreasonable to expect the boarders to answer their own phone so I don't have to go running up the stairs every five minutes."

"The phone's ringing now," I said, wondering how she had heard it the previous times.

"I think the phone is ringing right now," she said.

I picked up the receiver and said, "Plaut Boardinghouse."

"Peters," said a man. "I've been trying to reach you."

The voice was familiar but I couldn't place it.

"You've reached me."

"Two men are dead," he said. "The money is gone. It's not coming back. You want to live, tell Fields you're through, and find another client."

"Even if I quit, the FBI is after you."

"That's not your problem. Just take the warning."

"I appreciate the warning," I said.

Behind him I heard a voice shout in the distance, "Just tell the bastard I'll rip his head off and throw it and his lawyer out the window if he doesn't cooperate."

"Take it to heart," the caller answered and hung up.

I did the same, picked up my bag, and went to my room. It was neat, clean, the mattress on the bed with a colorful purple-flowered orange blanket with tucked-in military corners. The small sofa's pillows were fluffed up and the "God Bless Our

Happy Home" pillow rested in one corner. The Beech-Nut Gum clock on the wall told me it was nearing noon. I put down my suitcase and went to my small table near the window, where a soup bowl sat covered by a dish. A spoon rested on a nearby napkin.

I took off the dish and looked down at Mrs. Plaut's Aunt El-lendorf's red-brown peanut-butter rice pudding. The window was open about four inches. There was a scratch on the sill and Dash scrambled through the opening and leapt onto the table.

I tool a spoonful of the pudding. It looked like . . . but I was hungry. It wasn't bad. Dash sat and watched me.

"Want some?" I asked.

Dash looked at me blankly. He was independent, but I think we were friends. I didn't own him. He didn't own me. He just visited whenever he felt the urge, which was almost every day. Sometimes he slept with me on the mattress. Dash and I had met when he saved my life one day, jumping out of a closet onto the face of someone who had good reason for wanting to kill me.

I got a bowl from my small cupboard and scooped about half of what was left of the pudding into it. Then I put it on the floor. Dash jumped down, smelled it, and began to eat. He fin-ished and looked up at me for more. I poured him what was left of the oversized portion Mrs. Plaut had given me.

I took off all my clothes but my underwear, found a white T-shirt and put it on, and then considered whether I had to go through the trouble of pulling the mattress on the floor or just taking a chance and getting into the bed. Experience told me that, no matter how tired I was, if I wanted a working back, the mattress had to come down. I was home. I could get a few hours' sleep. Just one more chore. Pull the mattress down.

I managed, with Dash watching me from across the room where he was cleaning himself. I got onto the mattress and lay back. With the window open, there was enough cool air coming through to send me under the covers. I lay on my back, not want-ing to think about Fields and the case, but . . . why had the killer called and threatened me? I was nothing compared to the FBI, unless he thought I knew something, which I didn't think I did. I tried to place the voice, but I couldn't. And that other familiar voice in the background, talking about tearing off my head and throwing my lawyer out the window. My lawyer, Marty Lieb, weighs close to three hundred pounds. It wouldn't be a pleasant sight. And yet there was something about that second voice. I couldn't shake the feeling that the voice was familiar. And now I was beginning to think that the voice of the caller was also familiar. Half asleep, the only thing I could make of it was that the killer had a partner and I was too tired to make sense. I closed my eyes. Dash came to the bed and nestled against my side. I think I patted his back. I don't know. I was asleep.

I knew I was asleep because Koko the Clown was back, sitting on my chest. Somehow I knew I was a kid. From far away, a voice shouted, "Damn it."

Koko held a finger up to his lips and winked. He reached over and closed my eyes. I knew he wanted me to pretend I was asleep, which I was. A door opened and through my closed eyes I could see. I could see a shadow figure, the same figure from my last remembered dream, in a doorway about a dozen feet away.

"You forgot to close it again," the figure said. It was the man who had threatened to tear off my head. "I slammed it on my finger. My finger's broken."

He moved toward my bed.

Koko leapt into the air and began to fly around the head of the creature coming toward me. He was joined by Bimbo, Betty Boop, and Betty's grandpa. The creature tried to swat at the animations but he couldn't hit them. He was real. They were not. It was my dream. He backed off toward the door and said, "You're not sleeping. You hear me? I'll get you when you wake up. I'll break your nose again."

He backed out of the room, holding his throbbing thumb. Koko, full-size now, closed the door. Betty, Bimbo, and grandpa were gone.

"You get it?" Koko asked, turning to me.

"Get it?" I asked, sitting up, hearing my little-boy voice, look-ing at my little-boy arms.

"Look around," said Koko, rushing across the room and slam-ming into the wall.

He fell, landed on his back, and jumped up.

I looked around the room. It was familiar. It ought to be. I had slept in it for almost eighteen years while I was growing up. When my brother, Phil, was in the army fighting the Huns, it had become mine alone, and when he came back, he had moved out into a one-room apartment of his own. He had taken Kaiser Wilhelm, his German shepherd, with him, and I had been stuck with a tank of goldfish, most of which died within weeks, which made me stop giving them names. The last goldfish was alive for five months before I named him Hoot Gibson. He died a few weeks later. He had, like my phone caller, been better off anony-mous. But there, now, in a huge bowl, swam Hoot Gibson the goldfish, the size of a human. Koko jumped into the bowl and swam around with him for a second. Then Koko and Hoot looked at the closed door and said, together, in bubbly under-water voices, "Get it?"

Finally I did, but I didn't wake up. I had two more dreams. In one, W. C. Fields stood in his living room, billiard cue in hand, whirling around to keep away a dark faceless figure walking to-ward him. Fields was waving the cue around so quickly that it whirred and was almost invisible. The figure moving toward him paused and pulled out a gun. I was on the balcony over Fields's living room, looking down, no gun, nothing, helpless, watching. I tried to say something but no words came out, and then I was in the third dream. I was standing in front of another faceless man. This one was dressed in black and held a book in front of him. Behind him were a pile of small books, Fields's remaining bankbooks. John Neuenfeldt, the accountant, was sitting on a pillow, going through the bankbooks, looking for something. Then I was aware that someone had taken each of my arms. I looked. On my right was Anne, my ex-wife. On my left was

Anita Maloney, my high-school prom date, the woman I was now getting serious about. Anne and Anita. The names were alike. This was the first time I had noticed. I wanted to remember that when I woke up. The man in black coughed to get our attention and I knew I was about to get married to two women.

Neuenfeldt paused in his counting, turned on his pillow, and said, "Now do you get it?"

He was about to say more, but something woke me.

I sat up quickly, felt a twinge in my back from the sudden movement—I usually got up slowly, I had a ritual for getting up, to appease my unpredictable back—and looked up at Mrs. Plaut.

"Did you like the pudding?" she asked.

I nodded.

"You gave some of it to the cat," she said.

"The cat?" I answered groggily.

"Bowl's on the floor," she said. "You taken to eating from bowls on the floor?"

"No," I said. "The pudding was great."

"Plenty more," she said. "But not for cats."

I looked around. Dash was gone. He usually disappeared when Mrs. Plaut came into the room. He seemed to sense her coming. I looked at the Beech-Nut clock on the wall. It was after four.

"Another phone call," she said.

She left without another word, and I got up carefully and pulled on my pants. Then, barefoot and in my undershirt, I went out the door and to the phone.

"Peters," I said.

"No use," said Sheldon Minck, almost in tears. "Mildred said Violet goes or I can't come home."

"Then don't go home," I said.

"I love my wife," he said.

Mildred Minck was a plain-faced, overly made-up woman of average height and less than average weight who had made

Shelly's life a near hell. She bossed, threatened, punished, and twice that I knew of—once with a Peter Lorre imitator who she was later accused of killing—had affairs. Besides that, Mildred Minck hated me.

"Violet's not going," I said.

"Toby," he pleaded.

"Are you in the office?"

"Yes," he said. "I can't go home till I call and say Violet's fired. She doesn't buy the argument that Violet's working for you. Mildred doesn't care."

"See if you can find Jeremy," I said. "I'll be there in about an hour and a half."

There was a slight groan in the background.

"Got a patient under anesthetic," he said. "Wisdom teeth look like rotten apples. I'll find Jeremy."

I hung up and stood still for a few seconds, grasping at my dreams.

"Get it?" Koko had asked.

I got it, but I couldn't figure it out. The voice I had heard behind the killer who called me on the phone before I went to bed, the voice that threatened to tear off my head and throw it and my lawyer out the window, now had a face.

It was my brother, Phil Pevsner, the cop.

Chapter Thirteen

Thou shalt not use the name of the Lord in vain, unless you've exhausted all the four-letter words in your arsenal.

I had no trouble finding a place to park my Crosley on the street near the Wilshire Police Station. I had placed my .38 and the holster in the glove compartment and locked it. Even though I was within full view of the police station, I also locked my doors. The most logical place to find car thieves and other criminals is near police stations. Lack of evidence and a good lawyer will too often get a known offender out of lockup, onto the street for a good breath of air, and feeling ready for quick auto break-in and theft. A handy car on the street is ready-made transportation.

In my case, I was more concerned about the gun in the glove compartment. The Crosley was hardly prime material for window breaking and hot-wiring. There were plenty of better choices on the street, all a little farther away from the Wilshire Station.

A pair of hung-over sailors, one young, one not so young, came out of the station-house door and down the steps. Their uniforms were a mess and the young one had a closed black-and-red eye. They walked slowly down to the street.

Inside, the place was alive. People filled the benches, waiting to make their complaints to the single desk officer. There were mothers with little babies, a man with a beard babbling to another bearded man in a language I couldn't begin to identify. There were a couple of Mexican kids in zoot suits talking in Spanish and waiting their turn. One needed a shave. The other looked too young to shave.

The cop at the desk, Constantine Keratides, better known as

Connie the Greek, was a desk sergeant and had been for almost twenty-five years, which was fine with him. He was losing his hair, working on expanding his belly, perfect at dealing with whatever maniac appeared before him, and counting his days till retirement.

Someone ripped your son's ear off and shot your husband in the knee? Have a seat and I'll take care of it. Someone stole your ice-cream truck and gave away your entire stock to kids in the park? Have a seat.

I waved to Connie, who was patiently listening to the tale of a well-dressed couple who said they had been held up outside their hotel room. The couple were not happy. The couple were not young. The man was notifying Connie that he was a member of congress.

Connie was unimpressed. In his time, he had seen congressmen, movie stars, mayors, ministers, and world-renowned surgeons, all of whom had committed crimes or had crimes committed on them. Sometimes both. Connie nodded, took a few notes as I walked up the worn, wooden stairs that led to the squad room. I walked quietly down the hall past the door marked "John Cawelti, Captain." John was a redheaded, pock-marked cop who was sure the world was out to get him. He was right. He was one unlikable human being. Cawelti had replaced my brother, Phil, who had held the job of running the station for a little over a year. Phil had hated it. He longed for the streets and the criminals, not the public relations of dealing with the chief of police's office, local politicians, and the merchants' association. Phil was now back in his small office, back to being a lieutenant. As bad as Phil had been, Cawelti was worse and was barely hanging on to his promotion. Most, including me, figured his promotion had been a favor from a higher-up in the department for covering up something big.

I made it past Cawelti's door and met a detective I knew named Albergetti with a uniformed young cop. They were coming out of the squad room.

"I told you," Albergetti, a hound-faced veteran, was saying. "Never hit 'em in the face. It shows in the mug shot. Sometimes you can't help it, but the rule is 'never.' Stomach, chest, legs, high on the arms, ass, okay, but not the face."

The young cop nodded seriously and I went into the squad room. It was busy for a weekday afternoon. Busy and almost as loud as the downstairs lobby. There were familiar faces of weary detectives—Allen, Rashkow, Malloy, Davis. The smell was of sweat and carry-out food, with the faint lingering scent of not quite fully cleaned-up vomit. The windows were dirty. The floors needed more than the nightly sweeping and occasional mopping by the janitor, and the walls were covered with newspaper clippings, photographs, and memos stuck up with thumbtacks.

I knew that Cawelti had ordered the detectives to clean up the place and clear the walls. They had ignored him. Had my brother told them the same thing, they would have done it. No one wanted to be on the receiving end when Phil Pevsner went violent.

I made my way though crying women, pleading teenagers, old timers who sat with arms folded or at their sides, giving tired lies the detectives took down on their report sheets. Uniformed street cops were supposed to take care of the minor misdemeanors. If it got to the squad room and a detective, it was supposed to be a felony.

I looked around for Steve Seidman, my brother's partner for more than twenty years, but I remembered that Steve was gone. The tall, pale man, who always wore his hat and said as little as possible, had applied for a transfer when Cawelti took over. He finally got it. When Cawelti made that special mistake that he was sure to make, Steve would come back. Meanwhile, my brother was riding it out at the Wilshire, and Cawelti was smart enough to leave him alone.

I knocked at Phil's door and he said, "Come in."

Phil was leaning against the desk in his small office. The

desktop was filled with reports and notes and more waiting in his *in* box. His jacket was off and draped around the chair behind the desk. The collar of his wilted white shirt was open, as usual, and his tie was loosened to give him plenty of room to breathe. His sleeves were rolled up to the elbow. Phil was almost fifty-three. He was my height, built like a brick, and had short, bristly gray hair he liked to run a thick hand across when he was thinking.

Phil's arms were crossed and he didn't seem surprised to see me.

"I'm thinking seriously," he said, "of knocking Cawelti's head about two inches into the wall."

"I'd like to be here when it happens," I said.

"He took a bribe," Phil said. "I had a clean collar, felony, assault, Wally Range. And Cawelti let him walk after he talked to the perp's lawyer, Johnny Andrews."

"Figures," I said.

Phil looked at the wall and looked at me.

"Around noon today," I said, "were you in the squad room yelling that you were going to tear someone's head off and throw his lawyer out the window?"

Phil looked at me, arms still folded, thought for a few seconds, and nodded.

"I thought so," I said.

"What the hell is this about, Tobias?" Phil said.

"Someone in the squad room called me around noon and threatened to kill me if I didn't drop the case I'm working. I heard you in the background. That someone has already murdered two people."

"Lester Burton and Albert Woloski," said Phil. "You're working for W. C. Fields."

I walked over to the chair in front of Phil's desk and sat down. He was standing over me. There was a time not long ago when I took pleasure in pushing Phil into a temper blast, even if I were the target. But I had lost the urge over the past year or so with

Ruth's illness. Phil's and my relationship had gone through a se-ries of small changes. We got along a little better, but it was a lot less exciting.

"Who told you?" I asked.

"Cawelti brought in an FBI agent this morning," he said. "Cawelti turned him over to me."

"His name was Walter McEvoy," I said. "Tall, blond."

"Belongs in movies," Phil said.

"What did he want?" I asked.

"Information about Burton and Woloski," Phil said. "And about you and Fields. Any records we had. I gave him what we had, and he gave me his card and said he'd be in touch."

I must have taken on a strange expression, because Phil said, "What are you thinking?"

"Maybe McEvoy called me," I said. "Maybe he threatened me."

"An FBI agent? Why?" asked Phil. "Besides, I watched him leave."

"Okay," I said. "Then who? One of the detectives out there? I know their voices. A suspect being questioned? Detective walks away for a minute and he grabs the phone, calls and threatens me? Maybe McEvoy stepped back in just before you threatened to tear someone's head off?"

"Place was packed," Phil said. "I was shouting at Allen. I didn't look around, but I'd bet he wasn't."

"You'd lost your temper," I said.

"That's pretty obvious."

"Which means . . ."

"I didn't pay attention to anything but what I was mad about," he said. "All right, it could have been McEvoy. Maybe he just doesn't want you interfering with an interstate double murder and fraud."

"So now the FBI is threatening people with death if they get in the way?" I asked.

Phil shrugged. He had threatened many people who got in the way of one of his investigations.

"I know who was here," said Phil with a sigh. "Steve. He came by and went to lunch after he got me back to near sanity. Steve'll remember any unfamiliar face in the squad room. He's got a memory like a German camera." Phil turned, picked up his phone, and dialed a number. He handed me the receiver.

"Yeah?" came Seidman's voice. "Who is this?"

"Toby," I said. "I'm in Phil's office."

"Phil okay?" he asked with concern.

"Phil's fine," I said. "I've got a question. You were here at noon?"

"Yeah."

"Phil went a little . . ."

I looked at Phil, who shrugged, unfolded his arms, and moved back behind his desk, where he sat heavily.

"Cawelti is driving him nuts," Seidman said. "Between you and me, Toby, I'm doing some off-duty work on Cawelti. Finding his fingers in pockets. Trying to prove it. It's coming."

"Steve, when you were here today, was there a good-looking blond guy making a call when Phil started yelling?"

"McEvoy?" said Steve. "Phil introduced me to him, but he was gone when Phil started in."

"You sure?"

"I'm sure," Seidman said.

That killed one great theory. So I went for another. "Anyone in the squad room you didn't recognize?"

"Just suspects, witnesses, and perps," he said.

"Thanks," I said.

"Sure," said Seidman. "Keep an eye on Phil till I find a way to get rid of Cawelti and come back."

"I will," I said and we hung up.

"It's got to be one of the detectives, or a uniform," I said. "McEvoy was gone."

"It's not one of the detectives," Phil said. "And you know it.

And it wasn't Cawelti. He wasn't in the squad room, and you'd recognize his silly-ass chirp."

"Tell Ruth I might have to be out of town this weekend," I said. "If not, I'll come to dinner next week with Anita, if she wants me, and take the boys out to a movie or something."

"I'll tell her," Phil said, swiveling his chair toward the window, which had a beautiful view of a brick wall about a dozen feet away. His hands were behind his head. "Tobias, you know the story—O. Henry—about the leaf the artist painted on the wall across from a dying girl's room, painted it so it looked like it was on the tree. She thought it was real. She thought she was going to die when the last leaf fell. That's why he painted the leaf."

I think he had it a little wrong, but I kept my mouth shut.

"O. Henry did time," Phil said, looking at the brick wall. "And he could write stories like that. I'd like to find an artist to paint a leaf for Ruth."

"Ruth's okay," I said.

"No," he said. "She's not. She'll be fine for a while and then it'll start again. Doctor's told me. I'm telling you. I think she knows. If I take a long leave, she'll know why and it'll make things worse."

"I'm sorry, Phil," I said.

"I know," he said. "What I said this afternoon, about tearing off heads . . . I can't take the idea that there are worms walking the streets, hurting people, stealing, worms with healthy bodies who don't give a damn about anything, anyone. Yeah, I want to tear their heads off. You got anything else to discuss?"

"No," I said.

"Ruth asked me if we could take the kids to services," he said. "There's a synagogue not far from us. Off Victory, just before you hit Van Nuys."

"I know it," I said.

"I've never been," he said. "And I know you haven't."

"A couple of weddings," I said.

"That's not what I mean."

I knew what he meant.

"Our father never went," he said, "I don't think he was too happy with God when mom died when you were born. But I don't think they went to a synagogue before you were born either. I guess we'll go."

I had nothing to say except, "Anita and I'll see you, Ruth, and the kids this weekend, if I'm in town . . . I'll let you know as soon as I know."

And I left.

I didn't like Phil this way. I wanted the angry Phil back, the Phil who had broken my nose twice, the Phil who had tossed me around and who I could goad into an explosion. Jeremy once told me that Phil and I related the way we did because it meant emotion and contact—not particularly the most healthy contact, but contact. I thought he was right. Now we were losing even that.

I stood in the squad room looking at the detectives, uniformed cops, everyone. No one looked up at me but Big Buxbaum, who paused in his discussion with a skinny Mexican kid with tears in his eyes. Buxbaum gave me a nod, and then nodded at Phil's door and shook his head.

I nodded back in understanding.

It hadn't been Buxbaum who had called me. Buxbaum had a high voice and a thick New York accent he had never lost.

I gave up.

I made it past Cawelti's door, down the stairs, and back to the street, inclining my head at the overburdened Connie Keratides at the desk, who was now dealing with a huge woman who wanted the police to immediately go to her apartment and arrest her husband for beating her up. Connie nodded and let her talk.

Back in the Crosley, I checked my gun and headed for the Faraday Building. The lobby was eerily quiet. I checked my watch. It told me a lie, as it always had. I wondered if it had lied to my father. I was in no hurry. I took the elevator and watched the floors go by and looked down at the lighted lobby through the bars. The trip was long and I was trying to make sense out of what had happened, when the elevator stopped with a little jerk on the sixth floor.

I went to our office. The door was open. The lights were on and Violet Gonsenelli wasn't there. I went into Shelly's parlor. Shelly was sitting with his head in his hands, the top of his bald pate pointed at me. He was still wearing his white, bloodstained lab coat and holding a cigar between his fingers.

Beside him stood the massive Jeremy Butler, who raised an eyebrow at me as I stepped forward. Jeremy wore dark slacks and a short-sleeved blue shirt which showed the enormity of his muscles.

"How are Alice and Natasha?" I asked.

He said his wife and daughter were fine and that he had just written a poem about the toddler. I told him I'd like to hear it.

"Toby," said Shelly, looking up. "Pity."

His thick glasses were slightly cockeyed.

"Better than that, Shel." I said, and then I said to Jeremy, "The office next door, the little one the bookie moved out of?"

"Investment counselor," Jeremy corrected.

"Right," I said. "What's the rent?"

"For you? Twenty-five dollars a month, furnished."

"Wait," said Shelly, getting out of his chair. "I don't want you to move out. We're friends. Allies."

"I'll be right on the other side of the wall with Violet," I said. "I'll stop in every day and Violet will be right next door every day, so if Mildred drops by she'll know where to find her."

"That won't satisfy Mildred," said Shelly.

"I didn't think it would," I said.

"And who could I sublet your office to?" Shelly said mournfully.

"It's not an office," I said. "It's a broom closet with a desk and two chairs. When can I move in?" I asked Jeremy.

"Two days," he said. "Give me time to clean and paint it. Two months in advance is customary."

I had a wallet jammed with cash from Fields, and a fat account in the bank. People were threatening to kill me and I didn't know what the hell was going on, but I was making some money for the first time in years. I handed Jeremy two twenties and a ten.

"I'll sign the lease whenever it's ready," I said.

"We have no need for a lease, Toby," Jeremy said. "When you want to leave, simply give me a month's notice, and you have my word that I will not raise your rent or eject you."

"Good enough for me," I said.

"There's some furniture in the office," said Jeremy as Shelly groaned. "The tenant left hurriedly. You may keep what you can use with the stipulation that if he returns for it, you turn it over. Experience, however, tells me that we will not be hearing from the investment counselor."

Shelly had returned the cigar stub to his mouth and was weeping.

"Shelly," I said. "I've known you long enough to know when you're faking it."

Shelly stopped crying and looked disgusted.

"You can walk out on Mildred instead," I reminded him.

"Never," he said. "God help me, I love the woman."

"Love is not rational," Jeremy said. "Come, I will give you the keys."

"Betrayed," Shelly said. "By a man I trusted. A man I called my best friend."

"I'm moving right next door, Shel," I said. "Cheer up. I'll treat you to dinner at Manny's and a beer or two at Tucker's."

Shelly nodded morosely.

"I'll move everything out tomorrow," I said.

I took a second, went into my cubbyhole office, and picked up my mail and messages. None of it looked too important. I took it anyway.

"I'll be ready in five minutes," Shelly said sadly.

"I'll be back," I said, following Jeremy out the door and up the stairs to the apartment he and Alice had constructed out of three eighth-floor offices.

Alice was feeding Natasha at a table in the large studio that served as living room, dining room, and kitchen. To the left was Natasha's bedroom. To the right was Alice and Jeremy's bedroom. I had seen the bed. Jeremy had built it himself. The combined weight of the couple was somewhere between five and six hundred pounds.

In contrast, Natasha was a tiny, smiling kid who looked up at me from her high chair and extended her hand with a soggy biscuit. I took it from her and pretended to eat it. She watched. Alice paused and looked at me with the usual suspicion that I was about to put her husband in danger.

"Toby is renting six-thirteen," Jeremy explained, going to his desk in the corner for the keys.

Natasha made a gurgling sound to show that she wanted more food. Alice obliged as Jeremy returned and handed me two keys.

"I'll leave one on the ledge over the door tonight," I said. "I'll give Violet a call later so she can get started in the morning. You know, telephone, whatever she needs."

"We will be happy to assist her," said Jeremy.

"I'll do some straightening up when Natasha's asleep," said Alice.

"Thanks," I said. "You mentioned a poem about Natasha?"

Alice smiled up at Jeremy, who returned to his desk and opened his oversized notebook. He began to read while Natasha ate noisily.

> She smiles and I am blessed.
> How could I have guessed
> That at my age new life would come.
> She touches me and I am light.
> I hold her hand, but not too tight.
> And inside me, I hear a drum

Beating "Natasha." It's my heart
And it fills me with the surge of art,
Though her beauty nearly strikes me dumb.
To be or not to be is not a question.
Nirvana is no longer my destination.
My wife and I look at her and our souls hum,
Natasha, Natasha, more than heaven sent.
I touch my wife and we are both content.

"Beautiful, Jeremy," I said.

It was one of the few of Jeremy's poems that I had ever understood, and I really did like it. What I didn't like was that I was rushing toward fifty and had nothing in my own life like what I just saw and heard, and wasn't sure I wanted it.

"I've got to go. Bye Alice, Natasha."

Natasha grinned and did something like a wave.

I was determined to call Anita from Manny's, have a few quick tacos and drinks with Shelly, and see her.

Shelly was silent, resigned, as I led him slouch-shouldered and feeling sorry for himself down the Faraday stairs. At Manny's there were no other customers except Juanita, who was, as always, colorful and bangley, lingering over a cup of coffee and a double taco.

"Was I right or was I right?" she asked as Shelly and I sat at the counter.

"You were right, Juanita," I said. "Two men died."

"And Doc Minck just had some bad news," she said. "Not clairvoyance this time, Tobias, just looking at his face."

"Right again, Juanita," I said, hoping she would go back to her taco and wipe the spot of guacamole off her chin, which she did, but it didn't stop her from talking.

"Who was it?" she said.

"Who was who?" I asked before I could stop myself. I nodded to Manny for the usual.

"The man who made the call. The killer. He was in the room.

Somebody talked to him, helped him. He's dark, determined. And he wants more."

"More what? Money?" I asked.

"What are you two talking about?" Shelly asked.

"Who knows?" Juanita said with a shrug. "I can't control this stuff. I told you a hundred times. It comes. I tell you what I see. Bingo. Bango. You believe me. You don't believe me. We're friends so I don't charge you. And one more thing. You're going to a wedding. Soon."

"Whose?" I asked

"Don't ask," she said, opening her wide mouth for a bite of taco. "Just don't ask. Hold it. There's a black bag, like a doctor's bag, full of money."

"I don't suppose you could tell me where it is," I said as Manny brought us our tacos and drinks and went back to his stool to smoke, read *Collier's* magazine, and listen to the radio, which was playing music so quietly I wasn't sure it was on.

"No," she said. "Wish I could. If I could do that, you think I'd be in a dinky office in an old office building? I'd be finding money all over the place. Not that I'm complaining about my lot in life. Manny, I'll go for another double. The night is young."

I called Anita. She begged off on tonight. She'd had a long day and, as much as she wanted to see me, she needed sleep even more. Working a diner alone is close to working a chain gang.

About an hour later, over a third beer at Tucker's, about halfway down the block and across the street from the Faraday, Shelly's voice no longer made it into my consciousness. I just nodded as he professed his love of Mildred, the unfairness of life, and the ultimate end of the dental profession when someone finally discovered a preventive for tooth decay.

And suddenly, it came to me. A boom. A big bang.

The pieces fit. Sort of. And I had a fairly good idea who my killer was. I drank up quickly, hustled Shelly into a cab, and went to work. I had a hell of a lot of work to do and needed some help doing it.

Chapter Fourteen

*Never try to impress a woman. Because if you do, you'll be
expected to keep up that standard the rest of your life.*

I still had my key to the old office. It was after ten and I went in
as quietly as I could, groping my way in the dark past the reception room, across Shelly's parlor and into my broom-closet office.
I turned on the lights, and while I made my calls I looked
through my mail. The only thing of interest was a far-from-cheap
engraved invitation to the wedding reception of Anne Peters to
Preston Stewart at the Beverly Hills Hotel. No RSVP was necessary. Just show up. The reception was tomorrow. I wasn't invited
to the wedding itself but my name was. Anne's name, before we
were married, was Mitzenmacher. She could have used her second husband's name, but since he had been a murderer who owed
a lot of people money when he died, she used "Peters," when it
suited her. Like when she married someone else.

I put the invitation in my pocket and called Violet Gonsenelli.
Shelly had given me her phone number. He was more than a little soused at the time. Violet was home, listening to the radio
and about to take a shower. I told her about moving into the new
office and working for me. She asked for a raise. A small one. I
agreed and I told her she'd find a key to 613 on the narrow ledge
over the door. It wasn't the best place to hide a key, but I wasn't
really hiding it. There was no chance that anyone would be
breaking into 613 that night, and if they did, they wouldn't find
anything but old office furniture. I told her the first thing she
should do was get the phone working.

"I hope Doctor Minck will be okay," she said.

"We'll be next door to comfort him in his moments of need,"
I said.

"Met his wife the other day," said Violet. "Could see what was coming right away. Not the first time. Jealousy is a painful and incurable disease."

"You make that up?" I asked.

"No—Archie Bohanan, Angelo's trainer," she said. "He was talking about title holders, but the same thing applies. Know what I mean?"

"I know what you mean. War news is good. Very good," I said.

"Angelo'll make it," she said. "Juanita told me. At least I think she told me."

"See you tomorrow sometime," I said. Then I called Fields's house and a man answered. "Can I talk to Mr. Fields?" I said.

"He be sleeping in his barber chair," the man said quietly, in an accent that sounded like an Irish farmer in a low-budget feature.

"Wake him," I said.

"I be needing this job," he said. "Got one leg, a wife, and three kids, and I like to think I'm not a stupid man."

"How about Miss Michaels?"

"Went home hours ago," the man said.

"Is there anyone there who'd dare wake the great man?" I asked.

"No," the man said. "I'm just the handyman. Everyone else is gone for the night, and I'll be taking my leave when I finish packing my tools."

"Not unless you've fixed that damned leak," came Fields's voice over an extension phone.

"There be no leak," said the handyman.

"I'm inebriated, not deaf," said Fields. "I know a leaky faucet when I hear one. Years ago in Bombay I opened a fortune cookie that told me I would someday be plagued by a leaky faucet. The day has come. I should have known that one cannot escape an Oriental curse. Never ate Indian food again, though it was a Chinese restaurant. There is a leak. I hear it plop-plop-plopping in the bowels of this accursed hovel."

"I'll look again," said the man wearily. "I'll fix it. And then I'll be leaving."

"Back to the waiting bosom of your family," said Fields. "I see it now. Little Tiny Tim rushing up to you and leaping into your arms. The smell of lentil soup in a great pot over the open fireplace. Your red-cheeked wife giving you a tender embrace."

"I'll be fixing the leak," the man said calmly, hanging up the phone.

"Phone woke me, Peters," he said. "Phone and the dripping. Now I'll have to read and play some pool for a few hours before I do battle with Morpheus once more."

"Did you hide the bankbooks?" I asked.

"Brilliantly," he said. "No living being could find them. Put them all in an old box my dear mother gave me, brought all the way from England by my father, who was, I may have told you, of Cockney extraction, a race given to distrust nurtured by the realities of city life. The box and its contents are now sequestered in a location known to none but me."

"I've got a few calls to make. Then I'm coming over."

"Ah," he said. "Perhaps you'd like to engage in a few friendly games of Ping-Pong. Stakes of a pittance to make the joust interesting?"

"I think someone may try to break into your house tonight and take the books," I said. "If they don't find them, they may try to convince you to tell them where they are."

"Then call out the constabulary," he said. "And cling to the hope that they will be able to bungle their way through the night without accidentally shooting me."

"I've got no proof yet," I said. "The police aren't going to come out without a hell of a lot more than I've got. I'll get there as soon as I can."

"I'll have my trusty shotgun at my side while I sit enthralled by the adventures of *Peregrine Pickle*."

I had never called Steve Seidman at home, so it took me a few minutes waiting for the operator to track him down. I dialed; the phone rang. I let it ring and keep ringing until Seidman finally answered.

"Steve?"

"Yes."

"It's Toby."

"I'm in the middle of a shower," he said.

"Everybody's showering tonight," I said.

"American ritual," he said dryly.

"Life and death," I said.

"Always is," he said. "I'm dripping on the rug. Talk."

"Remember I asked you if there was a blond FBI agent on the phone in the squad room at noon?"

"Yes," he said.

"And you said you didn't see anyone in the room but detectives, uniforms, suspects, and witnesses?"

"Right," he said.

"Could you give me the name of every detective in that room at noon?"

"Yeah."

He rattled off the names of six detectives and two uniformed officers. I recognized them all and wrote the names on the back of an envelope containing a bill for a carton of Energine Cleaning Fluid, which I never ordered and never received.

"You have phone numbers for all of these?" I asked.

"You plan on telling them where you got the numbers?"

"No," I said.

"They'll figure it was Phil," he said.

"I'll say it was Cawelti," I said.

"He'll come after you when he finds out," Seidman warned.

"I'll risk it," I said.

There was a pause while Seidman put down the phone. Then he was back. "Rug's a wet mess," he said.

"It'll dry," I said.

He gave me the phone numbers of all eight officers.

"Thanks," I said. "You'd better get back in the shower."

Seidman hung up and I began calling. The first three I called all sounded suspicious, including Buxbaum, but they answered my question. I got no answer to the fourth detective's phone, but I hit pure gold on the fifth, Rocco Allen.

"Noon today," I asked him when his wife put him on the phone. "Did someone use your phone?"

"What kind of question is that?" he asked with definite irritation. "You get me out of bed with my wife when we . . . What kind of question?"

"I'm sorry," I said. "But it's important."

"And you couldn't wait till tomorrow?"

"No," I said. "When my brother came into the squad room yelling, were you at your desk?"

"No, I was getting coffee for us at the machine, in the corner."

I knew where the machine was.

"You said 'us.' There was anyone at your desk when you went for the coffee?" I asked.

"Yes," he said.

And then he told me who and why, and I had the biggest piece of the puzzle, one with a face on it. I thanked Rocco, asked one more question, got an answer, and apologized.

"What'd he do, make an obscene call while I got the coffee?" asked Rocco.

"Something like that," I said.

"You got me into something here, Peters," he said. "Now I've got to tell Cawelti about this call. If he finds out I didn't tell him . . ."

"Tell him, Rocco," I said. "Sorry about getting between you and the wife."

Rocco grunted and hung up.

I made one more call, long distance, and confirmed what I had discovered. It was all over but saving Fields's life and maybe getting back his money. Juanita had mentioned a doctor's black case. We'd see.

Something made me look up. Jeremy was there, filling the doorway, black slacks, yellow pullover. He had used his passkey and amazing ability, at his size and weight, to move quietly across the darkened reception nook and dental office.

"Saw the light," he said.

"Last-minute business," I said, getting up. "I'm done. Got a man who's about to be robbed and maybe killed."

"You want company?" he asked. "Alice and Natasha are asleep. I always go for a walk now."

"Alice won't like it," I said. "It might be dangerous."

"I have spoken to Alice," he said. "I have, I hope, convinced her that danger and even death are not to be hidden from. They surround us waking, sleeping, can come anywhere and anytime. To hide from them is folly. To face danger is to affirm the freedom of one's life."

"So you want to come with me?" I said.

He nodded.

I turned off the light and we left the office. He locked the outer door and I moved to 613 to put the key on the ledge over the door for Violet.

"I expect to be working in there before Mrs. Gonsenelli arrives in the morning," said Jeremy.

"I told her it'll be there," I said. "She's got some setting up to do."

He nodded his approval.

Our next stop was the glove compartment of the Crosley, where I retrieved my gun and holster. It was late, traffic was light. I unzipped my jacket, took it off, and put it on top of the car. Then I quickly put on the holster and gun and zipped myself back into my jacket. Jeremy said nothing. We both knew we were going to be driving in his car. He didn't fit in mine. His was a prewar Oldsmobile that he kept in humming condition.

"Who are we hurrying to save?" Jeremy asked as we drove and I gave him directions.

"W. C. Fields," I said.

"I've seen two of his movies," Jeremy said. "Is he like that?"

"The way he is in the movies? Yes. Even more," I said.

"Hiding," said Jeremy. "Each act of selfishness, each drink, each joke at the expense of another hides his fear of vulnerability. Getting close to him must be impossible. The walls he has built are too high, deep, and painted with a heavy coat of alcohol. He hides. He hides behind a persona that he has become trapped within and can no longer get out of."

"Could be," I said.

"I find his movies deeply sad," Jeremy said as we kept driving.

"I don't think he'd be happy to hear that," I said. "He thinks they're comedies."

"Comedy does not mean we must laugh," said Jeremy. "It is the reverse of tragedy. It suggests that life can continue with hope."

"Never thought of it that way," I said, unzipping my jacket so I could reach my .38 more easily.

What I was thinking about was whether I could shoot anywhere near as fast and as straight as the killer we might be about to face. I didn't think I could. He had had more practice.

It took us less than fifteen minutes to get to Fields's house on DeMille Drive. We parked in the driveway. I didn't see any cars I didn't recognize. Below us the city, which had blinked wildly at night before the war, was nearly dark.

We went down the tiled walkway. A bird cackled. A single light was on over the door. I knocked. No answer. I rang. No answer. I motioned for Jeremy to follow me and we moved around the house.

"Dogs?" Jeremy asked calmly.

"Fields hates dogs," I said.

We found a window. Locked. We found another window. Locked but with a small metal latch. I tried to push it up quietly. Jeremy touched my shoulder and I moved out of the way. He pushed gently but firmly, his hands on the glass. The latch strained and gave way with a small pop as it tinkled to the floor inside. Jeremy opened the window. We climbed in.

We were in a bedroom. At least it looked that way, with the little moonlight we had. There was certainly a bed in the room. I bumped my shin on it and reached down to feel the low bed-post and mattress. Light came through beneath the door. We moved toward it and I opened it as slowly and silently as I could.

We were in a hallway I recognized. Lights were on all over the place. Then we heard voices. I recognized both of them, particularly Fields's nasal whine, but I couldn't make out the words. I motioned for Jeremy to follow me as I took out my gun and moved to the living-room door. It was closed. I put my ear to the door but I still couldn't make out the words.

"I think we should go in," said Jeremy softly. "A man in there is threatening Mr. Fields and Mr. Fields is in turn threatening the man."

Jeremy hadn't even put his head near the door. The door was a two-part slider. I reached down for the handle and opened it quietly. The man whose back was to us was too busy with Fields to hear us, but Fields, dressed in his silk kimono with the drag-ons, was facing us. He was a pro, showed not a sign that we had entered.

Fields was holding his shotgun. The man with his back to us was holding a pistol. The pool table was between them.

"The bankbooks—you live," said the man. "Once more, where did you hide them?"

"You are in no position to demand my property," said Fields. "My weapon is as easily discharged as yours."

"Have you ever killed?" the man asked as we inched forward across the room.

"Birds," Fields replied. "Detest the creatures. I'd like to shoot a dog or two, and maybe a baritone, but I've never had sufficient legal excuse."

"I've killed more than twice," the man said. "I don't think you can do it."

"Perhaps we shall see," said Fields. "I'm a somewhat ancient but dapper codger whose entrails are perplexed and weary from years of alcohol. I could drop dead any second. Maybe right now. I can see my senseless head hitting the cue ball, which, if I fall correctly, will hit the nine, which, in turn, will hit the twelve, which will carom off the right side and have just enough left to cross the table and drop gently into the corner pocket on your right. It would be an honorable end. My only regret would be that it was not witnessed by someone who could report it to the press so it could appear in my obituary. I can see the headline: 'Fields Takes Final Shot and Calls It Right.'"

The man in front of us was tall. His hand was steady.

"I'll tell you exactly what I'm going to do," the man said. "I'm going to shoot you once in the gut and drop down below the table while you pull the trigger. Then I'll wait to be sure you're dead or dying. If you're alive, I'll shoot you again. Then I'll search all night till I find those bankbooks. You could save me time and work and your own life . . ."

"I'm giving it some thought," Fields said, stalling for us to make a move.

"It could have all been so simple," said the man. "Should have been. The lights were out. I came in with a door pick. I went to your office. And the bankbooks were gone."

"Then, after ransacking my office, you came down here to look, and I appeared like a silent wraith, gun in hand, risen from the pages of a fascinating tome of a time a bit simpler than our own by your noise," said Fields. "Unless I have suddenly become an ill judge of human nature, you intend to shoot me whether I give you my bankbooks or not. I'll make a counter offer. Give me back the money you've already taken and I'll turn you over to the cops for your day in court. You're a younger man than I, with much more to lose across the O.K. Corral Memorial Pool Table."

"And here we stand," said the man. "Let's count to three and you talk or we start shooting."

"Let's pick an even number like two thousand," said Fields.

Jeremy was within a few feet of the intruder now.

"One . . ."

"Do I get a last request?" asked Fields.

"What?"

"I should like to see Paris before I die."

"Two."

Jeremy leapt forward and grabbed the counting man's gun hand, turning it downward as he fired. The bullet hit the green felt of the table and screeched a two-foot path along it. Fields went to the floor, accidentally pulling the trigger on his shotgun. The pellets went into the already drooping ceiling, which instantly sagged even more, and, as Jeremy took the gun from the man's hand, a hefty piece of plaster and lath fell with a crash on the pool table.

Jeremy turned the man around. He threw a punch at Jeremy's throat. It hit the mark but Jeremy Butler had a neck that was all muscle. He didn't flinch or step back. He reached under the man's armpits and lifted the would-be thief into the air.

The man kicked at Jeremy's groin. Jeremy turned aside, taking the kick on the thigh. Ceiling plaster coated everyone but me. Fields was completely white and picking pieces of plaster from his hair as he looked up at the hole above us.

"Damned landlord should have had that fixed long ago anyway," he said, reaching for a ball on the pool table.

The man Jeremy was holding aloft and shaking threw a bent knee into Jeremy's face. Jeremy didn't let go or drop the man, but he did take two steps back. Before the man could throw the next knee, Fields let go with the billiard ball, hitting the intruder smack in the middle of his head. The man went limp and Jeremy dropped him on top of the plaster-covered table.

Jeremy had a distinct bruise on his cheek, but he ignored it and stood over the man.

"Dead?" asked Fields.

"No," he replied. "He'll wake up soon." Jeremy, in his

wrestling days, had seen more than one unconscious man. I trusted his diagnosis.

"Good," said Fields. "Wouldn't want to kill an FBI man, even if he was after my bankbooks."

"He's not an FBI man," I said, pushing the unconscious man on his side so I could get to his wallet and open it. "And his name's not McEvoy. The ID's a fake. I called the FBI locally and asked for McEvoy. They referred me to Washington, D.C. I called the office there. They confirmed that they had an Agent McEvoy, but that he was not available, though he could return my call. I described our tall blond here, and the guy in Washington said it wasn't McEvoy. Our fake FBI agent and his partner planned it fast and almost made it. First, he comes to you within an hour of our getting back, identifies himself, takes away your reason for calling the FBI, and takes away your reason for calling the local police or keeping me on the job. The FBI is on the case. He even checked in with the police as McEvoy, told them that he was working a case, and said he'd keep them informed if there was a local connection."

"Then who the hell is he?" asked Fields, coming around the table, shotgun in hand.

"Name is Knox," I said. "Mickey Knox. He's a detective with the Philadelphia Police Department."

I threw the wallet to Fields.

"Gus Belcher's partner," I said. "The helpful Philadelphia cop who said he wanted to work on the case, who said he'd call the FBI. Belcher went on a sudden vacation the day we left Philadelphia. It wasn't for one day. Belcher followed us. His partner covered for him, and whenever I called, Knox here took the call and had Belcher call us back from wherever we were. My bet is he called us from the same towns we were in. And we thought he was in Philadelphia."

"So Belcher killed Lester Burton and the Chimp," said Fields.

"I'd say so. And when he killed Burton, he went ahead to the next bank with a fake cast."

"The Chimp said 'police' when he was dying," Fields said. "He wasn't telling us to call the police. He was telling us the police had shot him."

"Makes sense," I said.

Jeremy stood at ease near the table. He didn't appear to be interested in our conversation.

"So, where is Belcher? Where is my money? And who is this giant?"

"This is Jeremy Butler, my landlord, friend, a poet, philosopher, and a husband and father."

"You remind me of the Great Bombini," said Fields to Jeremy. "On the circuit for years. Strongest man I ever met. Wrestled from time to time."

"I fought him twice," said Jeremy. "Strong but slow. Beat him too quickly the first time. The audience didn't like it. I let it go ten minutes the second time."

Knox groaned.

"I'll get some water and hit him in the face with it," Fields volunteered.

"Not necessary," said Jeremy. "I suggest you put your weapon away, drink some water slowly, and sit down."

"Excellent idea," said Fields. "I'll get a drink. Don't let him wake up till I get back."

While Fields was out of the room, Jeremy shook most of the plaster off his clothes, saying, "I think Mr. Fields was very frightened. He needs a few moments to calm himself."

"And a martini or two, or I don't know my man," I said.

Knox opened his eyes. A small piece of plaster or some plaster dust got in his right eye. He blinked, rubbed his eye, and tried to sit up. Jeremy reached down, put his right hand behind the man's neck, and lifted him to a sitting position on the pool table.

"Close your eyes," Jeremy said.

Knox looked at the massive bald head almost touching his face. He closed his eyes.

"Roll your eyes around and keep them closed," said Jeremy.

Something happened under Knox's eyelids. And then Jeremy's left hand came up open-palmed and slapped Knox's cheek, turning the man's head suddenly to the left. Knox opened his eyes. Tears of pain were coming out of his eyes.

"Tears should wash out the dust," said Jeremy.

We let Knox sit on the edge of the table. When he seemed to wobble as if he were going to fall, Jeremy sat him up again. In a minute or two Fields reappeared, rubbing his hands together, plaster gone from his face and hair. He was wearing a new robe, silk again, but with purple flowers on a red background.

"Two questions," I said. "Where's Belcher? Where's the money?"

"Not talking," Knox said weakly, blinking tears.

"Breaking and entering. Assault with a deadly weapon. Accomplice to murder. Impersonating a federal agent."

"During wartime," said Fields. "An act of treason. Firing-squad offense. I shall volunteer."

"Belcher's gonna take the money and run," I said. "Your bag is empty. His is full. Where is he? Where would he go? You're a cop. I was a cop. You know you didn't pull the trigger on those two victims. Get a good lawyer quick and make a deal to testify against your pal Gus. Might even get immunity."

"Who are you kidding? I'll get at least ten years, if I'm lucky. Wasn't supposed to happen like this," said Knox, closing his eyes and shaking more plaster from his face and hair.

"But it did," I said.

Knox shook his head and opened his eyes. There was nothing in them but tears.

"I've seen them get away with murder and I've seen them caught by bad luck and dumb mistakes," said Knox. "Gus said we knew enough to get away with it. I didn't expect the killings. He was just going to go after the money. I flew from Philadelphia to Chicago to Denver to here yesterday. I was on the job in Philly when Gus killed those guys."

"You want a deal?" I asked. "My brother's a cop. You met him. Pevsner. I'll call him and see what he can work out with the district attorney's office."

"I got a choice?"

"None I can see," I said.

"Gus is in the car," Knox said with a sigh and a cough. "In the next driveway, next door, that way, waiting for me. If I got caught, I was to stick with my FBI cover, say I had orders to confiscate the bankbooks, but . . ."

That was as far as he got. The window exploded. Glass crashed and Knox slumped forward. Jeremy grabbed him. Knox had a large wide red blotch of blood coming out of the bullet hole in his back.

There was a second shot. I think it was aimed at Fields, who was dropping to the floor when it came. Jeremy calmly laid the body down on the table as I took out my .38 and fired in the general direction of the broken window. I hit the wall about three feet above the sash. One of my better shots.

"He's running," said Jeremy.

"Knox?"

"Dead."

"Let's get the bastard," shouted Fields, grabbing his shotgun and digging a shell out of his robe.

I went for the window, hearing Fields behind me say to Jeremy, "Say, you wouldn't happen to know a cheap decorator, would you?"

I opened the pane and climbed out, careful with my back, begging it to stay with me. Belcher had a big start, but I saw him about thirty yards away in the dim light as he ran behind a row of bushes. I went after him in a half run, gun as ready as it would ever be in my hand.

Around the bushes, I stood in an open patch of grass. It looked like the green of a golf course, complete with a cup which caught my heel. I went down. My gun fired into the sky. A shot came from the shadows of three dark trees about forty yards away. Fields's lawn was the size of a small golf course. Belcher's shot took a deep divot near my head.

I lay flat, panting, and heard him running again. I got up and followed, crouching, moving a little slower, and headed for the three trees and then past them. Belcher or a figure that looked like his was down the slope, over a low gate, and heading for a dark car. I took aim with two hands, but before I could shoot, he spotted me and came within a couple of fingers of taking off my left ear. It was becoming quite clear that he was a hell of a lot better shot than I was.

He got in the car, started it as I made my way down the hill, and backed out of the driveway. I crashed into the fence at the bottom of the slope but managed to hold on to my gun. The lights came on in the big house at the end of the driveway. Getting over the fence was a big problem. My back told me it had had enough. It had cooperated so far, but this was it. I eased my way slowly and gently over the fence, knowing Belcher was getting away. On the other side of the fence, a man suddenly appeared, a big man, barefoot, without a shirt, and in a deep voice he said, "What the hell is going on here?"

I could have sworn the man was Anthony Quinn, but I didn't have time to take a close look or carry on a conversation. Jeremy's car screeched into view and halted at the driveway.

"No time now," I said, panting, as I tried to hurry to join the chase. "Fields will explain later."

"Fields? I should have known that old lunatic had something to do with this," said the man, who I think was indeed Anthony Quinn.

The passenger-side front door of Jeremy's car was open. I jumped in and closed it. Fields, still wearing his kimono and carrying his shotgun, was in the backseat.

Jeremy put his foot to the floor and shot forward. We kept Belcher's car in sight going down to the valley, and Fields said, "If you can just get close enough to the weasel, I'll explode his dreams of spending my money—with both barrels."

We went on for about four minutes and then Jeremy pulled over in front of an apartment building and stopped. "We have lost him," he said. "Too many streets to turn in to. Too many places to pull over on them and turn off his lights. I tried to watch the streets and keep pace, but . . ."

"I know where he's going," I said.

"Then what are we sitting here for?" asked Fields. "This damned vehicle doesn't even have a bar back here and I didn't have time to grab my thermos."

I told Jeremy where to go, hoped I was right, and hoped we got there before Belcher was gone. He was a cop, a detective. He had the experience and had worked out the plan. If we missed him, he could be on his way to Mexico, Brazil, Canada, or who knows where, probably a place where he could live cheaply and comfortably for the rest of his life on Fields's quarter of a million dollars.

Chapter Fifteen

*My associate doesn't know the meaning of the word "capitulation,"
but few do.*

The desk clerk was alone in the lobby. He was thin, with neatly
trimmed black hair, wearing a slightly shopworn hotel maroon
jacket, dark slacks, a bow tie, and a bewildered look. He was also
wearing double-thick glasses.

Before him stood a trio he would have had trouble describing
without people thinking he had dropped out of Alcoholics
Anonymous. There was no one in the lobby to help him. The
Coltrain Arms Hotel was not the home away from home of
movie stars, the wealthy, or politicians. It had always been a
slightly out-of-the-way refuge for those who were confident that
they'd soon write that great script, land the lead opposite Gable
or even Roy Corrigan, or direct Garbo in her comeback. There
were still a few like that, but the Coltrain was fast losing its rep-
utation and its willingness to buy new maroon jackets for its
desk clerks.

Fields was wearing his bedroom slippers, silk robe, and a
shotgun. I was powdered with plaster dust and looking like trouble, and Jeremy stood huge in dusty dignity, the bruise slightly
purple on his cheek.

"Augustus Belcher," I said. "Did he just come in?"

"Yes," said the clerk. "Five-twelve."

"We're the law," I said. "Don't call him and tell him we're
coming up."

"But he's a police officer," the clerk said.

"And we are escaped lunatics," said Fields. "To defy us is to
seal your certain doom."

"I won't call Mr. Belcher's room," the clerk said.

"I shall remain here," Fields said. "Brandishing my faithful musket to hold this myopic traitor to insure your safety during the apprehension of the varlet and the rescue of my cash."

Rocco Allen had told me about Belcher, told me that Belcher had been at his desk at noon. Belcher had given him his real name, said he was tracking a fugitive and that he might need help. He also told Rocco the hotel he would be staying at. I didn't think Belcher would lie to Rocco, in case Rocco tried to call him.

Belcher's mistake had been in trying to cover everything—the FBI, his own presence in Los Angeles, the threats. I had come to the conclusion that if Belcher got his hands on those bank-deposit books, he planned to kill me, Fields, and Gunther, and maybe his own partner, but not as soon as he had. He planned to get rid of everyone who might be looking for him so he could extend his vacation and quickly make another round of banks across the country. He could have walked off his job with a million or more, but now he had to figure that the nearly three hundred thousand would do.

Jeremy and I got in the elevator and, as the doors closed, Fields said, "Adios, auf wiedersehen, and get the bastard."

"What do we do when we get to the room?" Jeremy asked reasonably.

"We have options," I said, trying to sound confident. "We can knock, identify ourselves as Rocco Allen, and hope he opens the door."

"Unlikely," said Jeremy. "We have just chased him. He is certainly preparing to abscond. Identifying ourselves as the police would in all likelihood not deceive him."

"Right," I said as the elevator crept up. "We say we have a telegram?"

"Is he a fool?"

"No," I said as we passed the third floor. "I shoot the lock off. We rush in and make a citizen's arrest."

"He shoots far better than you, Toby," Jeremy said, eyes front, calmly thinking.

"You have any ideas?" I asked.

"We quietly approach the door. Listen. And then I break the door down. You come through right behind me, gun drawn, and aim it at him before he can obtain his weapon. The breaking of the door and the element of surprise should give you an extra second or two."

"What if you can't break down the door on your first try?"

"I will break it," said Jeremy, closing his eyes and folding his hands in front of him. "I'm visualizing the door. I'm watching myself hurl my shoulder against it. I see it breaking open, open wide."

I nodded, though Jeremy couldn't see me, as the elevator stopped at the fourth floor. We didn't want to take a chance on Belcher hearing it stop on his floor. We found the stairway, made our way up without talking, and opened the hall door on five. The hallway was empty. The doors we passed were wood and looked pretty thick to me. The real question was whether the locks were strong. The possibility also existed that Belcher had put something—a dresser, chair—in front of the door.

We found the door. I listened and definitely heard movement inside. I nodded at Jeremy, who closed his eyes again, breathed deeply, and moved against the wall opposite Belcher's door. He suddenly, silently lunged forward, hitting the door with all his weight and whatever his visualization had come up with. The door didn't pop open at the lock. It exploded into the room right off its hinges. I could see as I followed Jeremy into the small room that Belcher *had* put a chair under the doorknob. The chair had splintered into flying pieces of wood.

Belcher, or at least a leg, was just going out the window. He paused long enough to lean back and take a shot at us. The shot went through the front of my right shoe. I didn't feel anything. I hoped it had just barely missed my toes. I fired back, hitting a lamp near the bed a good four feet from the window.

Jeremy moved to the window as Belcher disappeared.

"Fire escape," said Jeremy, careful not to expose himself. "He's going up."

I went to the window. I could walk, but there was a strange feeling in my right foot. I looked down. The hole in my shoe was turning red with blood. I didn't have time to think about it. I took a deep breath and stepped out onto the fire escape, hoping Belcher would be in too big a hurry to take the time to try to deal with us. I was wrong.

Belcher was standing on the narrow, iron fire escape about five feet up, his gun trained on my chest. Before he could shoot, there was a loud boom from below us. Belcher hesitated and I went down on my knees. From below us in the alleyway, I heard Fields's voice shouting, "Churl. Assassin. Thief."

Fields fired another blast from his shotgun. He was probably too far away to hit anything except a few innocent windows on the second floor, but Belcher started up the fire escape fast before Fields reloaded and another fusillade came. I flattened myself against the brick wall.

While it wasn't likely that a shotgun blast would carry up five floors, Belcher and I weren't taking any chances. I knew Fields must now be reaching into the pocket of his kimono to reload for a second assault and that, if he decided to climb the fire escape and get a little closer, it might be as dangerous to me as to Belcher.

"Hold your fire," I shouted, getting up and listening to the sound of Belcher's footsteps hurrying up the fire escape. "Don't shoot."

"Drat," shouted Fields from the darkness below.

I got up, gun in hand, and started up after Belcher. I glanced back but Jeremy didn't follow me through the window. I had no time to wonder why. I climbed. My foot was definitely hurting by now. I thought it was my toes, or one toe. I couldn't tell. Up I went.

I could hear Fields cursing and muttering loudly in the darkness below, and I could hear Belcher's footsteps suddenly stop as he reached the roof. I ignored the throbbing of my foot and kept going, slowly. Belcher might simply be standing there waiting for my head to pop over the edge of the roof.

With no plan other than to keep going and ignore the pain, I went up another two floors to the roof, took a deep breath, held my gun up, and stuck my head over the edge, aiming in all directions.

Belcher was running toward the door to the interior stair. I fired. My shot went into the night sky. He turned to fire back. He came a hell of a lot closer than I had, even though he was running and I was standing still—well, as still as my wounded foot would allow.

Belcher was at the door now and I was hobbling forward. He turned, stopped, saw that I was alone, and took the time to aim more carefully. I had the feeling that he would hit something more vital than my foot this time.

Suddenly, the door behind Belcher popped open. He turned to see what was happening, and Jeremy Butler took a step forward, grasped Belcher's gun hand, and slammed it against the open door. In the light of the open door behind Jeremy, I could see Belcher's weapon fly into the stairwell and then heard it bouncing down the stairs.

Belcher was big, tough, fighting for his life, and more than twenty years younger than Jeremy. He didn't have a chance. He threw an elbow at Jeremy's face. Jeremy turned his head aside. Jeremy released Belcher's hand and turned him around as he had turned Knox. Belcher threw a punch. Jeremy blocked it with little effort. Belcher winced and took a step back.

"Stop," I shouted, gun leveled.

Belcher paid no attention. There were only three ways down for him—past me, through Jeremy, or over the side of the building, eight stories down. He made a lunge at Jeremy, who ducked. Belcher folded over Jeremy's shoulder. Jeremy stood, and Belcher, trying to catch his breath and looking like an insane ape, punched at the back of Jeremy's head. Jeremy ignored the punches, lifted Belcher, who came in, at least, at two hundred and twenty pounds, over his head. Belcher didn't give up. There was too much riding on this. He banged his fists against Jeremy's arms and tried to lean over far enough to bite the wrists of the huge bald silent man, who walked past me with his catch.

"You can put him down, Jeremy," I said, but Jeremy said nothing and kept walking to the edge of the roof.

I heard a sound behind me and turned back toward the door through which Jeremy had come. There stood the kimono-clad W. C. Fields, shotgun in hand. Jeremy didn't look back. He calmly carried the kicking and cursing Belcher to the edge of the roof, turned him over, and effortlessly dangled the killer over the edge of the roof, holding on with one hand to Belcher's right ankle.

"Don't drop the son of a bitch till he tells us where my money is!" shouted Fields. "Drat. Don't drop him at all."

"Jeremy," I said. "Put him down."

"Don't drop me," shouted Belcher into the darkness of the alleyway.

"What the hell is going on up there?" someone shouted from below.

"I advise you to get out of the way," Jeremy called back evenly. "A body may be coming past you in a moment."

"No," screamed Belcher.

"You killed three people," Jeremy said softly. "You shot my friend in the foot. You are a thief and a disgrace to your profession, to humanity."

"I'm a good husband and father," Belcher said.

"I sincerely doubt that," said Jeremy conversationally. "But the balances of human self and ego are constantly in flux and it is possible."

"Oh, Christ," Belcher shouted.

Fields was at my side. He looked me over for the wound Jeremy had mentioned and saw my bloody shoe.

"The hell with the money," said Fields.

"No," shouted Belcher. "I'll tell you where the money is. Pull me up."

"First you tell us where the money is. We check to confirm it and then I pull you up," said Jeremy.

"You can't hold me that long," cried Belcher.

"I'll switch hands," said Jeremy, "but even with that, you may be right."

"Car," shouted Belcher. "Parked two blocks south in front of the hotel. In the trunk. Black Buick. I don't remember the license number, thirty-four-something."

Jeremy nodded for me and Fields to go check while he stood calmly dangling Belcher. Fields, kimono flapping, shotgun in hand, was now moving a lot faster than I was. My foot was definitely in agony, but I followed through the door to the elevator which was waiting open, and down we went.

"Think he can hold him?" asked Fields.

"Jeremy's only killed one person in his life," I said. "And that was . . . a long story. He won't drop him."

We reached the lobby and I glanced at the dumbfounded, nearsighted desk clerk, who shouted, "What's going on? I'm calling the police."

"Then do it, fast," I said.

"You're trailing blood across the lobby," the clerk said.

I believed him but I didn't bother to look. We marched the two blocks. There weren't many people out—a man walking two dogs, a soldier walking with a girl. They tried to hide the fact that they were looking at the weird pair—a fat old man in a silk robe and clopping slippers with a shotgun in his arms, and a limping man with the face of a pug and a bleeding shoe—who passed them.

"Eureka," said Fields triumphantly, pointing his shotgun at the car.

"We forgot to get the key from Belcher," I said, leaning against the car behind the one whose trunk we were staring at.

"So we did," said Fields. "So we did."

He aimed the shotgun at the lock of the trunk from about four feet away, and I ducked behind the side of the car I was leaning against. Dogs barked, people shouted, lights went on. I looked at Fields, who was grinning delightedly. The trunk was open and Fields was holding a black bag in his hand, a bag that looked like a doctor's old house-call bag.

I made the V-for-victory sign. I didn't feel much like Churchill. I didn't feel much. It was about then that I passed out.

When I woke up, I knew immediately where I was—a hospital room. Jeremy was there. Fields, clothed in a pair of checkered pants and an almost-matching jacket with a white shirt and no shotgun, stood next to the bed on one side. My brother, Phil, clean-shaven, rumpled suit, tie loosened as always, stood on the other side.

"How long?" I said, my mouth dry.

"A few hours," said Phil. "It's morning."

"My foot?"

"You lost the little toe on your right foot and an inexpensive shoe," said Fields. "Knew a dancing kazoo player. Italian. Couldn't speak a word of English. Born with no little toe on either foot. Whole family. Walked perfectly straight. Ran faster than the baritone from Weehawken who chased him six or seven miles after the baritone caught the kazoo player in situ delicto with his wife, a voluptuous chorine of ample pulchritude but little talent. Kazoo player was running barefoot and bare-assed in the snow in Buffalo."

"Belcher?" I said, reaching for the glass of water on the table.

"Confessed," said Phil. "Already has a lawyer who's trying to save him from the executioner. I heard what happened. If I were Jeremy, I would have dropped him. He was a police officer, for God's sake."

"The money?" I said.

"Got it," said Fields.

"Since I know how you feel about Cawelti," my brother said, "I thought you might like to know he's already squirming about letting Knox pass himself off as an FBI agent without checking his credentials. With what Seidman already has on him, I'd say Cawelti's going to get a promotion out of the Wilshire and downtown behind a desk. He's got too much on too many people in City Hall to just get demoted. In two months in charge, he's made more mistakes than I made in a year, and I thought I'd set the record."

This was close to the longest speech I'd ever heard from my brother. He patted my shoulder.

A man in white, with glasses, white hair, and a stethoscope around his neck came in. "Awake," he said cheerfully. "Good. I suppose your friends told you you've lost your toe."

"They told me," I said.

"Sewed up the wound, gave you some blood, painkillers," the doctor said after listening to my chest and examining my foot. "Looks good so far."

"When can I go?" I said.

"Well, the bleeding's stopped. You've got color. No temperature. I'd say you should stay where you are for a few days, but you asked when you would be able to get up. Answer is right now, if you walk on your heel, but my guess is that it'll hurt like hell."

I tried to sit up. Phil and Jeremy reached over to help me.

"I've got a wedding to go to," I said. "Two days." I was dizzy.

"Good luck," said the doctor. "I spent a year in the Pacific on a destroyer. Saw men lose toes, fingers, and be back on duty in a few hours when they could have stayed in sick bay, probably could have gotten discharged. And I also saw men with little more than hangnails, saying they couldn't stand."

"Clothes," I said.

Phil moved to the closet in the private room and got my clothes. The same ones I had on the night before.

"I'll get the papers ready," the doctor said. "You can sign yourself out at the nursing station. I'd say you should see your own doctor in two days, change the dressing."

"Thanks," I said.

"Kept your toe if you want it," the doctor said, reaching into his pocket and coming out with a corked vial in which I could see a toe floating in clear liquid.

"Yeah," I said, reaching for the vial. "I think I will." I handed the vial to Jeremy as the doctor left.

"Let me see that," Fields said, reaching out his hand.

Jeremy obliged by giving Fields the vial. He looked at the toe, turned the vial around, held it upside down.

"A memento par excellence," he said. "What stories I could tell about this floating, slightly bent piece of humanity. I could leave it in my will to Jack Benny, who wouldn't have the heart to throw it away or the stomach to keep it. I envy you your war trophy."

"I'd rather have the toe where it was yesterday, on my foot," I said. With Phil's help, I dressed.

"Paid the doctor and hospital bills," said Fields. "Part of the expenses."

"Thanks," I said.

"And," Fields went on, pulling a white box from behind his back, "I prevailed upon a nearby merchant to open his establishment a bit early."

He handed me the box and I opened it. It was a pair of black slipper-shoes, one shoe about two sizes too large for me, and another identical shoe my size.

"Left one goes on the good foot," said Fields. "Right, with padding, goes on the bad one."

"Let's give it a try," I said.

Fields then produced a pair of white cotton socks from his pocket.

"My own," he said. "Fresh, soft as a baby's behind."

Jeremy helped me put on the left sock and shoe. I was a little dizzy, but all right. The right foot was different. Putting the sock on hurt enough for me to clench my teeth and try not to groan.

The slipper went on easier, padded with cotton Fields produced from another pocket. "Always be prepared," he said.

I stood up. It wasn't bad and the dizziness was almost gone. Taking a step almost sent me toppling, but Jeremy caught me and stood me up. I was more ready for the second step.

"It'll get easier," I said.

Fields threw the empty white box in the air. It spun around four or five times and came down behind his back, where he caught it. "You never lose the touch," he said, handing me a wad of bills. "Final payment and just a tad more. The tad more is a secret between those of us assembled. If word got out that I was being generous, it would destroy my carefully built image."

Fields walked to the door.

"I'm in need of a bit of libation," he said. "Our journey's been a jolt to my growing complacency. I shall stand in front of a photograph I have in my health room of me and Jack Barrymore in profile, and I shall toast the relative success of his joke and Burton's mission and tell the wide-eyed buzzard how much I miss him. I'll not invest the money I'm pulling from the banks in Beefsteak Mines, but shall gather the cash and stash it where none but I shall know of its location. And if I chance to expire before I tell anyone, I give you permission to seek it, keep it, and spend it. One final discovery I've made, my friends, and with it I leave you. The meaning of the journey is not reaching the goal but the journey itself. The irony is that we are doomed not to recognize this truth as we travel."

He threw the white box at me. I caught it and when I looked up, Fields was gone.

"Anne's wedding?" Phil said.

"Anne's wedding," I said, taking another step, this time on my own. It wasn't bad at all, if you can call screaming agony an improvement over horrible torture. "Think I've got anything to wear to a wedding?" I asked.

"No," said Phil. "I'll take you home. You can change. Tomorrow you can buy something at Hy's for Him."

"I called Alice a short time ago," said Jeremy. "I'm going home to work on your new office."

"What about sleeping?" I asked.

"I meditated while you were being worked on and then while you were unconscious," said Jeremy. "I am refreshed."

"Thanks, Jeremy," I said.

The bruise on his cheek was small, but definitely purple and slightly puffy.

"Friends, true friends, are few," he said. "And they must be given whatever we possess."

Jeremy went out of the room and I was left with my brother.

"I'll be right next to you," Phil said as I took more steps, each a little less painful than the one before, until I signed myself out at the nursing station and discovered that I was down to a continuing level of pain that I could live with, helped by the pain pills I had at home. They had been given to me by Doc Hodgdon for my back. The doc was seventy and beat me regularly at handball at the Y, though it looked as if I wouldn't be playing for a while.

I put a hand on Phil's shoulder to steady myself as we went down the elevator. He drove me home. We didn't talk much. We really didn't have much to say. We stopped right in front of Mrs. Plaut's Boardinghouse on Heliotrope. Phil started to get out but I stopped him.

"I can make it from here," I said. "You'd better get to the station. Cawelti might need some help packing."

Phil grinned at me. It was a real grin, not the kind I had been getting from him for years, the kind that meant I was about to go too far and he was about to erupt, but a real grin I hadn't seen on him except when he was watching his children do something that got to him.

"Best to Anne," he said as I opened the door. "And remember we want you on Sunday for dinner, early afternoon."

"I'll be there," I said, feeling the pain again as I stepped out. "I'm still planning to take the boys to a movie. If I can't drive, Anita will."

"I'll tell them," he said.

I closed the door and he sat there watching me walk up the cement path. I made an effort to look reasonably normal. Under my arm was the white box from Fields. Now it contained my holster and gun and a corked and sealed vial with the little toe of my right foot.

When I was on the porch, I turned and waved at Phil and smiled, which wasn't all that easy. He drove away and I went into the house, dreading the flight of steps.

Mrs. Plaut was standing inside the door, her arms folded.

"That was your brother," she said.

"Yes."

"Saw him through the window. You're walking funny."

"Someone shot off my right toe," I said. "The little one."

She was wearing a plain blue dress, and I could see that she was also wearing her hearing aid, the one Gunther and I had bought her.

"I don't see the point of that," she said.

"He was trying to kill me."

"Bad shot?"

"In a hurry," I said.

"You know the gun my Mister left behind when he went wherever he went when he died?"

"I know it well," I said, moving toward the long flight of steps. The gun was ancient, a huge six-shooter that looked enormous in Mrs. Plaut's small hands. I had seen her with it twice. I didn't want to see it again.

"Little toe?" she said.

"Right foot," I said, taking my first step up. "Like to see it?"

"My great-uncle Ryman," she said. "He lost a limb in the Indian wars. Can't recall whether it was an arm or leg or which one. He screamed, demanded it back, said he wanted it preserved so he could be buried whole when he died."

"Did they?" I asked, pausing to catch my breath.

"Did they what?" she asked.

"Preserve his limb," I said.

"As best they could though they charged him for the procedure," she said. "As I recall, they farmed it out to a taxidermist in Carson City. Uncle Ryman retained the limb, kept it in the basement, though he would drag it out at the slightest show of interest by a visitor. Eventually, he was indeed buried with it. I have never seen a digit not connected to a body other than that of Uncle Ryman when I was a little girl."

I leaned against the railing, opened the box, removed the vial, and held it up. Mrs. Plaut came closer and looked carefully at the floating toe.

"Looks considerably smaller disconnected," she said. "Far less impressive than a limb."

"I'll try to lose an arm next time," I said. "Maybe that taxidermist or his descendants are still in the business."

"You are given to far too much sarcasm," she said as I put my toe back in the white box.

"I know," I said. "I'm cursed. Now I think I'll go to my room and collapse into a useless pile."

"I'll bring you lunch later," she said. "Rabbit pie."

"I'll count the minutes," I said, deciding to hop up the stairs on my left foot while holding the railing.

Holding on to the box was the real problem, but I managed. Behind me, Mrs. Plaut said, "Calls are posted. I'm going shopping with Mr. Caton, and then he is returning here for lunch and conversation. We may even go to a movie. *Crystal Ball* with Goddard and Ray Milland."

I had introduced Lou Caton, the pianist at the Mozambique Bar, to Mrs. Plaut. He was even older than she was and more sarcastic than I was. They hit it off immediately.

"I'll be driving the Mister's automobile," she said as I hit the upstairs landing.

"That's nice," I said.

The Mister's car dated back to the early 1920s, maybe even earlier. Mrs. Plaut had kept it alive with her own hands and a determination far beyond my own. The door closed and Mrs. Plaut was gone. There were three messages on the board next to the wall. They were all from Anita. I called her at the diner and told her what had happened.

"Want me to close up and come over?" she asked.

"No," I said. "I think I'll sleep. Still up for a wedding reception?"

"Wouldn't miss it. Preston Stewart close up. I'll look great. Anne will be properly jealous."

"Not Anne," I said. "But it's worth a try."

"I'll come over when I close up," she said. "I'll sleep on the couch."

"Closer would be fine," I said. "I told Mrs. Plaut you were my cousin or sister. Tell her you've come to nurse me. She'll know it's a lie, but she likes you."

"Around ten," she said.

"I'll be here," I said and went to my room.

There was a note pinned to my door, written in clear perfect script. Gunther's. It read: "I will be in San Francisco for a few days. I hope you are well. I had a call from Gwen, inviting me. Please wish me good fortune." It was signed, "Your friend, Gunther Wherthman."

Gwen was about to get her graduate degree and move to Vermont. We had met her on a case in San Francisco. She had no lips, and eyes twice the size of normal. She also had no breasts and no sense of humor, but Gunther was smitten and I was glad she had invited him.

I staggered into the room, pushed the door closed, made it to the couch, where Dash was sleeping, and dropped the white box about a foot away from him. He opened his eyes, looked at me, and went back to sleep. I undressed to my undershorts, hopped to the dresser, got two of Doc Hodgdon's pills, hobbled to the refrigerator and got out an almost-empty bottle of milk. I drank from the bottle to wash down the pills and used what was left of the milk to make myself a bowl of Wheaties. When I was fin-

ished, I did a one-foot stand and got down on the mattress by
falling forward and rolling over in pain.

I took my shoes off but not my socks. There was no blood on
the white sock on my right foot and it hadn't been too excruciating to get off my padded right slipper.

With whatever they had given me at the hospital, the strain of
getting home, and what may have been the quick work of Doc
Hodgdon's pain pills, I was asleep in seconds.

All I can remember of my dreams of that morning was Koko
and Betty Boop arm-in-arm, sitting on Dash's back.

"Good job," said Betty.

"Don't lose any more toes," said Koko with a laugh. "Or your
dancing days will be over."

I slept until Mrs. Plaut came with a tray of rabbit pie and a
glass of milk with a cookie on the side. I finished it all while she
watched me eat and then she took the tray.

"Good," I said.

"Mr. Caton says hello," she said. "The stairs are a bit more
than he wants to tackle. You know he is not a young man."

"I know," I said. I think I was back asleep before she was out
the door. The next thing I knew I felt something soft against me.
It had no fur so it couldn't be Dash. I opened my eyes. It was
dark outside and I hadn't left any lights on in the room.

"Awake?" Anita said.

"I think so," I said.

"Hungry? I brought you a sandwich. In the refrigerator."

"Later," I said, turning carefully toward her, feeling her breasts
against my chest.

She laughed. "What are you thinking?" she said.

"You know."

"But your toe?"

"I don't think I'll need it for this," I said.

Chapter Sixteen

Putting one's feet up on the dinner table is not to be countenanced,
unless spats are worn.

In the morning, Anita was up early. She was dressed for work
and I was barely awake. She kissed me and said she'd close the
diner early and come back. I grunted and tried to get back to
sleep. A turn to the left showed me that Anita had put out a can
of tuna and a bowl of water for Dash, who was sitting near the
window, cleaning himself.

The pain pills and the hospital medication were still at work,
but they were fading fast. My foot was throbbing, but the pain
wasn't quite as bad as the day before. I managed to get up and,
helped by the couch's arm, was standing when Mrs. Plaut burst in.

"Breakfast," she said. "Last meal I serve in your room. You
look healthy enough."

I was, I realized, completely naked, my shorts somewhere
under the blanket. I looked for the clothes I had left on the
couch. Gone. Anita had put them away. The white box still lay
on the couch. I put it in front of me to cover as much as I could.

"I've seen naked men before," she said, placing the tray on my
table near the window.

"Bound to happen when you walk into their rooms without
knocking," I said. "How was your date with Lou Caton?"

She was back at the door now. "He'll have the Nazis on the
run inside a year," she said.

"Lou?" I asked, and then I realized she wasn't wearing her
hearing aid.

"Me?" she said. "Mr. Peelers, I'd say the loss of blood and toe
have given rise to delirium. I've made you tea with calming
berubi leaves my Mister brought over from the Orient in '02."

"I can't wait," I said, still holding the box in front of me.

"Well, your date will just have to wait," she said. "You're in no condition."

And she was gone. I rumbled around my mattress, hopping on my left leg, till I found clean shorts. Then I ate. All I was sure of was that the bowl contained a warm, sweet, pulverized grain that didn't taste half bad with a touch of sugar on it. The berubi tea could not be saved by the entire sugar industry of Cuba working full time for a week. I gulped it down, expecting nausea, but it didn't come. My head became light and my mood was suddenly good. Before I stood I was wondering what berubi was.

It took me fifteen minutes to finish dressing. Getting the socks on would have been the big problem, but with the help of berubi tea, I had not taken them off. I tried not to think of what it would feel like when I did. I took the vial containing my toe out of the white box, put it in my pocket, and put the box with my .38 on the shelf, after taking out the bullets that were left. I tried to pull the mattress back on the bed, couldn't do it, and gave up, panting.

I waved to Dash and made my way out the door, walking on my left foot and my right heel. I may have looked like an idiot, but I could walk, and at the bottom of the steps I tried to take a real step with my right foot. I could do it, but the pain was still there. So was Mrs. Plaut, a huge metal toolbox in her hand.

"Something's wrong with the pistons on the Mister's car," she explained. "I'm gong to work on it. Louis didn't notice."

I assumed Louis was Lou Caton. I almost made the mistake of answering, but nodded my head and smiled instead.

"I admire a man who has the spunk to get up and out the day after losing a foot," she said, looking at me.

"It was a toe," I said before I could stop myself.

"Well, I don't see how you could move fast under the circumstances. 'Jehosaphat,' as the Mister would say. 'Jehosaphat.'"

I nodded and limped for the door. I pointed upstairs and

said, "I couldn't move the mattress back. Sorry. And thanks for breakfast."

"I'm up in years," she answered, shifting the heavy toolbox, "but I see what I see. That woman is not kin."

"Woman?"

"One who came last night," she said. "Had to let her in."

I didn't know what to say, so I said nothing.

"I like her," she said decisively and walked past me toward the back of the house, toolbox jangling.

Driving the Crosley wasn't the hard part. Getting in was the problem. There was no way I could do it without my foot touching something. Once I was in, I could press on the gas with the heel of my right foot and I was off.

I parked in the no-parking zone in front of the Faraday and scribbled a note on a piece of paper I tore out of my pocket notebook: "Driver is recovering from a foot wound. Office 613 if you wish to check." I signed it, hoping that the police, if they showed any interest at all, would think I had a war wound and show leniency. I didn't think I could park in the back and make it all the way around the building.

I had almost as much trouble getting out of the Crosley as I had getting in, but I made it and went through the doors of the Faraday. The lobby, as always, had the strong smell of Lysol. I liked it. I was feeling reasonably good.

I made it to the elevator just as Juanita, colorful Carmen Miranda costume flowing, long dangling earrings, dyed hair in natural ringlets, and face overly made-up, stepped off.

"Don't say anything," I said. "Don't tell me what I'm thinking or what's going to happen. You were right about everything."

She shrugged. "You're limping," she said.

"Yes," I answered, moving past her into the elevator.

"You lost your little toe," she said, "but you still have it. I don't get it. How can you lose it and have it?"

I pulled the vial out of my pocket and showed it to her, closing the steel door of the elevator. She smiled triumphantly.

"Knew I was right," she said, heading for the front door. "By the way, he's crying."

"Who?" I asked as the elevator started up. Her voice echoed through the eight-story lobby.

"Shelly," she said. "Not psychic stuff. Heard him when I came down."

When I got to my new office, the door was open and the place smelled like fresh paint. Violet was polishing a desk in a reception room the size of a reception room, with a file cabinet in the corner and a typewriter on a small table. She had put up a poster over her head on the white wall. It was the fight card for the Olympic on a night three years ago. Topping the bill was Angelo Gonsenelli against Red Roy Remington. Violet was brightly dressed and in a good mood when she turned to face me. Violet was indeed a lovely young woman.

"Looks pretty good, huh?" she asked.

"Looks pretty good," I said.

"Your foot hurt," she said. "Mr. Butler told me."

"Hurts," I said. "Getting better every minute."

"Mr. Butler must have been up at four in the morning," she went on. "The whole place was painted when I came in."

She pointed to the poster.

"Okay? I mean, can I leave it up? There's no window."

"Okay," I said.

"Angelo won with a K.O. in the third," she said, looking at the poster. "Remington wasn't half bad but he had a slow left jab. Angelo slipped it every time. I think the judges thought Remington was connecting, but Angelo showed them."

She looked at the poster proudly. My office was separated from the reception room by a wooden wall with a pebble-glass window you couldn't see anything but shadows through, but some light was making it from my office window into the reception room. My office door was solid wood. I opened it and stepped in. About three times the size of my old office. Desk with a telephone, at the window. Neat small pile of letters in my *in* box. Wooden swivel chair, and two chairs for clients. Jeremy had moved all my things. On one wall was the big Dali painting of the woman and two babies. On the opposite wall was my license and the fading thirty-year-old photograph of me, Phil, our father, and Phil's dog.

I went behind the desk and carefully sat in the swivel chair. I was going to like this. There was a knock on the door and I said, "Come in."

Violet said, "Phone with a new number will take a few days. They're working, though. Old tenant didn't turn off the service. But it's still his number, and I've already gotten a few oddball calls. We'll have our own number in a week maybe. Meanwhile, Dr. Minck doesn't mind taking messages, and I'll talk to the mailman."

I took the vial out of my pocket and placed it in front of me.

"That your toe?" she asked.

"Yep."

"Can I see?" she said, moving forward.

"Sure," I said.

She moved across the room and picked it up. "Kind of cute in a weird way," she said.

Like you, I thought, but I didn't say anything. I liked Violet and I didn't want her filling up a corner of her mind with insults from me to turn over to her husband when the war was over.

She put the vial down. "Man just came to put your name on the door," she said.

"Just tell him to make it 'Toby Peters, Private Investigator' in black. Letters don't have to be very big. We don't get my trade from people passing by on the sixth floor of the Faraday."

Violet nodded.

"And send this," I said, handing her the vial, "to W. C. Fields with a note saying, 'The trophy is yours.'"

Violet nodded again and took the vial. I gave her Fields's address.

"I get paid by the week?" she asked.

"When times are good," I said. "Might be some lean months, but you'll always get paid. Two dollar a week raise. You can read on the job, do your nails, write poetry and letters to your husband, and handle whatever business comes our way."

Violet smiled and left. I called Anita and told her I was in my office. She said she couldn't talk, early lunch customers, a crew working on the sewer down the street.

I checked the window. Same view as from the cubbyhole in Shelly's office: the alley, some wrecks. No people.

I was tired before I even did anything, but I went through the mail and messages. Messages from No-Neck Arnie, a man named Walter Simmons with a scrawled "insurance salesman" under his phone number. There were two that might have been clients. The letters, six of them, contained no checks or cash. A few former clients still owed me money. I didn't really expect to ever see it. Three of the letters were bills. One was an invitation to visit an exciting new subdivision in the valley, deep in the valley. The letter said the value of the houses would triple when the war was over. Servicemen would be coming back, moving their wives out of small apartments, or getting married, wanting to have a real home. It was, the letter assured me, a great investment. The war will be over soon. Don't wait till it's too late. I junked the letter, put the bills in a pile, and put the other two letters in another pile, the possible clients. One wanted to know if I could come to San Diego and find out if her husband was cheating on her with a Wac. She had heard of me through a mutual friend she didn't name. It was a possible, a two-day job at the most. The wife's number was in the letter. The other letter was more interesting. It had been hand delivered. No postmark. It simply had a telephone number. Below the number was a signature—Cary Grant.

I was already tired, in no condition to talk to an important potential client on the phone, if the letter wasn't a joke. I'd call in the morning. I limped into Violet's reception room, which now contained four wooden chairs and a very small table against the wall opposite her desk.

"For clients," she said. "We thought we'd surprise you."

Four people waiting to see me at one time merited inclusion in *Believe It or Not*.

I told her it looked great and that I'd be back the next day. I moved past the man in white, paint-stained overalls who was putting my name on the door and headed past Shelly's office. I couldn't stop myself. My name had already been removed from the door. I walked in. The waiting room was empty. I walked into Shelly's chamber of horrors and there he sat in his dental chair. His glasses were on the end of his nose. The cigar in his fingers was down to a stub, and his white lab coat had a few fresh coffee stains. He wiped his eyes and looked up at me.

"Toby," he said. "You lost your toe. Jeremy told me. You know they're doing experiments on sewing toes and fingers back on wounded soldiers."

"Too late for that, Shel," I said. "Look, I'll be right next door. I'll stop by, see you, have lunch once in a while, and you can come and see me."

"That's not why I was crying," he said. "Mildred wants to come and work here half days. I can't stop her. She's on a mission. She says she can straighten me out, make calls, get patients, make money, keep Violet and you from visiting. Toby, she'll be here half the time. She won't let me smoke my cigars. She'll . . . I can't stop her. Look what you've done."

The prospect of seeing Mildred Minck almost every day didn't appeal to me either.

"She won't let me have lunch with you," he said. "She won't let me eat tacos at Mann. She won't let me go in your office, past Violet. She may, if I behave, let me breathe once in a while. She wants your old office and I'll have to go back to taking care of the waiting room. Think of something. Save me. I love Mildred, you know that, but this is my sanctuary. You've heard me sing while I work. The singing'll stop. Mildred says I sing like an iguana. What the hell does an iguana sing like, I ask you?"

"I don't know, Shel," I said. "I'll try to think of something to change Mildred's mind."

"No use," he said, sagging and adjusting his glasses. "Once she decides . . . no use. All because you moved out."

"I'll work on it, Shel," I said.

He nodded, a nod without hope, and I left.

Two days later, Anita and I went to the reception after the wedding of Anne and Preston Stewart. I wore a new suit from Hy's for Him on Melrose, picked out with Anita's help. I was walking a little better, but I had to wear the slippers. Doc Hodgdon had changed the bandage on my toe the day before and he had given me more of the pain pills.

Anita had gone all out. She looked great, wore a blue suit and her dark-yellow hair piled on her head in the latest style, like Mary Beth Hughes or Ann Dvorak. The hotel ballroom was filled with movie people, a few I knew from working for them on cases, most I recognized—Paul Henreid, Danny Kaye, Joan Crawford were the big names—but there were character actors, directors, producers, and, in one corner, looking uncomfortable with a drink in one hand and a little piece of cake in the other, was Harry Cohn himself, surrounded by Columbia yes-men.

We made our way through the crowd and across the dance floor. A small band was playing and a few people were dancing. I found Anne, congratulated her, kissed her cheek, and shook the tuxedoed bridegroom's hand. His golden hair bobbed boyishly when we shook. Preston Stewart had a great, friendly smile.

"Glad you could make it," he said. "Anne's told me a lot about you."

I looked at Anne. She was dark, beautiful in a white dress, her hair down. Her eyes were pleading with me not to say anything. I introduced Anita.

We were a study in contrasting couples. Anne was dark. Anita light. Anne was a few years younger, but neither looked her years. Stewart was smaller and thinner and younger than I was, a lot younger.

"Anita and I have to take off soon," I said, seeing relief on Anne's face, a nod of thanks and a small smile. "Good luck to both of you. And if you ever need a private detective, I'm in the book."

I suddenly got an idea and headed Anita toward the dance floor.

"I like her," Anita said.

"So do I," I answered, slightly elbowing Bill Demarest.

"You did fine," Anita assured me, squeezing my arm.

The band was playing what I thought was a fox-trot. I had recently taken lessons from Fred Astaire for a job I did for him. I couldn't hear the beat and I was, he had said, not likely to compete with him for roles, but I could dance. I led Anita to the floor, which was not particularly crowded.

"Dance?" I said.

"Your toe?"

"I'll ignore it," I said.

"You want Anne to see," she said as we stepped onto the floor.

"And I want you in my arms," I said.

"That's a Preston Stewart line from *Brigands of Bengal.*"

"I know, but it's true anyway. Just tap me on the beat so I know where to start."

The band was playing "Long Ago and Far Away." I ignored my toe and danced, hearing Astaire's advice in my head, ignoring my feet and counting on them to do the right thing, keeping my back straight and my arms up, being sure to give Anita the right leads. Over her shoulder through the break in the crowd I could see Anne looking at us past Dorothy McGuire, who was talking to her. Anne's large brown eyes were filled with what I took for disbelief. The Toby she knew couldn't dance. The Toby in front of her was moving around the floor in the right direction, going backward and forward, executing turns. I didn't make a mistake, if you discount the stupidity of dancing with a recently missing toe.

When the song ended, the crowd applauded politely and I led Anita out of the ballroom without looking back.

"I'm taking you out to dinner," I said in the hotel lobby. "We're all dressed up and there's no point in wasting it. Name the place, any place."

"You're kidding?" she said.

"Nope," I said. "Name it."

"The Brown Derby," she said, and the Brown Derby was where we went.

When I got home that night after taking Anita to her place, I gave in, walked on my heel, and as I walked past Mrs. Plaut's door, her hand came out with an envelope in it.

"I'm in my nightie," she said, closing the door.

I took the envelope, and as she closed the door I could have sworn I heard Lou Caton's voice inside say, "Where did I put it?"

I made it up the stairs to my room. Dash was out for the night and Mrs. Plaut had made up my mattress and left it on the floor. I took off my slippers and, with a pain greater than I had imagined, removed my white socks. A trickle of blood had stuck my right sock to my foot where my toe used to be. I eased it off and went to the kitchen alcove in my shirt and underwear. Even though I had just eaten at the Brown Derby, I prepared a bowl of Corn Krispies while I read the note in a scrawling script that took me some time to decipher:

Thanks for the gift. I shall display it enigmatically in my office and change the subject when anyone tries to probe me with questions of its history. Might scare off a few pests from time to time. The plasterer and window repairman recommended by Mr. Butler did a job worthy of the Pope's ground crew. Thanks again for the toe. Best gift I've received since I performed before the Maharaja of Wonderpar, who gave me an elephant which I donated to the Fort Worth Zoo. Got the elephant for juggling six burning Indian clubs from the Maharaja's private collection. Juggled them blindfolded. Juggling was easy. Getting blindfolds on burning Indian clubs, however, was no mean undertaking.

The note was signed, Snidely J. Whiplash.